This edition, issued in 1953, is for members of the Companion Book Club, 30 Bedford Street, London, W.C.2, from which address particulars of membership may be obtained. The book is published by arrangement with the original publishers, Michael Joseph Ltd.

THE NET

"A blessed companion is a book"—JERROLD

THE NET

*

JOHN PUDNEY

THE COMPANION BOOK CLUB

LONDON

AUTHOR'S NOTE

To the scientists and research workers of Great Britain who have been screened for security, the author offers his humble assurance that Port Amberley is a calculated fiction. Real people and actual projects are necessarily excluded from this otherwise true tale.

Made and printed in Great Britain
for The Companion Book Club (Odhams Press Ltd.)
by Odhams (Watford) Limited,
Watford, Herts.
S.953.V

PART ONE

Because Hornets are very great,
They easily passe through the net;
When as the sillie little flye
Is taken therein continuallye.

JOHN NORTHBROOKE
Spiritus est Vicarius Christi

CHAPTER I

THE first time Lydia was unfaithful to him in her heart was at a dance in the Recreation Centre of the Research Station which is internationally known as Port Amberley. She and Heathley were both members of the organising committee, and most people agreed that their energy in particular had contributed to the success of the evening. Hers because she liked to do everything well. His because it was an opportunity for once to be working with her, and because it was a matter of policy to make the dance go with a swing.

Sir Hereward Cruddock, the Director, had stressed the need for more "get-togethers." It was essential to create some internal warmth to compensate for the social isolation of Port Amberley. It was necessary, too, to find some sort of social basis upon which that strange assortment of human beings could blend. As a departmental head, Heathley knew only too well how difficult it was to mould together the personalities and the work of men and women of several nations and many contrasting backgrounds. Lydia, he knew, found it uphill work to bring together their wives and relatives, a task

7

she dutifully attempted from time to time. Lydia saw such social problems as clearly as Heathley himself. "The poor things all feel that they are exiles; and in some senses they are right."

Open to the four winds where it sprawled on the blind, empty marshes, even the everyday life of Port Amberley was cordoned off from the humdrum world. Its isolation in the social pattern of the twentieth century was not only a matter of geography, but of top-level policy. To the people who worked there, the place was not a chosen sanctuary but a retreat insulated by expediency.

Most of the people at Port Amberley had little sense of mission. They had not dedicated their lives to some cause or bound themselves over by spiritual vows. Their talents, their ambitions and, here and there, some specific enthusiasm had assembled them from quite unrelated sources to serve the interest of science. They were not prophets or visionaries. Most of them were average human beings working at what they considered to be ordinary jobs. Among them, certainly, were men and women of genius, of specialised gifts, of high academic attainment. A few of them could hardly be unconscious of a sense of latent power. There were certain exceptional individuals who were consumed by missionary zeal, and received precious little encouragement when they spoke of it. Taking them as a whole, however, whatever stirred their hearts and their minds, whatever their potential and their aspirations, they had all been screened by the authorities.

Because of that mesh, they were different from others, although they seemed to Lydia, as the dance began to go with a swing, such very ordinary people. Too ordinary a company, surely, to have provided the occasion for that unfaithful fluttering of her heart.

Much too ordinary to cause the slightest defection in a well-developed sense of duty. Lydia was a colonel's daughter and her mother was a colonel's widow, so they both understood duty in that sense. Team-work. Getting the chaps together. Healthy relaxation. Lydia had submitted to such phrases all her life. Like her mother, she had long since learnt the obligations and the need to make them look like a pleasure. Was it not all the more disturbing, therefore, to be surprised by a flutter of the heart in the midst of such a function, with a husband fetching a glass of the claret-cup which one had spent half the afternoon making?

The cause of the disturbance was Brian Jackson, that self-possessed young specialist, who looked like a Red Indian, but who was, in fact, a local boy-made-good. That was surprising. It was shameful, too. It took her unawares. You are old enough, Lydia, to be—not perhaps his mother, but his aunt. You must think of your position. You must remember your own mother at home looking after the children. You ought to consider your husband. His status in this pattern of official and social distinctions. This damn silly pattern . . . but what was she daring herself to think instead of considering Heathley?

"Come along now, Brian, and talk to Lydia! And you, Lydia, for heaven's sake, don't disillusion him. The world needs scientists like him, complete with their illusions," joked Heathley, handing her the drink. He gave his own to Brian Jackson, who took it in an off-hand, awkward way instead of refusing it, which would have been more decorous.

"Thanks, Heathley." He spoke jauntily, with that healthy warm voice which belonged to the country, the deep country of the Sondings which lay beyond the perimeter of Port Amberley.

"I'm sure my illusions are safe with Lydia."

"Why not, Brian? I've got my own. Don't you worry," said Lydia a little too sharply, a colonel's daughter aware of standing orders.

"Why on earth," said Heathley, "don't we have these shows more often? One sees people quite differently. Look at the Deputy. He's making a night of it."

They sat there grouped upon the three hard chairs as if somebody had posed them for an informal photograph. The people, thought Lydia, looked, as usual, ill-assorted and undistinguished, at once very bourgeois and very brainy. They were full of cliques but they were always ill at ease. Out of the corner of her eye, she admired the square sunburnt wrist of Brian Jackson and smiled at her own wickedness. She listened for Brian's voice and sipped her claret-cup, wishing that it were a large brandy.

Heathley was even more ashamed of his thoughts, for he was wishing that the Deputy Director might fall down and break his neck. Perhaps just a bone would do. Something painless, of course, but incapacitating. The Deputy was a bear of a man with a long unhappy matrimonial past and a well-controlled appetite for spirits. He revelled in not being loved, but could never quite succeed in not being liked. He was one of the most able administrators in the service but scientifically he was reactionary, time-wasting, obstructive, devious. . . . Heathley sighed and pulled himself up. He touched Lydia's hand. That brought him to himself at once. How she saved him from himself. How easily he might have become too immersed in it all to enjoy the essential stability of life.

How typical of Heathley, Brian Jackson was thinking, to be so perfectly matched. How enviable was Heathley's assurance, his effortless manner, his accept-

ance always of all that was best. Just as he would un-
erringly pick out essentials in the laboratory or on a
test bench, whether one agreed with his general
premises or not. Just as he would handle the physical
aspect of a problem in the air, with an unhurried ease,
as if he were for ever wearing gloves in order not to
sully himself with the obvious. It was almost unfair
that a man should be such an outstanding, if contro-
versial, scientist while possessing such an abundance
of other gifts. He longed to explain away his growing
dissension from Heathley over the next phase of the
M.7 project and emphasise that there was nothing
personal about it. But sometimes, in the presence of
Lydia Heathley, he felt himself a lout. Because of her
smile, he felt that too much was expected of him. He
might have gone on dancing with Ilse and remained
more at his ease had it not been for the conventions to
be observed at parties like this. Ilse was a colleague and
there was mutual respect, tempered by the right
amount of frivolity. One dared not let a personal
relationship like that get out of hand unless. . . . But
no: there was not that kind of response in Ilse, no
warmth behind the pleasant frivolity. Even as his blood
rioted sometimes, he would be constrained to face her
over a conference table with some such remark as, "I
trust Dr. Leon's calculations will bear me out." He had
had to say it that very morning, wondering why the
words did not choke him; and now, off duty, he could
hardly keep his eyes off her, even as he paid his social
respects to the Heathleys.

"For heaven's sake, go and dance with her," Lydia
said with a desperate playfulness which shocked him
into saying like a fool, "Dance with whom?"

"Dr. Leon—Ilse . . . I mean," Lydia Heathley
said. "The poor girl's looking slightly anxious

11

and the Deputy's simply hogging all her dances."

Brian started as if the words had been a comb drawn across his scalp. He had only let his thoughts dwell for a moment upon the pleasure of dancing with Ilse and Lydia Heathley had pounced as if he had spoken out loud. "She doesn't look as anxious as all that," he said jerkily, with a kind of schoolboy terseness.

"Brilliant girl," murmured Heathley, his eye still following the Deputy, watching him as he went nosing up to Ilse like a bear, before she could possibly find another partner.

"Do you think so?" Lydia stifled a pretty little yawn and puzzled them both, for it was impossible to tell at whom the remark was aimed.

"Her brother's very able, too," parried Heathley.

"I agree, Heathley. You'd have to look a long way to find anybody to touch Alex, though it's a limited field," Brian said.

"Shop!" snapped Lydia, like a child playing cards. Then she smiled at them both: "I've vowed that whenever it starts I shall yell *shop*. It's our only hope of staying sane."

"Excellent idea," Brian said simply. In fact, it made him even less sure of himself in her presence and even more determined to put a bold face on it. "Alex Leon's teaching me to play chess in return for my teaching him golf."

Some madness in her eye went on looking at his wrist, drawing out of its shapeliness a whole character, an idealised image. She laughed and said, less to Brian than to his image, "You could give me a stroke a hole. It might improve my game. But I can't offer you chess in return."

Heathley said: "She slices her shots mercilessly. You might be able to cure her, I can't."

12

The playing of golf was another activity which had had official encouragement. To Cruddock, it meant fresh air. The staff needed to be "taken out of themselves," just as much as they needed anything which would "get them together." So Felix Tatham, the Personnel Manager, had organised it. Along the coast at Cresham Strand, there was a nine-hole course, with a faded blue corrugated-iron pavilion. Major Tatham had come to terms with the sad Scots idealist who ran the place. Port Amberley people had special terms. A modest transport service had been started between the Recreation Centre and the club-house.

"It's ages since we played," Lydia said with a blush which surprised her, made Heathley think the room was hot, and went unnoticed by Brian Jackson. "What with the children, and running a house, and the extraordinary hours the Professor's been keeping . . ." she rattled on.

"Let's have a game on Wednesday morning," Brian said. "I know I shall have the morning off as the . . ." He stopped and glanced meaningly at Heathley. The first batch of M.7 prototypes would be fitted that morning, and that would provide a break for everybody but the mechanical staff. Heathley would know that. Ilse and Alex would know that. It was official knowledge. Lydia Heathley, however, must not know officially, even if her husband might choose to talk about it in bed. Lydia was in the mesh, too; but not that far in, formally at least. Brian's sentence must end in the air. Indeed it would have been better left unsaid.

Sentences were left in the air all the time at Port Amberley. That was Security. That was Colonel Bord. Nobody knew, especially since such cases as Fuchs and Pontecorvo, where the activities of Dennis Bord began and where they ended—what was the shape and density of the mesh. There were times when Heathley, who had spent most of his adult life on secret work, found the whole thing irritating, and times, too, when the Colonel's blood in Lydia declared it to be amateurish. Nevertheless, demands of Security had grown to be like the prevailing winds which blew across the shack-city of Port Amberley from the marshes and the Sonding market gardens behind them, blowing with teasing persistence across the laboratory blocks, the secret waterside sheds and slipways, the curdled mud flats, and the desolate experimental target areas of the open sea, a domain whose only boundaries were marker buoys and lines drawn on charts.

Beyond the half-hearted coastal settlements such as Cresham Strand, were full-blooded resorts like Flimby and Ruxtable. Inland lay Tollbury, a cathedral city, slicked-up for tourists but also booming with light industry. It was in Tollbury that Brian Jackson had had his opportunities. Scholarships took him there and passed him on thence to his brilliant academic career. To him, Flimby, Ruxtable and Tollbury still savoured of high life. In one or another of them, he had first tasted alcohol, bought his first made-to-measure suits, learnt to drive his first car.

His return to take up an appointment at Port Amberley had been Heathley's doing. Heathley, who, in his bachelor days, had lodged with Brian's parents on the farm at High Sonding while Port Amberley was in its early stages of development. A younger, less steady, less assured, less secretive Heathley, who had shocked the villagers with his left-wing sympathies but mollified them by his high scores at cricket. A heroic figure in Brian's youth, a man of known achievement, an intellectual leader, a contentious, sometimes commanding but always even-tempered colleague. Yes, a colleague because they shared fields of research and their work was often complementary. That was what was so exciting and absorbing. That was why he had expected Heathley to give him some signal, however ambiguously, when he had spoken of Wednesday morning. It had not occurred to him that Heathley had not heard the words at all, that the man was unaware of his presence or even of the presence of Lydia, that the hand which held the claret-cup trembled slightly not because of the heat but because of an abstraction. It was a pattern of thought in which the M.7 project was, of course, the central focus, but it was one in which the clumsy figure of the Deputy Director was jostling everything into a corner. A man who need only fall down, something painless, of course, but incapacitating, to enable certain unsupportable theories to be applied to the project, theories which could only be tested to the breaking-point of human lives. Theories which only needed proof to change the nature of the M.7 project from a side issue to a reality of decisive importance. There was nobody to share such thoughts, to sympathise with such an abstraction.

Lydia was aware of its existence without beginning to understand it. She had been brought up with strict ideas about the limits of a woman's influence in the masculine routines of soldiering. There were certain primitive male mysteries, like manoeuvres or rugby football, expedient, healthy, and as established as the Prayer Book. It was conceivable within such a conception that the women might have the initiative and the brains. Battles, as her father had loved to say, might be won on the playing-fields of Eton, but they could be lost in the bedrooms of Camberley. It was a crude but practical outlook which at Port Amberley had served her well. Her faith in Heathley's work was unquestioning. She admired the scope and capacity of his character. Heathley, she told herself, she told him, she told everybody, was a big man.

It was typical of both of them, and also of the community in which they lived, that she nearly always spoke and thought of him as "Heathley." They had first met while she had been working for the Ministry of Aircraft Production, and never at any time did she hear him called by any other name. Nor was he, for all the character and personality which he carried so easily, a man to whom anyone could conceivably fit a nickname. When she had found out his first names, she had tried calling him Arthur Vivian for fun. Then she had noticed the impatience with which he took the joke. She discovered that the few surviving members of his family used "Arthur." It sounded stilted when they said it; but she had brought some warmth into it by saying it over and over again, intimately to herself and then intimately to him. Even so, it had soon lapsed into being a private special word, to be used only purposefully when no other word would do, at times when Heathley was palpable, revealed.

The thought, which was no more than a numbness deeply seated in her senses, was that Heathley was becoming less palpable, less and less revealed. It sometimes seemed as if their very love was being sieved in the interests of security, as if Heathley's generous nature was being screened. She sensed that in his life there was a climax building up which was greater than lifesize. She was too well trained to be jealous of his work. She was even prepared for their love to miss a beat. She was not prepared, though, for this unfaithfulness in her own heart.

It sprang upon her like the breeze which had

16

dropped and left the smell of spring lingering upon the asphalt paths of the Research Station. It had soared like the lark-song above the corrugated-iron skyline. It was, perhaps, typical of that strange pitch to which they were all attuned that she should mind so much that Colonel Bord should have joined them without her noticing, that she should feel that he had surprised her in some unspeakable thought. It was absurd that he should notice the glances which had fallen upon anything so unlikely as Brian Jackson's wrist. Yet she started, and for a split second she forgot to smile. She said, a little defiantly, "We were talking about golf. The idea is that Brian Jackson is to cure me of slicing."

"I was just saying that we might have a game . . ." Brian began.

"On Wednesday." Dennis Bord finished the sentence for him, smiling in his affected over-precise military style. He took no trouble to conceal the fact that his profession was Security. Even the soft speech which proclaimed his Irish origins had a genially sinister omniscience about it.

Lydia, ignoring the interruption, which could only have been smart if it were not clairvoyant, said boldly: "I can't really manage any other day."

Heathley was out of earshot when she said it. Brian Jackson could take it as a tactful piece of rescue work if he pleased. She meant it as a small defiance to Dennis Bord and, as such, she knew it was folly, particularly when he treated it as small talk and dismissed it with an Irish "of course." Then, with his usual precision, he stepped aside to bring forward a companion and said: "You may not perhaps have met an American colleague of ours, Sam Seagram—Major Seagram—Mrs. Heathley."

"Glad to know you, m'am," Sam Seagram began with

17

brisk Texan courtesy; and that little crisis which perhaps Lydia had taken too seriously was over.

She stood up, tall and gracious, serenely aware that her beauty and her poise could dominate that gathering, but that she was mature enough not to assert herself, to realise that that was no part of a function designed as a "get-together."

When the band played *God Save the King,* she invited Bord and the American to come home for a night-cap. She omitted Brian from the invitation, but boldly chaffed him about not forgetting Wednesday. Heathley joined them and said: "I'm going back to the office to turn off the taps"—a phrase he used when he went to speak to people who happened to be working on night-shift or when he had something on hand which needed a last look. It meant a brief absence. When he said he was going to "run the taps," it meant a night's work, and Lydia packed up food and drink. It was domestic shorthand, a code not designed to deceive anybody in the know. Sam Seagram declared it to be the neatest piece of domesticity.

Bord looked preoccupied and suggested that the American should go along with Lydia and that he himself would follow after checking on a point in his office —"turning off a few taps myself." So, partly for the sake of decorum and partly because she fancied he looked so lonesome, they picked up Alex Leon on the way out.

The Colonel's widow, her mother, was waiting up with her indomitable perkiness, a weapon as ready as a loaded gun. This good humour, and the real pistol she had kept under her pillow ever since she had been through a frontier incident, were the signs of her ritual faith in Kipling's India where the *memsahib* shared a part of the white man's burden. The Colonel had called her Mem, and now they all did—even Central Europeans like Alex and Ilse Leon, who thought it was an abbreviation by which the English aged were especially honoured.

"How that poor man works!" she boomed when she heard that Heathley had gone off to turn off the taps. "But we all know what it means to the country," she added with an inscrutable nod toward the American major.

"We do, m'am," he answered with just the right emphasis, as if they had all been saluting the flag.

"Splendid!" said the old lady, permitting Alex to kiss her hand. "Thank goodness you've all had an evening of relaxation without having to leave the camp."

"Not the camp, Mem," Lydia said. "Remember we've all agreed not to use that word. The Director says it gives people a trapped feeling."

"It certainly gives me the creeps," Alex supported her with a polite continental shudder.

"I know, I know!" Mem said, with cheerful perception. "I mustn't use the word, must I? In my young days, of course, a camp was quite different. Plenty going on. Most agreeable. I expect you still have them in America, Major Seagram?"

It was one of the Memsahib's foibles that the United States of America was a society which had just reached that happy state of nineteenth-century imperialism from the roots of which she had drawn her own massive good nature. She was spending the evening of her life upon the fringes of people and projects which of their very nature were ahead of their times. Kipling's India had been mourned and lost. Nevertheless, she was convinced that modern America was just a façade behind which the traditional splendours, graces and austerities of the white man's burden were ever bright and

19

resplendent. Behind the plangent sound-track of American life, she never failed to hear distant nostalgic bugles. She was as obstinate in this as she was in her devotion to Heathley whom she had romanticised into a sahib of the scientific age, a translation which she had never attempted to justify or explain.

Sam Seagram, with his Texan manners, was, of course, just her man. Her questions about America were mostly rhetorical, and assertive. Before he could begin to answer them, she dazed him by her suppositions about the polo and the big game "in the interior."

Lydia handed out drinks. She was exhilarated by the innocent escapade of her heart—and, unaccountably, by the dark cool admiration of Alex Leon's eyes. Alex Leon, of all people! She smiled at herself for having thought of anything sinister in the omniscience of Dennis Bord, as she ushered him into the room. He looked, she told herself, so typical of the administrative side of the Station. So typical of the spirit which had promoted the dance, his gingery dog-like alertness, the red, rigorously conventional moustache, a little at variance, perhaps, with the magnified colourless eyes, but surely unremarkable none the less. The dance had been a success. As one of the organisers, she was pleased about that. It had done them all good. She urged her guests to stay on until Heathley came in.

Then she answered the telephone. It was one of the Security detail wanting Heathley urgently. She suggested calling him in his office, but the man said he had already tried that. "He must be on his way back here . . ." she had begun to explain when she noticed Bord at her elbow. It was not surprising that he should offer to answer any call on the internal telephone system; but she was startled by his alacrity. He might have been awaiting the call.

"Tell him the Professor will be in at any moment," she said, handing the instrument to Bord with a twinge of annoyance. "It can't be as urgent as all that."

"You have to get used to the telephone at all hours over here, Major Seagram," Mem was beginning to explain. "Life is lived at such a pace and my poor son-in-law, Professor Heathley . . ."

"The Deputy has had an accident," Bord interrupted, replacing the telephone. "He's apparently fallen off one of the slipways. He's unconscious. I shall have to go down there. When the Professor comes in . . ."

The telephone went again. It was Heathley himself saying that the Deputy had had an accident.

The wind that blew through the house as the front door opened belonged to the winter. Alex Leon looked helpless, but he left just after the others. The Deputy, he explained, was not just an individual involved in a human mishap. He was part of a pattern affecting everybody. Alex drifted off apologetically, leaving behind him a trace of charm like some rather exotic masculine scent.

What a pity, Lydia thought, another anxiety when he is already so busy. Then she wondered if it would affect Wednesday, not listening to her mother's cheerful gambit about the accidents that had happened, like the time the Major-General went overboard in Bombay.

CHAPTER II

HEATHLEY trembled slightly as they waited in the sick bay for the doctor to report on the Deputy.

"Cold, sir?" said Sam Seagram, who had come along with the rest.

Heathley shrugged his great shoulders and smiled. "Just thinking," he said. "One is always thinking a couple of moves ahead—or trying to, Major Seagram. I hope my mother-in-law gave you a good impression of America?"

"The Memsahib had me beat, Professor. I thought I could hold my own on the subject of the United States, but when she got round to what she calls the native problem. ..."

"He's in a coma," said the doctor from the doorway. "There's nothing anybody can do. I shall have to move him to Tollbury. Somebody had better telephone the Director, who's at Farnborough, I believe."

Everyone looked at Heathley, but it was Dennis Bord who moved to the telephone, saying: "Probably best to reach him through our security people."

"Good idea," Heathley said easily. "Let your people contact him, then I'll speak to him myself. I may as well use the scrambler telephone in my office. We'd better get Tatham to deal with the relatives, if any."

The assurance with which Heathley took command implied no special self-assertiveness. It was quiet and controlled. The doctor acknowledged it. "I'll let you

22

have a progress report, Professor," he said as Heathley went to the door.

Alone in his office, waiting to be put through, Heathley trembled again. He was glad that there was nobody to ask him if he felt cold, for the spasm was due to excitement. He, who never betrayed any feeling in the laboratory, at the test bench or in the air, should have been able to face up to this situation without a tremor. If it had been an abstract problem, he could have done so. It was not, in fact, a problem at all. It was a flesh and blood approach to internal politics. He resented having to withdraw his faculties from the M.7 project for this test of nerves. He had identified himself with it for so long that it cost him an unnatural effort to stand back and narrow the view of it down to administrative detail. For the last ten days he had had to argue about it as if it were just any routine enterprise which Port Amberley had been scheduled to carry out. He had been overruled by higher authority upon this point and that, small issues which did not alter the pattern of the work which had been categorised as Phase I. Upon the larger issues concerning the trials which would be Phase II, he had tried to stand his ground—and had come into conflict with the well-documented obstinacy and the reactionary obstruction of the Deputy. It had been a conflict about methods, rather than fundamentals. For that reason, Heathley had resented it all the more. Younger men like Brian Jackson found is easy to embody the details of administration in their approach to a project. Brian was never distracted by it. That was the result of a more modern training in which such practical considerations, however irksome, had always been taken as a matter of course, or, as the Deputy loved to say, "as the constant element in the co-related planning."

Neither his exasperation over the administrative problems nor his obsession with the abstract thought had caused Heathley to lose sight of the potential influence of this creation of his upon human affairs. If it succeded, it would be of incalculable importance. To whom? To his side. To his organisation. To his country. That alignment of realities he took for granted. To himself also, though materially that seemed of slight importance, for he had never been in material need, or lacked prestige among the people who mattered. Could he deny, though, that it was not a matter of life and death to himself that this, his own creation, should remain in his control?

He looked down at his hands, strong and well-kept. They were uneasy as they waited by the telephone. Not because of that ultimate responsibility to himself, to the human race, to God: but because of the conversation he was about to have with his Director, Sir Hereward Cruddock.

Cruddock must see his point that the only way to handle M.7 was his way. It could not wait and it certainly could not be supervised by a man in a coma. It was a pity that there had not been more direct contact with Cruddock, who, though he was an outstanding Director, had developed a fancy for moving in very high circles indeed, and strenuously living up to his reputation—which, to do him justice, was most impressive. Probably he had had excellent reasons for delegating so much to the Deputy; but it had brought about an intolerably leisurely tempo. Heathley was over-conscious of his own vigour and it distressed him to see it sidetracked and dissipated. How dissipated it had become was borne in upon him when he observed his own excitement as he picked up the emerald green telephone which automatically scrambled conversations with the outside world, enabling him to talk to the Director confidentially, frankly, cogently, putting the case which only the Deputy's removal made possible. In the air while on test he frequently had to act on the spur of the moment. Here was a case for instant and ruthless decision in the dreary world of administration.

"Sorry to hear about the Deputy, Heathley."

"You've heard already, sir?"

"Of course, the Security people told me."

It may have been a case of the proper channels, but it infuriated Heathley because it took the wind out of his sails in an unexpected way. The whole of the work of the Research Station, to be sure, was at issue, but for the moment the Deputy's significance lay most of all in the one sphere of M.7. Heathley had long ceased to bother to think in the terms of seniority, but he supposed that he was the proper person to speak of the Deputy's accident, rather than an administrative officer such as Bord whose position in the chain of command was so nebulous.

"And I've just had a word with the Medical Officer," Cruddock went on.

"I could have given you his report. I waited for it before telephoning," Heathley said irritably.

"Security thought I'd better go through to him direct."

"Did they?" said Heathley with a sigh which Cruddock, whose perceptions were attuned to the moods of individualists, recognised as combative, excited, a little out of control.

"Just routine. Don't let that worry you." He spoke soothingly enough to infuriate Heathley. But Heathley managed to contain himself. He said: "I'm upset, naturally, Sir Hereward, but not worried. We shall go ahead on schedule. I shall tackle the Phase II air tests in my own way just as I've planned to do all the way along. The Deputy and I were almost in agreement about that." *Almost.* It made him sweat to say the word. It was an untruth, but, by God, wasn't his cause just? He could not remember having lied before. His ideas had been too big for that. Why was he lying now? Enthusiasm, fatigue, exasperation? Was he taking a too-easy short cut? Was he risking his integrity? The voice boomed back demolishing these scruples. "Carry on for the time being, Heathley. Let nothing interfere with M.7. Naturally it has priority. Carry on just as you are for the time being."

"For the time being?"

"I shall be back just as soon as my present commitment is through. I shall have to get everything into perspective. You'll have to manage till then."

"I shall carry on with the air-testing, of course." Heathley strove to keep the excitement out of his voice.

"Just stick to the schedule for the time being. . . ."

It was not surprising that he jumped to his feet guiltily when the door of his office began to open. "Get to hell out of it," he said, as he put down the green telephone. Then he saw it was Ilse Leon standing in the doorway with a cigarette cocked in her mouth in that provocative, over-confident way of hers.

"It's usual to knock," he said, frowning, damping down his excitement.

"Sorry, Professor," she said. "It's only a personal visit. I was anxious about the Deputy. I knew you'd be the one person who would know. . . ."

"What on earth are you doing in the Experimental Block tonight after a dance?"

"Oh, the dance stimulated me, I suppose," she said

—and she too seemed to be lying. "You know that plastics problem you put me on to? It suddenly began to work out. We'll go ahead on schedule with Phase II, I suppose?"

"Of course. Why not?" Heathley was himself, self-assured, genial, looking down into the restless intensity of her eyes. She was one who never took anything on trust, he had always noticed. It was a useful quality in the laboratory, but it was exhausting in personal relationships.

"You didn't say how the Deputy was, Professor," she said, using his ash-tray.

"He's in a coma. Going into hospital."

She blinked at him as if she were sharing some confidence. He switched off his desk light. He wanted to hurry back to Lydia, though he was too excited now to sleep. Thank God there was Lydia to take him out of himself, and the Memsahib to fuss over him, and the children, secure in their sleep, to renew that sense of tranquillity without which life was not worth living.

"This is a ridiculous hour of night for a keen scientist," he laughed, going round the desk and patting Ilse in a heavy, avuncular manner. "Why doesn't brother Alex look after you and take you home?"

"Alex leads his own life. I lead mine. We've never known what you call a family life." Her eyes darkened. She had not responded to his smile. Without her glasses, her face took on a piquancy, very alien, very demanding, almost predatory. Heathley remembered her record, the dispersal of her family by persecution, the academic brilliance and the concentration camp upbringing. It had made her hard. Without her spectacles, she was like a person seen for the first time out of a familiar uniform. There were unforeseen qualities, but they still seemed to be hard. Before he could think

27

of any gallant answer, she was saying: "But I needn't tell you that. Everything is known about all of us in this place. You probably have my life history in that filing cabinet."

It was true. He kept a précis of the records of all the staff in the department. From every point of view, hers was one of the most satisfactory. She had been fearless and single-minded. She came of a great scientific family and, in spite of all that she had been through, she seemed to have inherited their best qualities. As a worker, she was worth two of her brother Alex. Though he had proved amenable to the discipline of research and she had been too questioning, too eager, too awkward, she was the more creative. That was all in the Personnel File in the cabinet.

Heathley smiled and said: "Yes, my dear, it's an astonishing filing system."

He was reaching for his hat, dismissing her politely, when she said, her voice vibrant, sharp, urgent: "But you'll be able to have your own way over the M.7 project now, won't you, Professor?"

"I won't discuss matters of policy," he said, with aggressive coldness. He lifted down his hat and bowed formally toward the door. She had forfeited her rights as a woman. She was a member of the staff and the interview was at an end. Heathley curbed the turbulence of his own excitement, within a show of formal courtesy. "Good night now," he snapped, holding the door. "We shall issue a statement about the Deputy tomorrow."

She put on her spectacles before she left the room. She seemed to shrink back into herself. She did not apologise or make any move to meet his official attitude. She hugged her briefcase and said, "Good night, Professor," with that synthetic correctness of English which

28

may have come from any country in Europe. He was left with the lingering feeling that she had put him to some test, that her alertness, her appeal, her dignity had been calculated. He thought about it for a full minute, standing there by the door wearing his hat. Then, like a man acting out a dream, he went back to the green telephone and asked for the Security Officer.

"You may think it a bit odd at this time of night, but I'd be glad if you'd make a check-up on Ilse Leon. I've nothing whatever to report. No panic, old boy. Just a precautionary thought. I knew you'd still be in your office, otherwise I'd have left it till the morning."

Bord answered crisply, just as if it were a matter of daytime routine. Heathley put down the telephone and found himself wondering why he made the call. It was not out of irritation or any vindictive spirit. He had simply felt puzzled about Ilse Leon and one checked up automatically when one was puzzled by anybody—why?

He put down the telephone, went to the door and switched off the light. But almost as soon as he had let himself out, he was halted in the corridor by a sense of incompleteness, as if he had been thinking and talking too much and had left some practical thing undone. The corridor was brightly lit and empty. Ilse had gone. Yet just for a moment the feeling came over him that he was being watched. He shook that off at once but he went back to his office to see if everything was locked up. How jittery he was! He had, of course, locked up hours ago before the dance. He had gone back to the office only to use the green telephone. How could anything be unlocked? But there was that absurd sense of excitement which he could not quell.

His conversation with the Director had left his own approach to Phase II of the M.7 project wide open. He could give himself entirely over to his own methods, though the Director's go-ahead had been so cautious and conditional. His own methods were risky. Inspired experiments often were. He was not that kind of extremist who would urge that human life was expendable. Nevertheless, he was enough of a realist to calculate the millons of lives that the successful application of M.7 would affect, to measure his human risks in these terms.

He mooned round the room, and smiled at the photograph of Lydia. Such an evening as this would have been intolerable without the thought of her. That thought might have become a habit, but it was the one reality amid the ever-changing values of the abstract.

He switched the desk light on and off idly and then he noticed the glint of the key by the wastepaper basket. He had been right to come back after all. He picked it up, then fished out his own key-ring and found it was the key of the filing cabinet. Probably one of the nightwatchmen or the office cleaner would have found it. But it was not the sort of thing which the head of the department should have left lying about. Heathley yawned, slipped it in his pocket and left the office. He would tell Lydia that he was slipping if she were still waiting up.

The finding of the key, in fact, did Heathley good. He strode down the corridor jingling it in his pocket, whistling to himself. If it had been part of an unpleasant nervous tension to go back into the room, the small discovery had enabled him to throw it off. He was a fit man both from choice and necessity. The rigours of air-testing demanded a high standard of physical fitness, in spite of long hours of theoretical study. Heathley breathed in the night air and with it a hint of spring. He had assimilated his excitement and he felt good.

Lydia's voice was cold and there was a strange wariness in her eyes.

"You shouldn't have waited up, darling," he said, delighted that she had done so.

"I just wanted to make sure that everything was all right." Her smile was brief and nervous. She waited impassively while he told her about the Deputy. Then she said: "I hope it's not going to mean a lot more work and responsibility for you."

For some unexplained reason, he was disappointed when she said this. He brushed it aside. He was even a little brusque in his large hearty way. They went to bed, talking about the success of the dance, feeling that something had been left unsaid, their voices subdued not to wake the children.

CHAPTER III

WHEN Bord put down his telephone and said: "Heathley wants to check up on Ilse Leon," Felix Tatham whistled and said: "That's a case of mind-reading. Sam Seagram was asking about her."

"Just a hunch I had as we were driving back here to your office." Sam stood up and yawned.

"I suppose we'd better have her file. I've got it in the next-door office." Felix languidly slid off the desk to get it.

"Isn't it a kind of an odd time of night to ask for a check-up, Colonel?" Sam Seagram wondered.

"Anything can happen at any moment in any twenty-four hours in this place," the Security Officer explained, with a touch of pride. "Security is fortunately timeless. You'll soon see that there are no real office hours in this show. I'm only too pleased when departmental heads like Heathley ring up all of a sudden at some odd hour. If it does nothing else, it shows that they've got the right idea about Security being a round-the-clock business."

Sam Seagram stretched his long leathery body. "I guess you fellows are picking things up all the time. Even at a get-together like that dance tonight. I may have got bitten in the end by the Memsahib, but I figure that party taught me a lot. I like to take a look at them when they're relaxed—and I've got a mighty big job weighing people up around here."

"Pity we've a near-corpse on our hands just as you

32

arrive," Bord said. "You may get some idea of how we tackle things, but it gives a completely false first impression of this god-forsaken brain-factory. For months and months nothing whatever happens at Port Amberley. Everybody gets on with their job. Everything ticks over nicely and discreetly, as it has done for years. Everybody has 'flu in the winter because of the climate and the central heating. Now and then some unlucky type gets knocked down or caught up in the machinery or something. But, apart from public convulsions like the Fuchs or Pontecorvo rows, we haven't a thing on our minds. Then the moment you come and I introduce you round as a harmless personnel Liaison Officer, the Deputy walks off a slipway and finishes up in a coma."

Sam Seagram laughed. "And you all turn on the new boy and ask *did he fall or was he pushed?*"

"Until he wakes up and gives us the answer himself, that's what we're bound to ask. We've got a man at his bedside all night who'll call out if he snaps out of it suddenly."

"That's fair enough. You can't take anything for granted in a set-up like this. And you know your man. Egocentric, as you say, self-opinionated but a first-class administrative scientist. Much too egocentric for suicide. Not important enough for murder, or is he? It would take a master spy to tell us that. But there, he's not even dead and tomorrow, maybe, he'll start looking sheepish and tell you he just fell over."

Dennis Bord gave him a quick look of discreet suspicion. He had frankly resented the arrival of a Personnel Liaison Officer, particularly an American, even after the Director had "made it all right" by pointing out that such projects as M.7 were an international responsibility.

"If this were just an ordinary factory," he said, "making spades and buckets, and one of the Directors took a header after a staff dance—and, by the way, both the Doc. and our own check-up agreed that he'd had quite a few drinks—it really wouldn't mean a thing. The local papers might like it and probably they wouldn't get it. But just because this is Port Amberley, where the destiny of the human race is being chucked about by a bunch of all too human if slightly absent-minded scientists, our melancholy task is to behave like stage detectives." At such moments, his Irish rhetoric got the better of Dennis Bord, and he enjoyed himself.

Sam was relieved. He was beginning at least to get behind the stiff upper lip. It had crossed his mind that both Bord and Tatham might be over-dramatizing a fairly straightforward misfortune. Any accident involving the Deputy Director might have serious repercussions upon closely integrated routine work. There seemed little point, nevertheless, in prolonging the present session.

So far the facts, as Bord rather dogmatically set them out, were unexceptional. There was a group of slipways about equidistant between the Recreation Centre and the Experimental Block. The two nightwatchmen on duty in that part of the Station had not paid any particular attention to the Deputy's motor car which was parked, as it often was, at the head of one of the slipways. It was only when one of them had noticed a door of the car standing open that he had walked over to investigate. Probing around with his torch, he had discovered the Deputy lying a few yards away in shallow water and mud.

Did he fall or was he pushed? There were no signs of a struggle. He had not been robbed. He was given to fits of abstraction when he would stand or sit looking out to sea. Only a few steps from the door would have taken him to the side of the slipway.

"It seems to me," said Sam, "that you boys have got to work hard to get anything sinister out of this."

Bord shrugged his shoulders. "Anything that happens to anybody connected with M.7 must be rated as sinister, until the opposite is proved. Of course I don't have the operational knowledge to assess the Deputy's exact value, but my guess is that his dropping out, even if it proves to be temporary, will leave a big hole."

"Which Professor Heathley will fill?"

"You bet Heathley will fill it."

"I wonder if that was what Heathley was thinking about when he was watching the Deputy during the dance, when you were introducing me to his wife."

Bord shot another half-suspicious, half-irritable look. "Come, come. We may have some fanatics around here, but not Heathley. He's been in the service since he was an apprentice at Farnborough. He's not the sort who would want to go and push a superior officer into the drink. Who was the Deputy dancing with to cause Heathley to stare?"

"The physicist girl—what's her name?—Ilse?"

"Here's her file," said Felix Tatham through the open door. "Does the plot thicken?"

"What's she been doing to worry Heathley beside dancing with the Deputy?"

"She's been to Oxford twice. Her uncle's there and he's all right. A few concerts in London. Telephone calls as innocent as the day. No mystery tours. No love letters abroad. All in order up to this evening—stop-press." Felix Tatham threw down the file. "This

35

dossier business sometimes makes me just a little sick, between ourselves."

"It wouldn't be too bad," said Sam, thoughtfully, "if it were just the routine stuff that mattered. The sickening side of it is what really matters is how people are leading their lives. From what I've seen of this bunch tonight as an outsider with an objective view, I'd say that your Deputy just fell. . . . But I wouldn't like to leave it at that."

"If he comes out of his coma," Bord said tartly, "he'll probably agree with you. Perhaps he'll even explain that he got out to relieve himself after rather a good party and toppled in."

They left it at that, and Bord was very nearly right. When the Deputy regained consciousness during the night, he murmured to the watching Security man: "Entirely my own fault." Then, to the dismay of everybody, he said no more and died.

CHAPTER IV

WHEN Brian heard about the death of the Deputy, caution rather than sensibility prevented him from feeling pleased. He frowned when Alex Leon blew out cigarette smoke and said in his clipped synthetic English: "Now perhaps we may all move up one."

Brian himself was thinking just that. "He'll leave quite a hole certainly," he said without turning to look at Alex. "Poor old chap! What a ridiculous thing to happen—after all the flying he's done."

"Accidents will happen," Alex was never at a loss for the exact English phrase. "At least I suppose it was an accident."

Brian started. "What else could it be, Alex?"

"My dear boy, if you had seen as much sabotage as I have, you'd believe in fairies before you believed in accidents."

"Sabotage is the result of bad security," Brian argued automatically, "and in any case you're talking about equipment, not people."

Alex sighed. "There are times when human beings are almost as important as equipment. Trained people, that is. An act of sabotage, or an accident, involving an important man can be terrifically important—but terrifically...." He rolled the r's, relishing his favourite adverb.

"Not if a programme is well enough organised," Brian argued. "This business won't have any fundamental effect upon M.7. Even if it were sabotage—

which, of course, it isn't—there would have been precious little object in it. It would need somebody to blow up the whole lot of us. And that would only mean promotion for a lot of other people who are probably hoping that one day. . . ."

He stopped speaking because he was beginning to think aloud. He sometimes saw himself as a promoter might view a large-scale enterprise. His integrity as a scientist was the basic treasure, to be guarded with his very life. His capacity as a scientist was something to be promoted. His brain and his body were functional elements powering the whole enterprise. It was this self-analysis which sometimes made him talk of himself like a third person, breaking through his shyness and unexpectedly impressing people.

Brian scrutinised the Port Amberley organisation with the clarity of an efficiency chart the moment he knew that the Deputy would never come back to work there. He weighed all the moves, calculated all possible surprises and did not hesitate also to measure the event in personal terms. There was little enough reason for him to be resentful about the outspokenness of Alex, but he belonged by blood to a people who always calculated, but always were reticent. The bland surmises of Alex outraged him slightly.

The man's good-humoured volatility, he knew, concealed strength and intelligence. Alex wore his charm, like his expensive clothes, with a worldly but self-conscious air. He appeared too anxious to be considered an ordinary man of the world, it might well have been because he had emerged from unspeakable darknesses of body and mind, fighting every inch of the way.

Brian could admire a colleague, trust a friend, revere achievement. He was not lacking in generosity, but he needed always to measure against himself. He had travelled alone, wary as a cat. One day, he was prepared to allow, love might change the feline singleness of this focus. He had thought much about that, too, with a great show of objectivity, but he had long been mature enough not to trust theories. The unpredictability of his own passions scared him. Passions? Sometimes he seemed to be able to dismiss them as lusts, but he was never sure.

That was a subject in which Alex revelled. He would talk with equal delight and precision about what was coarse and what was delicate. Just as he had deliberately mastered the language, he had found some lasting poise between passion and affection. It might look like cynicism, but it was too vital for that. From the very beginning, Brian had been attracted by Alex, not only because he admired his abilities, which were in fact exceptional, but because of that mature alien nature of his. The spoken English might be smooth, the clothes might be just right, the manner easy and assured; but still that nature was tempered by suffering. Brian had begun by being sorry for Alex and Ilse. They had lost a way of life, a family, a language. Even their name was a convenient abbreviation of something or other which was too long for the English to pronounce. Neither Alex nor Ilse, however, would tolerate pity. They knew their worth. They stood on their feet. They did not even rely upon each other, though their work had kept them together. They lived with a sister who kept house for them, a curiously foreign establishment with heavy vulgar modern furniture mingling with their few personal possessions, a transitory encampment rather than a home, with the stout elderly sister padding about all day in carpet slippers.

His sympathy rejected out of hand, Brian soon

39

recognised the wary appetite for life which existed behind the slick tailoring of Alex. It sometimes seemed indeed as if Alex carried about with him the experience of more than one lifetime. It was impossible to judge his age. His dark lithe body was that of youth. His blowing of smoke rings and his closing of heavy-lidded eyes, on the other hand, sometimes suggested one who was timelessly old. His self-assurance in the laboratory or on the test bench was that of the matured scientist in his prime.

It was because of the many contrasts between them that Brian and Alex got on so well. But even as he winced at Alex's blatant talk about people moving up, Brian was assessing the exact position of Alex in relation to himself. He thought, too, of all the thousands of qualified, ambitious people in the background ready and available to take over. This thought perhaps was a little fevered, but it was part of his inner insecurity that it loomed like a recurring childish nightmare.

"Sabotage is a singularly potent weapon," Alex was saying from some depth of his own experience. "Its greatest effect is in the elimination of some vital part, or, if you like, some individual. Neither need be of top significance. That sort of thing may well be more damaging than the blowing-up of the whole which is often too heroic to be sinister. No, it is the throwing out of gear of the great works by the small discrepancy —the tiniest of spanners in the biggest works—by which sabotage gets home. The same applies to people. A small treachery, a trifling accident"—the eyelids drooped like brocaded curtains over those consuming too-bright eyes—"the little spanner of a single man's life can have terrific results—but terrific!"

Brian laughed. He was meant to: but Alex's eloquence on one of his favourite subjects sent a peculiar shock through him. His outlook and training resented the implication that such things were possible here and now in Port Amberley. Yet it was in fact true that the next phase of M.7 would be affected by the news they had just received.

The conference called by Heathley confirmed this. Heathley began with a formal announcement of the death of the Deputy. He looked almost nervous, but he spoke dogmatically to the little gathering of specialists concerned with M.7. "In case there are any of you who may not have heard. . . ." Alex smiled at this, and Brian could see his lips forming the words "as if any of us wouldn't." Brian himself thought it odd that the Professor made quite such a solemn opening; but soon he guessed that it was a cover for some excitement or tension which Heathley was hoping to conceal.

"This unfortunate event will not, of course, affect the work on this project," Heathley declaimed, peering at them almost as if he expected some opposition.

"I spoke to the Director himself on the telephone last night after the mishap and he at once agreed that our plans would go forward in the ordinary way. Naturally I had to speak to him again today to break the news. As you may know, he has gone to the Aeronautical Research Establishment on attachment to the same very important mission which came here. It's not possible for him to break that commitment immediately though, of course, he wishes to return here at the earliest possible moment, if not in time for the inquest." Heathley lowered his voice on a carefully controlled note of reverence. Then he drew a deep sigh, as if to let out his real feelings, and continued more briskly: "Now I needn't remind you that we're ready for the beginning of Phase II in our programme. This is an opportunity I must take, since you are all

41

together, to express a word of appreciation for the teamwork and patience which has brought us so successfully to the end of Phase I. I know that the Deputy himself had meant to say that. He told me so during my last conference with him on the procedure we shall adopt. Phase II will be more exacting for all of us, particularly for those concerned with the airborne tests. The programme for these was mapped out between the Deputy and myself as recently as yesterday. There are two methods of approach, as you know. The more orthodox one is to build up our data wholly on instrumentation and ground control. We have everything prepared for this. A less orthodox, speedier and more effective approach, is by human participation outside the limits imposed by ground control."

They stirred uneasily. Alex's lips formed the words: "Now we're coming to it." Brian, though he was hanging on every word, became absorbed, too, in a kind of counter-point contemplation of the features of Ilse Leon, who had taken off her spectacles, whose warm colouring defied the bleak tobacco haze. She puzzled and disquieted him. She was the one individual in the room whose immediate thoughts he could not interpret. She was one whose support he most craved.

The others, he knew, would be divided upon the question of method, which Heathley, in spite of the excitement he was suppressing, propounded so lucidly. Brian himself had always sided with the orthodoxy from which the late Deputy had never budged. Now, even before Heathley had come to the point, he could see why everyone in the room was stirring. Was Heathley going to take immediate advantage of the Director's absence to insist on having his own way? Or was it possible that he had really persuaded the Deputy to countenance the plan? Brian respected Heathley above all men and he was ashamed of the doubt in his mind. His respect, his admiration and his gratitude amounted almost to a worship for Heathley's character. Nevertheless, it was reasoned enough to observe Heathley's actions judicially. As the tempo of Phase I had increased and the prospect of Phase II had come nearer, it had been clear that Heathley was becoming increasingly restless, uncompromising and ruthless.

"We shall carry out Phase II tests," Heathley was saying, "by both methods, but the direct method of human participation will be tried first and will predominate." He looked round again and smiled, both with an undertone of aggressiveness. "We all understand one another, I hope. One likes these meetings to be an exchange of confidence. Do not hesitate, anybody, to raise any issue of general principle while we are all here." Heathley stressed this informality by lighting his pipe with a steady hand.

Brian found himself speaking with a moment's premeditation, as if some conflict within him had resolved almost in spite of himself. "It might give us a great deal of additional confidence if we had the positive assurance of the late Deputy that this policy has the full backing of the authorities."

"You mean you lack confidence, Brian?" The match did not waver. Heathley swallowed and blew out smoke, his eyes excited and demanding.

The Scots engineer called Baird, who rarely spoke, started nodding his head energetically, throwing out his elbows and muttering: "Aye, but there's something in what Brian says."

"It's not a question of lacking confidence in yourself, obviously, Heathley," Brian said. "But so much of the administration of this project has depended upon the Deputy's relationships with higher authorities that I

43

thought that if he had left any explicit instructions. . . ."

"You've been in this service long enough, Brian, surely, to realize that such a job as this, with profoundly important international implications, is not one which depends upon the authority of a single man. Phase I has been successful. Phase II and Phase III have been authorised." Heathley leant back and folded his arms. "Need I say any more?"

He was clever like that. He could always present a long view, making it seem that others were immersed in detail. Brian wished he had not spoken. He was ashamed that the uneasiness which he shared with several others in that room had got the better of his native caution. Heathley continued to grin at him, grateful perhaps for his having provided just the opening he needed. Others glanced quickly at him; and he knew they were supporters. Brian half turned to watch Ilse, but she gave no sign.

Over the murmur of conversation, Heathley raised his resonant voice once more. "Before we circulate the schedule and go into details, are there any other general questions from you people?"

"Just a word about the air tests, sir," came the rich, grumbling voice of Baird. "We shall need a very full instructional period with the test pilots. In fact, sir, I am bound to say, now that we're all here, I'm wondering if it's right—and by that I mean *morally* right—to ask them to take it on?"

"What chaps you Scotsmen are for morals," Heathley called back, over people's heads. "But the question of morals is hardly likely to arise in the opening stages of Phase II on Thursday. I'm going to carry out the tests myself."

There was a silence: then everybody talked at once.

44

Heathley was as well qualified as anyone in the world to carry out the Phase II tests. There were even good reasons for his doing them. There were also a hundred reasons for him not to. Before any one of them could bring their minds down to any cogent or persuasive comment, Heathley was striding athletically away up the corridor in the direction of the testing sheds.

CHAPTER V

JUST as they submitted to the exigences of Security, everyone at Port Amberley accepted the element of danger which went with the routine work of the Station. Airborne and waterborne trials often involved exceptional risks to the specialists and test pilots who undertook them. The whole community would be keyed up when such special tasks were in hand, though these undercurrents of anxiety rarely showed themselves. There was nothing abstract or spiritual about this self-discipline. It was simply recognised that Port Amberley existed to test machines and equipment to breaking-point. Human beings were not there to be tested to such extremes. Any human risks involved were accidental. Cruddock had always said that human risk needed even stricter control than any other aspect of air experiment.

Though direct references were rarely made to them, at home, Lydia usually guessed from Heathley's manner when a special test was in the offing, for there were a number of small personal clues. He would be suddenly obsessed with physical fitness. He would give up alcohol and become pernickety about food. He would show the strain of his responsibility, whether he was flying himself or not, in over-acting his unconcern. Sometimes he would betray himself by acts of small elaborate tenderness toward Lydia and the children.

Even before Lydia perceived such signs, the Memsahib unfailingly foretold them. She claimed that she was aided in this by second sight. In fact, she relied upon her comprehensive knowledge of other people's affairs. Her voice would take on the vibrant note of pride of a woman accustomed to seeing menfolk off to the crusades: "We all know that there's no true service without danger. There's nothing new or even unusual in men accepting risks for the Good of the Cause. Think of the number of times the Colonel exposed himself to danger on the Frontier, when so many others were playing polo or, worse still, twiddling their thumbs in England. Mind you, Lydia, I'm talking about a time when India was India. . . ."

It was with such admonitions that the old lady greeted the return of Heathley from his morning conference. He came in quietly and joked about the Memsahib's encounter with Sam Seagram. Her attitude towards America was famous, and the story had already gone the rounds with the morning coffee, as did all the domestic anecdotes of Port Amberley. He said nothing about the Deputy. He insisted upon there being plenty of time to go out and play with the children in the sandpit before lunch. It was almost as if there were not all that much time left to play with the children.

"I think it's one of those days, Lydia, when you and he should have your lunch together in front of the fire and leave me to cope with the young," Mem suggested. "He ought to be allowed just to have a quiet time. Obviously he'll want to talk to you about the Deputy. . . ."

Lydia was grateful. There were times when the old lady's instincts more than compensated for the days when she told her dreams, flung herself into the Good of a Cause, or remembered half a century of garrison life. Yet, even as Lydia agreed with her, she felt a deep uneasiness amounting almost to panic. There was no

47

good reason for it, but she did not want to be alone with Heathley. She did not want to know about the Deputy, and how his mishap would affect the work in hand. She was afraid of the easy subterfuges by means of which Heathley would cover up the urgency of his real feelings. She dreaded the strain of pretending not to know how he would take advantage of the accident to press forward his own schemes.

That was what narrowed life down. That was what was confining her heart which had leapt with the spring breeze. It had been an act of loyalty to accept the isolation of that community devoted to ends which were never revealed. That isolation and the reticences which went with it were constantly closing in. Even the idea of their lunching alone, because there was "something in the wind" gave her a momentary repugnance.

"Lydia, dear! You mustn't quake like that," her mother said. "We must all do our best to make things bright and cheerful for Heathley. I expect it's such a worrying time."

Over lunch, they talked, of course, about the Deputy's death. Without knowing why she did so, Lydia wept a few tears for him. "He was so utterly unlikeable," she sighed, "so stuffy, so tiresome. He thought he had the spirit of eternal youth, too, which was such a bore. That's why he kept dancing with Ilse Leon, telling her, as he used to tell all of us, that he wished he had not become such an administrative cog." She blew her nose and Heathley let his hand fall on her shoulder. "Don't take any notice of me, Arthur. I'm always sorry for people when they're such bores."

"You're really sorry for him because he's dead." Heathley kissed her forehead, not thinking of the Deputy at all but only of Lydia herself, his shared happiness, his very hold on life.

48

"I should not be sorry for the dead, but I am."

Heathley laughed. "I suppose I'm too concerned with the living. . . ."

"But aren't you sorry for him?" she cut in quickly. "To have been so painstaking about everything, then to have fallen into one of the slipways. He probably was just an administrative cog, but I'm sure he would rather have gone on being that than——"

"How do you know, Lydia, you silly? I can't bear the idea of your getting morbid."

"It's all right for you; with your analytical mind, I wouldn't expect you to see it the way I do." She spoke without bitterness. "To you, it's just another worry, I know. When's the Director coming back?" It cost her an effort to ask this question for it led directly to the tricky question of who would be the Deputy's successor. With characteristic partisanship, she had already begun to think of a thousand reasons for Heathley being the only possible choice. It was not, in fact, a foregone conclusion. Another man might be chosen from among the senior specialists at Port Amberley. A man might be brought in from another establishment, though this seemed on the face of it unlikely because of the specialist character of M.7 and the progress which had already been made. The creative impulse had been Heathley's, though so much of the work was of necessity shared with others. Then Heathley was a natural leader . . . hadn't he assumed leadership in the absence of the Director? Lydia wanted to speak openly about this. Her duty was to encourage and support him. Yet, when she made the effort to lead up to the subject, Heathley only hedged, concealing his real ambition, that undefined force which sometimes caused her such disquiet.

"We shall carry on just as before, until the Director

comes back," he said, "and I don't suppose even a new appointment can have any immediate effects. It's an unhappy business, of course. Everybody was very upset about it at the conference this morning. There will be some sort of inquiry and an inquest. But Felix Tatham and Dennis Bord will handle all that between them." He kissed her again carefully and added: "Sorry, Lydia, I didn't mean to talk all this shop at lunch. You've got your golf match with Brian tomorrow. How would it be if we drove into Tollbury tonight for dinner?"

Lydia smiled. The forward planning of social events was a sure sign that Heathley was about to give himself up to some special test. She longed to break down his reticence, to be frank and open with him, for it was so obvious that he was still drawing so much from their life together, and yet there could be so much more for both of them. All that she said was: "I'm afraid we can't make it this evening. Mem has one of her Guild meetings in the village. I'd hate to interfere with that."

The way she said it was disappointing. She could not seem to get the flat tone out of her voice. Heathley knew it would be unreasonable to look ruffled. Instead he forced himself to suggest cheerfully that he would cook an omelette and that afterwards they might invite the new American in, and perhaps Ilse Leon and Brian Jackson. Even though he said this on the spur of the moment, there were threads of purpose in the working of his mind. He needed to weigh up the newcomer, Sam Seagram. He needed to satisfy himself that there had been nothing behind Brian Jackson's question which had given him the opening at the conference that morning. He needed to compensate Ilse in some small measure for his perfunctory dismissal of her from his office the night before.

The sun came out. Heathley opened the glass doors leading to the garden. They stood there counting the first spring flowers. His large hand closed over hers. He said: "Just as soon as things have sorted themselves out, we'll take a holiday. It's quite time that you had a break from all this. It's so easy for one to get too absorbed."

She knew then that he had noticed that flat tone which she had been unable to keep out of her voice. "Getting away will do us both good, I suppose," she said, "but it isn't only a respite from the place and the people. . . . What you need is to step right back from it all, to give yourself time to be an ordinary man—and I don't mean a dull man. Don't think I'm running down that sense of duty the Memsahib is so keen on. She brought me up to understand its value. What she means though, is simple and humdrum compared with this . . . this strain of detachment. The trouble is that we're both getting so used to it we don't notice how ugly it is. . . ."

She left the sentence in the air because she did not know where it was leading her. She was only aware of the compulsion to probe Heathley, to probe beneath the great solid handsome personality of the man and force some answering simplicity, the simplicity which was the essential balm her heart desired.

If Heathley, overwrought, over-excited, over-stimulated by anticipation had not winced and dodged and withheld from her at that moment, the sickness in her heart might have eased. Instead he answered her with a warm but facile sympathy. "You always have such a complete understanding of these things, Lydia. You have a greater talent for objectivity than a good many scientists. Of course, I understand what you mean. Abstract thought is a kind of prison in itself. It is only your understanding which rescues somebody like myself from a life sentence. I acknowledge that and I'm grateful for it. It keeps any work in some kind of perspective. It would otherwise be so easy to be blinded, to think too much about ultimate effects." He sighed, looking across the garden toward the gentle slopes to the fields and the villages inland. "One is too involved, and the work is too important. To break it suddenly would be like a doctor giving up healing or a preacher changing his cloth. But that won't prevent us from going away, from having time off, away from it all, even from thinking." He squeezed her arm and laughed. He liked these confidences. He was not even conscious of how much he was holding back.

She laughed, too, in spite of her inner confusion. She was intelligent enough, but she was not an intellectual. She was not articulate beyond the immediate limits of day-to-day life. There were feelings which she knew she could not explain. She could not even begin to mention, for instance, the deep unpredictable glints of wanton happiness she had experienced, the ecstasies of trifling disloyalty. She remembered the Red Indian look of Brian, the soft resonance of his voice. She despised herself but she still remembered them.

"It's good to have talked, Lydia. It clears the air," Heathley said, standing out on the lawn. "It saves one from being too circumscribed by all this . . . the mesh." He waved toward the living quarters which crowded in upon their flank.

Theirs was an end house, a little larger than most because of Heathley's status and the size of their family. It had an upper storey, which in Port Amberley was such a mark of distinction that Felix Tatham sometimes amused himself by talking about "the upper-storey snobs." Because they were all keen gardeners, they had contrived to give the place some character, though the front of it faced an uncompromising concrete roadway and the end of the garden was divided only by tattered boundary wire from the belt of fallow land which sealed off the Research Station from the surrounding country. By obstinate and relentless cadging, the Memsahib had created a rock-garden out of broken concrete. Heathley had made a lawn and a children's playground. Lydia had laid out flower-beds and vegetable patches. In that synthesis of uprooted people and prefabricated buildings, their patch, with its ugly squat house, had an atmosphere all of its own. They had brought a sense of well-being and leisureliness to one corner of the upstart place.

Port Amberley was raw and incomplete. Whenever Lydia looked out of a window, there were workmen starting or finishing jobs. They would be laying drains, fixing cables or planting the domed shrubs which the Director referred as "amenities of the future." Trucks would drive out over the shiny soft grass of the waste land beyond the garden to dump rubbish. The concrete bungalows stood out like teeth upon the skyline to the east where there might have been a view of the sea. They were occupied by people who lived there for expediency, not choice; who earned good money and were content with their families and their possessions but who rarely spared any thought for their surroundings in spite of the Green Finger Committee who organised garden competitions.

"But why are they digging holes over there on the other side?" Heathley said, pointing with his pipe. "You'd better keep an eye on that, Lydia. The construction people are mad enough to put up anything anywhere."

"They often dig holes," Lydia said lightly. "But if

they come anywhere near our garden boundary wire, Mem is on them like a knife."

"Shall I have a word with the construction people when I go back to the office this afternoon?"

"Don't bother. You've such a lot of more important things to worry about."

He frowned. "I don't want you to get the idea that I'm worrying, Lydia. I can't afford to worry."

She did not weigh up how seriously he spoke. She did not think about the words at all. She felt them. They entered right into her, clamping down upon her spirit like an occupying army. *I can't afford to worry*. The phrase kept repeating itself senselessly long after he had kissed her goodbye. She dealt with the children. Then she went outside again, idly watching the men digging holes, and waving to her mother who was setting off purposefully, in black silk, to take the bus to High Sonding.

She had come to hate not just the uncouthness of the place, but that remote, withdrawn, secretive element in Heathley's character which was so obsessed with power that it made him say that he could not afford to worry. Yet it was power, something inhuman and ungodly but infinitely compelling, causing Heathley to live upon two levels, only one of which she could ever share. This was an hysterical thought, perhaps. It was born of being so close to so much which was elaborately secretive, of hearing people speak in the disguised language demanded by Security, of the nagging tension of research and experiment always experienced at second-hand. Was it not in fact life lived at second-hand?

There! The thought reached out and touched her as she stood by one of their horticultural treasures, the early prunus whose buds were like reddish bruises against the sullen pallor of the sky. She had been un-

54

faithful to Heathley in her heart and now, alone in the chilly contemplation of the afternoon, she had found an afterthought to justify herself. An afterthought and not a sudden defiant notion? No: because it expressed the mounting hysteria of discontent which caused that flat tone in her voice.

She watched the men lugging along concrete posts. To have gone over to ask them what they were doing would have broken her sense of reverie. Very likely Heathley would appeal to the construction people after all. It would demonstrate his efficiency, his attention to detail. In any case, the Memsahib had probably found out already, for she rarely let a job as close as that pass without investigation. She thought of Brian Jackson again as she went indoors to prepare the children's tea. She did this deliberately to steady her restlessness, to salve the flutter in her heart. Then came the discovery which made her bite her lip and stand there looking at the frosted glass of the scullery window as if it revealed a vista she dare not take her eyes off. There was a paradoxical duplicity about her thoughts. Her dream-world blazed with a double image. The superficial attraction of Brian Jackson and the reality of Alex Leon— his texture, enigmatic, opaque, but triumphantly assertive.

Alone in the kitchen, she laughed. It was so fantastic, this discovery. It was like going to the jam cupboard to steal—she had done it in her teens at Camberley— and becoming recklessly drunk on a heady port wine. The justification lingered, but it did not explain the enchanting madness. She had felt that life was beginning to pass her by; then she had swung to the other extreme and given way to this intoxication which was falling in love with love.

She told herself that she ought to make some kind of

confession to Heathley, perhaps even to laugh it off, though it involved loyalty, and her world was girdered with loyalties. But what a monstrous thing to try to tell Heathley, at a time when he said he couldn't afford to worry. She answered the telephone. She attended to the children. Usually she could absorb herself in pleasant chores, but today a glimmer of restless defiance came back. He could afford to let her be half alive but he could not afford to worry. Why should she worry about her wayward enchantment? Why should she not find ways out of this . . . he himself had called it a mesh? She trembled with a kind of exultation as she called to the children.

Evidently they had sneaked away to the sand-pit, for they answered from outdoors. A moment later Giles, with Heathley's blue eyes and rich ruddy colouring, came storming in through the back door. "Do you know what the men are doing, Mummy?"

Lydia squatted quickly and took him in her arms. She had forgotten the workmen. She closed her eyes and smiled, because she knew that she was not disloyal to her family, to fundamentals. "I expect Mem knows what they're up to. We'll ask her when she comes back, shall we?"

"But we can see, Mummy. We've been watching." Giles had seen her smile and thought she was being coy. "We know what it is. It's to make us safe!"

"What is? Mummy hasn't been watching, darling."

"Come and look. Elizabeth's still out there watching them. They're putting up prickle-wire."

It was a barbed-wire fence, outside the garden boundary, but hemming them in, with jagged lines across the view of the distant villages. Lydia saw it through a blur of tears. She could not speak for the rush of frightened protesting sobs.

"There's Colonel Dennis," cried Giles, "coming in with Elizabeth."

Bord loomed against the amber western sky. He was talking to Elizabeth but he smiled steadily toward Lydia as she waited shivering on the lawn.

"What is this beastly thing they've put up?" she called hysterically.

"Sorry if it's rather unsightly. It's just a security measure. Hope you don't mind my coming through your garden. I saw the children and I'm more or less wired in myself!"

Lydia tried to quell the physical panic by turning her back on the wire and inviting Dennis Bord to have a cup of tea. "Can't afford to take any chances, you know," he barked as he entered the house. "Sorry if it's upset you."

"I'm not really upset, only startled."

"Don't want to upset Heathley either." He ignored her rather shaky protest. "He looked a bit strained, I thought, when I saw him this morning. It's a worrying time...."

Lydia rallied herself. "Heathley just can't afford to worry." She spoke graciously but coolly, pouring tea with a deftness which was a challenge in itself.

CHAPTER VI

THE villages spaced out along the high ground over-
looking Port Amberley were known collectively as
the Sondings. At one time the coast road had gone
through Little Sonding, Abbot Sonding and High
Sonding; but the arterial highway built during the
'thirties skirted them and cut them off from the low
land over which Port Amberley had mushroomed
inward from the tidal creeks.

Nevertheless, High Sonding was near enough to be
spoken of always as "the village." A bus service connected it with several other villages, with the Research
Station and with Tollbury. Many of the Port Amberley
workers had found homes in and about High Sonding.
The Research Station had brought work and trade to
the place. Yet the crossing of the arterial road was still
the passing of a frontier. High Sonding was aloof, down-
to-earth, with a bleak character all its own which
grudgingly admitted the presence of Port Amberley as
"that place down yonder."

Country traditions said that all the Sondings were
peopled by dark men who were strangers to the rest of
the countryside, a close race who did not mix or even
trade with their neighbours. The people of the Sondings were market-gardeners, not farmers. For many
generations, they had traded with the London markets.
Since the development of truck-traffic, they had pros-
pered. Their holdings were not large. They worked
intensively and they did well. They turned their

weather-boarded farmhouses into bow-windowed villas surrounded by solid yellow brick-built, slate-roofed outbuildings. They lived warily, suspicious of amenities, of each other, of the London markets and of the new-fangled, disguised blessing which was Port Amberley.

The home of Brian's parents at High Sonding was near the old church of Saint Botolph's, which was in all the guide books. It had been called Chestnut Lodge since old Herbert Jackson, in a fit of vanity, had gouged out the front of it to fit a set of sash windows and a portentous gabled porch as his contribution to the megalomania of the nineteenth century. Its ancient name, Clumbers, still lingered, however, among Sonding people, in spite of the monkey trees which old Herbert had planted, and the draughty packing sheds erected by George Jackson, his son and Brian's father, that great card whom all the Sondings in their grudging fashion revered.

The Memsahib pushed open the creaking wrought-iron gate and picked her way up the weeded but untrodden garden path of Chestnut Lodge. She was well aware that everybody in the Sondings had used the side-door in the yard for nearly a generation. Yet she clung to the formality that ladies must use the front door when visiting people of uncertain status—or, as she put it, "the non-com level." The door knocker was so rusted that it dropped with a silent thud, but she thought nothing of accompanying her formal approach by loud cries of "It's only Mrs. Loose. . . . It's only me. . . ."

In the porch behind the door in a musty twilight of stained glass and potted ferns, there was much shuffling, scraping of chains and turning of keys. There were also squeaks of recognition and delight. These

59

welcoming sounds were made by two singularly small shrunken and faded sisters, Mrs. Jackson, Brian's mother, and his aunt, Miss Stilwell.

"It's only me," roared Mem for the tenth time as the door grated open. "I thought I'd just pop in on my way to the Guild."

"Oh, Mrs. Loose, how good of you. You came on the bus, I suppose? You'll have a cup of tea now you're here, won't you? And how's the Professor, and your daughter and the children? Was the bus crowded, I suppose it was as it's market day in Tollbury. Richard's out, of course, somewhere on the top field. Isn't he like his brother Brian in looks, but so different in everything else? You know Brian by sight, of course, down yonder?"

The soft patter of nervous questioning was a duet. Sometimes they spoke in unison. Sometimes they shared a sentence. Most of the time they achieved a kind of rhythm like a part-song without beginning or end. The Memsahib had her own methods of dealing with them. She simply threw herself into the rhythm of statement and question and turned it into a trio. "The bus was dreadfully crowded as usual. Half the women from Port Amberley seemed to be rushing into Tollbury. Where they get all the money to spend, I can't think. Yes, I saw your Brian the other day. Such a credit to you, by all accounts. Did you try the very hot bath with the Epsom salts? And what did the Doctor say about moving him? I wondered which of you is coming along to the Guild today? It ought to be such fun, I think. . . ."

The Memsahib needed a village just as a child needs playmates. As soon as she arrived at Port Amberley to establish herself with the Heathleys, she found High Sonding. "I'm sure there's a lot of Good Work one can do here, although this is such a dreadfully modern, complicated place," she had explained. "But I like to feel that I'm in the swim and I must find a place with a church, even though nobody goes to it." So she had adopted High Sonding as her parish, entering the life of the village in her usual resolute manner; and the odd thing was that High Sonding had dropped its traditional reserve and taken her to its sparse, suspicious heart.

This might perhaps have been explained by the lack of native gentry, by the extinction through time and circumstance of ladies with the grand manner, abundant sympathy and enough leisure to support these virtues. The former land-owning families of the Sondings had long since been bought out, bankrupted or dispirited by building development such as the arterial highway, Port Amberley itself and the packing stations of the market gardeners.

Such a village as High Sonding was dedicated to hard work and material progress. Many of the farmsteads, the cottages and the little shops had, nevertheless, been in the same hands for as long as anyone could remember. A closely knit village life existed, but it was undemonstrative. The Settlers from Port Amberley sometimes complained that it was like living in a foreign country. The Memsahib, who had collected villages all her life, had a knack for such things. "I'm Mrs. Adderley-Loose," she announced urbanely, "my name is hyphenated, but you can call me Mrs. Loose for short. I have come to stay in these parts for some time and I feel sure that we shall all get on very well together. I think the village has got such character—in spite of the appalling amount of litter which seems to be left about—and I do hope that you will count me in on all your activities. I shall be at church most Sundays.

61

I've always been a member of the Women's Institute, and I daresay you'll want me to give a little talk on India, where I spent so many happy years. I always support youth activities and I'm a very keen gardener. . . ."

It was formidable; but High Sonding found it stimulating and in a roundabout way flattering. Within a few weeks of her first visit, she acquired a nodding acquaintance with nearly everybody. She was on visiting terms with a number of most unlikely people. She was Vice-President of the Guild and a member of the committee of several organisations which came under the heading of Good Causes. By sheer personality, she had created an Anti-Litter League, with a committee of reluctant tradespeople and bewildered smallholders.

She was very pleased with High Sonding, and often said that she would consider being buried there—always her favourite tribute to any village which had taken her fancy and fallen under her sway.

To the Jackson family, her flying visits were momentous. Since Richard had taken over the land and Brian and the girls had left home, the old people, worn out by the hard but careful life they had always led, had settled into a bemused retirement. They read a newspaper every week. They became fanatical listeners to broadcast light music. They listened with reverence to the views of Richard and the younger men upon markets, prices, crops and land. They spoke in hushed voices of Annie, the daughter who had called herself Annette and gone to the bad. They spoke with satisfaction of Lucy, who had married a doctor and who enjoyed, unscathed, the gay life of those twin coastal resorts Flimby and Ruxtable, sometimes known to the

Sonding people as Sodom and Gomorrah. Their attitude towards Brian was proud but bewildered, for everything about him was so unlike themselves. Since he was quite a young boy, he had not given High Sonding a glance as a future prospect or as a way of life. He had never asked for any help or any advice. He had always been self-possessed and competent, though obedient and amenable in the domesticities of home life. When it had become obvious that his interests did not lie in the Clumbers land, and the schoolmasters had reported that his intelligence was above average, old George had in turn suggested that he might become an auctioneer, a wholesale agent, an agricultural implement salesman and even a veterinary surgeon. These were professions of substance and honour in the eyes of old George. They were fitted for the brainy one of the family and he was prepared to put down good money to ensure his son a start. In this, however, Brian had proved to be quite intractable. He had refused both guidance and financial help. He had drifted completely out of their lives almost before they had had a chance to worry about him. They had never had any conception of what he really did, for old George resolutely refused to believe that research was work and always referred to him as some kind of special engineer.

Though he might be preoccupied by such alien things, Brian's warmth of affection both for the family and the place was deep. He was particularly attached to Richard, who was a couple of years his senior. He would walk all over the land with Richard, taking a cursory interest in the crops, and puzzling Richard by the detailed recitals of his aims and achievements. He was completely satisfied if Richard grunted approval from time to time.

The first big building programme down on the

marshes at Port Amberley and the arrival of Heathley as a gay, turbulent bachelor paying guest had had a profound effect upon all of them. In the beginning, they had looked upon Heathley as something of a windfall in extra money. It was not the habit of the Sonding people to turn good money away. Though old Herbert Jackson had left them rows of freehold cottages about the village, besides property in Tollbury, invested money and the Clumbers land in good heart so that they had never known a financial anxiety in all their long lives, they had welcomed the extra work entailed and had accepted Heathley gladly. He had astonished them with his zest for living, his easy manners and his knowledge of the world. He had alarmed them with his advanced political views and his prophecies about the wars of the future. It had been fun having Heathley as a lodger, a never-to-be-forgotten memory. The truly remarkable part of it, however, had been Brian coming home from the University and talking to Heathley in his own language. From that moment, there could not be the slightest doubt about the brilliance of Brian. They accepted him as one of those who had stepped out into another world beyond their imaginings. Heathley had been the most impressive figure from that other world—and Heathley had been impressed with their boy Brian. "Leave him to me," Heathley had said. "The lad's a genius. He's gone an astonishingly long way for his age already. That's nothing to the long way he'll go in the end."

The Memsahib had, of course, heard the whole story a dozen times. She had heard it in the parlour downstairs, at the unpretentious kitchen table round which the family still gathered, and upstairs in the bedroom where old George lay helpless, sharp-tongued and reminiscent. Only Mem could have initiated the "little

64

chats" which had become events of such importance during his last illness.

"It's all so typical of Heathley, that great and good man," she would say. "I've never known him to give a false opinion of anything or anybody. You're a lucky man, George Jackson, to have a son like you've got. And you're lucky to have had my son-in-law for a lodger."

"Ah! But I needed one like Richard too, Mrs. Loose. If I thought there wasn't a boy of mine out there working my land, I'd pull myself out of this bed, even if it killed me."

"No gadding about now, George Jackson. I've some experience of land myself, in this country and out of it, and I'd have you know that I've very rarely seen it look so well for the time of year. Not too forward, mind. There's plenty of cold wind about. But, of course, up here in High Sonding you've got reasonable protection. Now down in the Camp . . . as I can't help calling it . . . I mean the Research Station. . . ."

"That's dead land, that is. No good ever came out of that. Poor soil and as sour as the sea."

"You should take a look at my rock garden in about a month's time before you say that."

"You know as well as I do, Mrs. Loose, I shan't see no more gardens."

They both looked out of the crooked window on to the tops of budding apple trees. They both knew that old George would look upon apple blossom this year for the last time. He always waited until his own womenfolk were out of the room before he spoke of this. It was a secret reality he shared with the incredible old lady who had rustled into the evening of his life almost imperiously, as if she had some right to be there.

"Tell me what it's like in that place down yonder,

Mrs. Loose," he said, his mahogany-brown eyes which Brian had inherited, returning from the tree-tops and the sky. "I know the gardening must be rough. I've got a fair idea that things will be pretty lively with that son-in-law of yours as one of the head ones. I've never been no kind of saint myself—in fact, they talk of me round here as the devil's undertaker." He guffawed softly, merrily, a little defiantly because she was church and he was chapel. Then he drew together the white tufted eyebrows whose shape was so clearly marked upon the features of Brian, and whispered earnestly: "Are they up to any good, down yonder, Mrs. Loose? That's what I've begun wondering. Aren't they trying to find the best way of killing millions of people and destroying all the crops? Aren't they going to make God angry before they've done, Mrs. Loose? Isn't it something young Brian ought never to have got mixed up with, for all his brain and for all the wonderful talk of Heathley?"

She let him exhaust himself by finishing. He expressed a doubt which she had sometimes dared herself to contemplate. She had never lied to him and she spoke now with complete sincerity when she said: "They're doing it for the Good of the Cause."

He was more alert than usual because of the green buds of the apple trees. He demanded the simple statements of childhood. He said that which not even a child had said to the Memsahib for half a century. "What good of what cause?" he said, closing his eyes which had never looked out upon any wider horizons than those of the Sondings or upon any causes other than those of his land and his livelihood.

The Memsahib was taken aback. She snorted and said: "To begin with, God is on our side. . . ."

"God don't take sides, Mrs. Loose, if you don't mind

66

me saying so. What about that Christmas in the trenches in the First War when Jerry and us sang carols to one another? Yes, and sometimes we sang the same one! Funny how things come back when you know you're going to go over the hill. . . . No, I don't reckon God takes sides, but that's not to say that people don't work for the devil. And I don't suppose that's what you mean by the Good of the Cause."

"If God wasn't on my side, I shouldn't want to fight," said the Memsahib simply. "And to believe anything else is blasphemous or worse."

Old George grinned. "I shall get punished soon enough, won't I?"

"That's not for me to say, George Jackson. As I see it, your son Brian and my son-in-law are working for their fellow men. It's not only work, it's duty. It's no different from duty as I've understood it all my life. That's what I mean by the Good of the Cause. There's everything to be proud of and nothing to be ashamed of."

Old George nodded, but he was only half convinced. "There's nobody I'd ever talk to like this but you, Mrs. Loose. My women have never been taught to understand things. . . ."

"Your women, as you call them, are really sweet and gentle."

"That's as it should be. They've worked hard all their lives and they don't want to be bothered now by asking and answering questions. But while I've been lying here alone, I've thought a lot about Brian. I know Richard is all right. He's steady and he don't drink as much as I did at his age, not by a long chalk. But Brian I'm really proud of. He's gone his own way. He's always been straight with me. He's come out on top. I've never understood what he's up to and it's only these last few days I've begun to wonder whether he's really up to any good."

The Mem stood up and patted his hand lightly. "He's working for his country and for civilisation."

"Ah, I wonder how many people he's going to kill in the end? Do you reckon they ever think about things like that in that place down yonder?"

The Memsahib forced a reassuring smile. She had never heard such things discussed, but she knew her own intellectual limitations. Several times she had had to reject her own timid doubts on this very point. Old George's words disturbed her. The smile which she mustered was only half an answer. "If I don't go now, I shall be late for the Guild Meeting," she said. "I'm taking either your wife or her sister with me."

Old George could not move his right hand very far, but he raised it in a little gesture to retain her. "Not a word about any of this to the women, if you don't mind, Mrs. Loose."

"We've got plenty of other things to talk about, don't you worry."

"But there's one very important thing that I'd like you to say for me. They'll never listen to me. I want to be brought downstairs."

"Not on your life, George Jackson! Have you forgotten what your stairs are like? Why, they must be hundreds of years old and I have to cling on to both banisters myself."

"That's just why I want to be brought down. Perhaps Richard and a couple of men . . . if you said so . . . they'd listen to you."

The Memsahib glanced at the great powerful body lying so inert and helpless, so clearly shaped by the neat white quilt. His features were shaggier than Brian's but they had the same aquiline Red Indian look. The

68

Mem had never seen old George upright, but she supposed that he stood every inch as tall as his son.

"I think it would be mad," she said, "and I don't really think that it is any of my business. It's the sort of thing your family ought to talk over with the doctor."

"I know it's not your business, Mrs. Loose." There was distress in his voice. "I'm sure you've been very kind coming here, as a newcomer. You've made all the difference to me."

"It's very nice of you to say so. But you ought not to give way to worry, you know."

"When you go back to that place down yonder, you could mention it to Brian, if you like. He's a clever chap. He'll be able to talk to the doctor, no doubt. I do worry. And I'll tell you for why. They're never going to get me down them stairs in a box. My old Dad was nothing like as big as me and they couldn't get him down in a coffin, however they tried. I reckon that when this old place was plain Clumbers, it wasn't built for dying upstairs. I don't want to go out in a box through the window like my Dad, with a rickyard rope and tackle. You speak to young Brian about it. He comes up here to see us most weeks. . . ."

Nobody saw the tears in the Memsahib's eyes for the crooked stairs were dark and she took her time, though the two sisters were patiently chattering below, waiting for her to come down. It never occurred to her, as she went off to the Guild Meeting with Mrs. Jackson, that her capacity for mingling with the lives of other people was in any way exceptional. There may have been a tinge of arrogance about that formidable outward appearance of hers, but her nature was illuminated by the inherent modesty by which she measured all human values.

She offered to the Guild a number of recipes for

making curry, and made a fervent appeal on behalf of
the League of Pity. Then she took the bus back to the
floodlit centre of Port Amberley, feeling that she was
stepping out into another world but pleased also that
she had established herself in "a place with a church
in it."

eyes_or Ilse—or_his conceit? He was identified with the M_2 project nearly as wholly as Heathley. He had contributed a substantial share under Heathley's leadership. He was becoming equally committed. For all his present uncomfortable sense of opposition, they were partners, ...es rather than master and pupil, leader and follower.

CHAPTER VII

BRIAN looked up from his work and was at a loss for an excuse when Heathley stood there inviting him to come in for a drink in the evening. He was amazed at himself for wanting an excuse. "Just yourself and Ilse Leon and that new American fellow, the Personnel Liaison Officer. I thought it would be a chance for you to fix up the details of your golf with Lydia tomorrow. And we'd all better have a working knowledge of this Sam Seagram, who's important, and a very nice fellow by all accounts. Come straight on from the canteen, say about eight or so."

Excuses stuttered through Brian's head and remained unspoken. "Thanks very much, Heathley," he murmured, judging correctly that it was one of the semi-official occasions when prefixes were dropped.

"Splendid!" Heathley said, giving him a long steady look before he turned away.

Brian felt trapped. His advance work on Phase II would obviously continue until nearly seven o'clock. After that, he would have to remain on call. Nothing would have induced him to leave the vicinity when the technical preparations were about to begin. Why in any case did he suddenly feel the need to sidestep the company of the Heathleys? Could it be because of Ilse, because the presence of Ilse would inhibit him? Why had he thrown out that embarrassing question to Heathley during the conference? Might it not be, after all, that he was emphasising his own integrity in the

71

eyes of Ilse—or his conceit? He was identified with the M.7 project nearly as wholly as Heathley. He had contributed a substantial share under Heathley's leadership. He was becoming equally committed. For all his present uncomfortable sense of opposition, they were partners, team-mates, colleagues rather than master and pupil, leader and follower.

It was Heathley's ruthless seizure of the advantage of the Deputy's death which had taken him by surprise. It was going to force him into open conflict with the man to whom he owed everything. The issue was keen and personal. The ultimate success or failure of M.7 might not be in the balance, but its immediate effectiveness was. It took a giant's confidence and courage to break away from the orthodoxy which the Deputy had always demanded and maintained. Brian was neither pleased nor sorry that the Deputy was out of the way. He had simply been shocked by the triumphant swiftness of Heathley's reaction. It looked almost as if Heathley had foreseen the mishap and had had his course of action planned.

Heathley's unorthodox approach to Phase II laid too great a stress, Brian knew, upon personal factors. It admitted the possibility of human error at too early a stage, when the experiment was poised between calculation and exactly ascertained technical data. Heathley's own experiments and that of such crew as he chose to take with him, would be of their very nature incomplete. They probably meant testing men's physical capacities to breaking point just as the frames of aircraft might be tested in the laboratories.

M.7 was a craft which combined deep-water navigation and supersonic flight. The precision with which the two elements of air and water had been blended was and still is the secret which gave it such a significance both as a revolutionary transport development and as a potential weapon. The purpose of Phase I had been the completion of enough prototypes to carry out the practical experiments of Phase II on a large scale.

Who would Heathley choose as crew-mate, Brian wondered, as he watched him turning away. Would he dare to make any choice? Whether he was right or wrong to attempt such a test at all at this stage, it was an act of personal courage and of outstanding self-assurance to do it himself. It would also be an act of over-confidence amounting almost to arrogance to go alone. It was just like Heathley not to ask anybody to do anything he would not do himself. It would be quite in character if he were to say nothing more to anybody and to go alone.

Though he opposed the whole idea in principle, this thought absorbed Brian as he watched Heathley with his springy step leaving the room. He could have held back his own reservations and supported Heathley wholeheartedly; but it would have been dishonest. He might still back him part of the way out of loyalty. His own ambition nagged him to go even further than that. Why should Heathley alone obtain this vital experience? Why should he alone with his cool domination force the pace by placing himself in the lead? Without the Deputy, and with the uncertainty of that unfilled place, Brian felt he had been quite justified in expressing his doubts in finding himself opposed to Heathley's methods. But had he been wise to blurt them out in that almost damaging way at the conference? He had hated the overbearing egotism and the sense of frustration and intrigue which had surrounded the presence of the Deputy. While the Deputy had been in control, there would have been little hope of progressive action, or even of promotion. Heathley himself would agree with him in this. For Heathley had suffered more than his fair share of frustration. With the Deputy gone, however, Brian might have been wiser to have held his hand. It was this very hesitancy which embarrassed him when Heathley offered the invitation for that evening.

He was so lost in these thoughts that he did not notice the presence of anyone else in the room until Bord from one of the high stools against the drawing-boards at the far end chided him with the remark: "It must be wonderful, Jackson, to have that degree of detached concentration."

"It must be valuable to you to have that talent for noiseless movement, Colonel."

Dennis Bord laughed and stretched himself as if he had been there for a long time.

"Send me away, if you're unbearably busy. I happened to see Heathley come out just now and I imagined that your thread was broken. It didn't occur to me that I'd surprise you. I've just prowled in for a cup of tea with Lydia Heathley. She's pretty mad about our new barbed-wire ring fence."

"Barbed wire?"

"Just a detail of the Security tightening up . . . on account of all this work you're doing." All the while he had been speaking, Bord had been moving across the room towards Brian. He reached the spot where Heathley had stood, and joked: "To keep you men in, of course, rather than to keep malefactors out."

Brian remained steady, though he felt a tightening of his heart, rather as if he had just heard of people taking precautions against his stealing. "So it's holy ground indeed?" He laughed. "Marked out and protected by the Ministry of Research and Development?"

The Security Officer put on a smile meant to indicate

a change of subject, but it was bleak and perfunctory. He said: "After the dance last night, you presumably went out to your car which was parked behind the Deputy's. Did you see anybody get into the Deputy's car?"

"I wasn't looking. I was going to the Aerodynamics Department to check over the final results of the wind-tunnel tests on the B prototype modifications."

"Your overdoing the detail, Jackson. I'm not a technical man. All I need is a straight answer. There's going to be an inquest. The Coroner's Officer and the police are in charge, of course, but naturally they're working with me. There were fingerprints of yours on the Deputy's car."

Brian took a deep breath and said: "I had to move the Deputy's car when I came in. Otherwise the back of my car would have stuck out into the roadway."

"And when you came to fetch your car?"

"I just drove it away."

"You didn't by any chance open the door of the Deputy's car to have a word with him?"

"No."

"You didn't see who was inside it?"

"I couldn't. I. . . ."

"Then there was somebody inside it?"

"What the hell is this in aid of, Colonel Bord?" Brian leapt to his feet. The ruddy colour of his face deepened. Dennis Bord noticed the strong veins in his neck. "Why do you come in here and cross-examine me when I've still got work—important work. How in blazes do you know that there are fingerprints of mine on the Deputy's car?"

"Don't worry. There aren't any now. But yours were there. It's a matter of Security routine, as you may remember, to have fingerprint records of everybody."

75

"Like a bunch of criminals," Brian snorted. "Finger-prints and barbed wire! What about shackles for a little light relief?"

"Charming thought," murmured Bord, looking toward Brian steadily, admiringly, but with a kind of detachment as if he were looking at a specimen. "Pity to get yourself all excited, Brian Jackson. I came here to save you trouble. I realise that all you specialists are a little worked up at the moment. And with good reason, though it alarms me when it verges upon mass-hysteria. . . ."

"It seems to me you do your best to put everyone on edge. In any case, you've got your bloody psychologist to sort it out. Why don't you get Felix Tatham to try a little mass psychiatry? That might be one way to get people to do their best work in these conditions." Brian was quite unable to calm down. He knew he was rattled. This inquisition and the need to defend himself had come so unexpectedly on the tail of those thoughts about Heathley. He had been taken off his guard; and his show of bluster was the measure of his weakness.

Dennis Bord offered him a cigarette with a gesture which meant: "We're really all pals together, but I've got my job to do." It was one of his neat professional tricks. The recognition of that steadied Brian a little and he answered bleakly: "I don't smoke in here." Then he sat down, without the usual formality of offering the Security Officer a seat. Bord ostentatiously drew towards him the full ashtray, lit a cigarette and sat down.

Brian frowned and pressed together his fingertips, a habit of concentration with him. He must control his temper at all costs if he were going to have to lie to a man as formidable as this. Almost at any other time in

76

his career, he would have felt quite equal to meet these questions. He had fooled himself into believing that they would never be asked. Now that the much larger issues had been forming in his mind, urging him to volunteer to accompany Heathley on the air test, the once important and disturbing events of the night before had seemed trifling. The pressure of his finger-tips increased as he smiled and said: "I'm sorry to go off the handle like that, Colonel. One way and another, this has been quite a harrowing day. I've no need to tell you that we're just starting Phase II. There's been a lot to do, and I still shan't have finished for another hour."

"And there's been just a shadow of disagreement between you and Heathley, I imagine?" Bord spoke carefully, treating it as a foregone conclusion. To Brian, that exaggerated casualness came as an advantage. It meant that there was something that Bord wanted to know beside the details of what had happened after the dance.

"Disagreement with Heathley? Why, of course. . . ." He gave away nothing. "If there were not the attrition and stress of disagreement, we should get nowhere. You didn't suppose that we all thought alike, surely?"

"As you are all such great minds, I didn't," snapped Bord, conscious that he was losing his position. "But I gather that Heathley's unorthodox methods are causing a degree of dismay, almost amounting to unrest?"

"In a minute you'll have worked up again to mass hysteria," jibed Brian.

"I hope you don't think I came here just to amuse you, old boy." Dennis Bord smoothly changed his tack. "I've got my hands pretty full at this moment and I know that you have. I asked you that question quite deliberately not just as a piece of gossip. I'm used to

77

dealing with people who are highly strung and who from time to time do not hesitate to show it. I have no operational authority, though, as you realise, my job would be useless if I didn't collaborate closely on all operational matters. I explain this because I want you to understand that I'm not an interfering busybody getting in the way of you specialists. On the contrary, I respect your work and try to keep you free from extraneous worries so that you have the best possible conditions."

"Why not come to the point, then?" said Brian, taking the pressure off his fingertips and fondling the work on his desk.

"I'm not beating about the bush, my dear fellow. I believe Heathley's taking on very grave responsibilities. I have an idea that he has let himself in for quite exceptional strain. Your influence in this is important. You don't need to explain to me the depth of your disagreement with him about Phase II. Probably I shouldn't even understand it. But I do understand that you have a greater influence than perhaps even you suspect." Again he gave Brian one of those appraising looks. "You have a lot of support. I think you should be very careful how you exert this influence in the next few days, at least until the Director returns and the Deputy's post is filled. I know it's a damned impertinence of me to say this, Brian"—it was the first time he had used the first name—"but I want you to take it in the spirit in which it's offered."

"I'm going to support Professor Heathley." The slight formality of the sentence countered the first-name business.

"I thought you would. It's essential at this stage," Bord stood up and patted him lightly on the shoulder. He had become not only a colleague but a supporter.

There was a hint of something sinister about the warmth of that support, and Brian decided overtly to ignore it.

It was just as well. For Bord offered what could only amount to a sly *quid pro quo,* a cunning token of reward. "Now about this other business of last night, Brian." He spoke briskly and paused, as it were, to let the first name sink in. "Our view is—and I have spoken to the Director on the telephone myself—that it must be allowed to pass off as quietly as possible. It would be disastrous to focus the attention of the press and the public on Port Amberley at the very moment when you people are just entering upon Phase II. It's essential, too, that people like yourself and Heathley should not be distracted at the very moment when you are stretched to the full. Am I right?"

Brian, a little taken aback, murmured: "I see what you mean, of course. It's obvious that if Port Amberley became the scene of a public sensation, we should have to pack up—and we simply can't pack up at this moment. Too much depends on this."

"Right, we're agreed on that, at least. I've got the Coroner's Office and the police to deal with. They're coming here again tomorrow, when you're playing golf with Lydia Heathley."

Brian started. The man seemed to forget nothing. Though he had been at such pains to declare himself an ally, there was something untrustworthy about his omniscience, something almost suspiciously ambiguous about even his most commonplace remarks. "I'd almost forgotten that myself. Thanks for reminding me."

"You need all the relaxation you can get. You'd better take it. I gather you've most of the day clear. I shan't need to bring you into the investigations. The

Coroner's Officer seems disposed to agree with the Doc and myself that it was a case of heart failure."

"I imagine it was, wasn't it?"

"It's for the Coroner to say. But, as far as you're concerned, you went to fetch your car before going to the Aerodynamics Department to check up final results of the wind-tunnel tests. If I was forced to call you in, I imagine that's your story and you're sticking to it."

"It's the truth, Colonel Bord. . . ."

He did not seem to hear. "We shall forget the fact that you touched the Deputy's motor car, or that you saw who was inside it. Is that agreed?"

Brian took a deep breath. The Security Officer's washy blue eyes did not flinch. He went on staring into them until Bord blinked and said: "Surely we understand one another, Brian? I don't want to stand here wasting your time. Is this thing agreed?"

"Agreed," said Brian.

He watched Colonel Bord's military gait, so precise, so measured, so sinister by contrast with Heathley's. He wondered what sort of story Ilse had told. He wondered what other fingerprints they had identified on the Deputy's motor car before they had wiped the evidence away. He wondered if he had lied in vain.

Then the dark realism of the Sondings of his birth came to his aid. First things must come first. He would worry about what he knew. He would concentrate his trained faculties on the work in hand. Afterwards he must concentrate upon the human factor which had become all important in Phase II, with which, after all, his whole future and fortune were linked. The human factor was, of course, Heathley.

CHAPTER VIII

THE party at the Heathleys was like any other at Port
Amberley, where such gatherings could hardly fail to
resemble one another. The folding back of the double
doors separating the two standard living-rooms created
a long, slightly too narrow, space, familiar to every
home occupied by a departmental head or higher
executive. That articles of furniture were supplied by
the Ministry, if required, also tended to standardise
the scene. Heathley's books and sports trophies, Lydia's
eye for period furniture, even the Memsahib's
souvenirs of foreign travel, somehow failed to let the
room break out of the official pattern—as Lydia was
only too well aware.

There were often modest gatherings like this. To
save domestic fuss, people came in after the evening
meal. They never failed to chide each other about talking shop. It was inevitable, however, that there was a
vigorous currency of gossip and that this easily drifted
into shop. The social structure was fortuitous in throwing together individuals of such diversity; it was
arbitrary in creating a synthetic society which could
never be wholly at its ease. Though the basis of all
effort was teamwork, there was also an underlying spirit
of competition which could at any moment threaten
community life. The limitations of the place and of the
work, the standardisation of buildings and working
habits, at once emphasised the need for social relationships and made them difficult to achieve.

81

The Heathleys were good at these things. They mixed well and effortlessly put people at their ease. Though he was such a newcomer, Sam Seagram guessed that the little gathering that evening was not without purpose. The room was bright and warm. There were drinks on a trolley. There were special recordings played upon the radio pick-up which was one of the hobbies at which Heathley excelled. Yet, perhaps because he was a stranger, Sam Seagram's perceptions told him that there was a perplexing and unexplained intensity there which forbade anybody to relax.

To Lydia, the event had become a crazy adventure ever since she had committed the folly of challenging her own sense of guilt by asking Alex Leon to come round with the others. "Heathley has asked your sister, I believe, and one or two others," she had telephoned, with a tremble in her voice which Alex, in his office, had mistaken for suppressed laughter.

"You talk as if I mind my own sister," he had laughed back. "But Ilse can always be trusted to look after her own interests while I pursue mine."

The stilted gallantry had pleased Lydia out of all proportion to its merit. She had always been disposed to join Heathley in a little good-natured private mockery of the continental manners of some members of the staff, including Alex. Now she chose to interpret them as a personal compliment. She began to believe that there might be compensation for the barbed wire outside, to counter the Security measures, the pale eyes probing, it seemed, for weaknesses in a victim.

Because of the hysterical boldness of this otherwise ordinary invitation of another guest, Lydia had mismanaged her announcement of it to Heathley. "I don't remember exactly whom you said you were having

82

round this evening, but I thought we might have Alex Leon."

"But he was here after the dance last night, wasn't he?"

"That can't matter surely." The flat tone returned to her voice. She made it sound as if she did not care who came or went. "For that matter, Sam Seagram, the American, was here last night and you said you were going to invite him."

"I thought you said you'd forgotten whom I was going to invite?"

It had developed into a weary wrangle, without any suspicion in Heathley's mind that there could be any reason for her inviting Alex except that she had wanted to show her independence in some trifling way. It nettled him to have to conceal the reasons for his own selection of Brian, Ilse and Sam Seagram. He became more and more obstinate in his determination to make out that this choice was one of chance or casual social necessity. He had surprised himself by working up Lydia into a fury of self-justification. He had made himself angry too by telling her that she was over-tired and by returning to the subject of taking a holiday. Lydia had banged out into the kitchen then in one of her infrequent fits of weeping. He had been left by the prepared drink trolley, feeling self-righteous and a little guilty. That indignant shame had only left him when she returned, as she had sometimes done before, apologetically and calmly. She had blamed it all on the barbed wire.

Now, as she had promised herself for the last two hours, Lydia was turning her head from Brian Jackson and staring straight into the politely mocking eyes of Alex Leon. Heathley was saying: "This barbed wire fence idea is really the last straw. I don't wonder Lydia was upset about it. I can well imagine that we shall have to hold the Memsahib down when she sees it in the morning, or she'll be out there with my wire clippers. But there it is, I suppose it's justified. There's been all the row in the papers about picnickers walking into top secret research stations. The only trouble is that barbed wire, surely is so archaic. Why didn't Dennis Bord go for high-tension wire while he was about it?"

"I've just been asking him why he doesn't fix shackles on us and have done with it," Brian said.

"All we need now is for the Ministry to make an issue of whips and I shall feel that I'm back where I started," Ilse's voice was brittle as if she felt that she must make that sort of jest at all costs.

She was a tawny blonde colour which contrasted with the blue-eyed, Anglo-Saxon, mousey blondeness of Lydia. Because she was a research specialist of outstanding talents, and was, moreover, the product of a distinguished European family of scientists, she tended to emphasise her femininity off duty. She followed fashions pedantically, but adapted them to her slight figure with skill. Her changes of hair style were so frequent and sometimes so dramatic that sweepstakes were not unknown among masculine colleagues upon how long any one style would last. If there were slightly uncompromising signs of glitter and ostentation about her, in such details as the long cigarette-holder, the bizarre built-up shoes and the strident use of perfume, she managed to carry them off with such an air that few women ever quite forgave her and few men ever quite ignored her.

Lydia Heathley behaved better than most women by declaring that Ilse was not her style and extending toward her a generous protective compassion. It never occurred to Ilse to resent this. In fact, it touched her heart. She saw qualities of calmness and magnanimity which brought out in herself an ardent admiration. In her eyes, Lydia was perfectly civilised, domesticated, poised and English. She herself was not a woman's woman, but neither was Lydia. They had nothing much in common save only this vain generosity on the one part and envious adulation on the other. It was a sympathy which did not inhibit Ilse from a profound, almost platonic, interest in Heathley.

Though her abilities were universally recognised and her relationships on duty meticulously conventional, Ilse was quite unable to leave people alone during the hours of leisure. She had time to make up. She had to live down the tragedies of the past. She had to compensate for the unemotional exercises of her faculties which were her professional life. Nothing had ever been allowed to trespass upon the integrity of that. She was prepared to sacrifice any emotional attachment to it, except love, the deep lasting love of her dreams.

She was every bit as sophisticated as her appearance suggested. The uneasiness which Lydia detected and which she saluted with her compassion, was that restless fear of Ilse's that she would never in fact catch up with life, that she would never attain stability without love, or any purpose without faith. Even if Lydia could have said as much, there would have been no occasion for saying it.

Ilse delighted in confidential chats about scandal and about clothes. About her amorous encounters, she had no reticence whatever. Ilse would drink in the sympathy, the calm of Lydia even though she would persist in asking leading questions about Heathley. The tragic race against time which went on behind the elegant femininity and the scientific accomplishment was never revealed.

Even as she joked about whips, Ilse was wondering how Lydia came to be so animated upon what was, after all, such an ordinary occasion. Was it possible that Lydia, of all people, had stepped down from her pedestal to participate in some sort of rivalry? Ilse, off duty, was acutely conscious of rivalries.

She found Brian Jackson attractive. There was a rugged directness about him which put her in mind of an intelligent peasant in her own country. His work was in a class of its own. She acknowledged that, for she was capable of an exact assessment. It was his physical presence which she now looked at for the first time, dispassionately, she liked to think. She did this only because she had intercepted Lydia's look and had been startled by it. Brian's features had an aquiline symmetry which she had previously admired. His forcefulness was not coarse and predatory, like that of so many of the men she had preferred. It was potent, drawing on some steady reserve of blood and experience.

It was characteristic of Brian, she thought, that he should have formed about him, with little more than the asking of a vague ambiguous question, the allegiance of men like Baird who opposed the methods of Heathley but who was too buried in his subject to do more than grumble at conferences. She revered leadership but her interest in Heathley went far beyond his achievement as a scientist and departmental head. She was magnetised by his authority as a human being.

Nevertheless, she was hunting for qualities which were more simple, at once sensual and noble. Qualities to justify every sacrifice. Now, because Lydia had looked at him in a certain way, she began to wonder if Brian, who danced with what reminded her of a peasant grace, might not after all be. . . . She did not demand a paragon. She had no intellectually worked-out conception, indeed, no word for that ultimate quarry. . . .

As for Brian, he was ignoring her. He was absorbed in manoeuvring Heathley aside into a corner; and Sam, the American, seemed determined to make his number with her. "You never gave me that dance last night, young lady," he began, courteous and yet seeming to be looking at her from all angles.

"I'm sorry about that, Major Seagram. A certain amount of duty came into it."

"Duty well done too, I should say. You must have given the late Deputy a lot of pleasure, poor man, on his last night on earth. . . ."

It was one of those disconcerting, uncomfortable remarks. Both the Heathleys happened to overhear it and both rated it as deplorable bad taste. But Ilse turned down the corners of her mouth and greeted it with mock-tragic gusto. "So long as nobody makes out that I gave him the heart attack that finished him, I'm happy. I think that he enjoyed his last night. I've seen plenty of people go who didn't."

"Is that so?" Sam said, his long grey face keeping its fixed smile which, if anything, underlined its solemnity. "And you think it was a heart attack?" He spoke mildly, but even his mildness, she suspected, was alert.

Ilse hesitated and covered her hesitation by a characteristic flourish of her cigarette-holder. "What else could it be, Major Seagram?"

"I wouldn't know, of course. Though I can well imagine how it must have come as a shock to a lot of people. I can well imagine that."

"Your gifts include imagination then?"

"Imagination comes in handy when I employ what you call my gifts. It certainly does. I should be lost without it." Then, without altering his conversational tone, he added. "But you're not wearing the same perfume that you wore last night, if you don't mind me saying so."

"I'm flattered with the attention, Major Seagram. Your nose for these things must be quite exceptional, or else your imagination must be over-stimulated. I seem to recollect that we only met for a few moments at the bar, and I never wear perfume of that sort at functions. It stimulates all the wrong people."

"But how it lingers, such a perfume as that. How it lingers. Why I've known a perfume—not as elegant as that one—to hang around in an automobile for hours."

"You really have a nose, Major Seagram, haven't you?"

"It's the way some automobiles have fabric upholstery, I suppose. Yes, that's what makes a perfume linger."

Nobody in the room was listening to them any longer. Ilse glanced round to make sure of that. She could talk to him in the manner which best suited her. She said: "I believe you're putting two and two together, Major Seagram. Mathematics is another of your gifts, eh? Well, you'll need all your imagination to work that sum out."

"I don't quite get you!" He screwed up his eyes. His effort to look stupid was a signal failure.

"I think I get you, Major Seagram. You see, I'm accustomed to using my head, and I believe I know what you're driving at in your nice natural way. You're trying to discover—out of kindly curiosity or because a thought has just struck you—how it came about that

88

this perfume which you admire so much happened to linger in the Deputy's motor car."

"You jump to some pretty neat conclusions, young lady, and I. . . ."

"Well, we're not all fools, brother. Let's begin from there."

"And where do we go?"

She teased him with a grandiose gesture of the cigarette-holder which, made by anybody else, would have looked comic and affected. "The Deputy took me for dinner into Tollbury the night before last when we had finished the final stages of Phase I in the Aerodynamics Department. As we were both agreeing just now, it's extraordinary how perfumes have a way of lingering. That's a particular favourite of mine called *Shocking*. I'm delighted that it pleased you so much as to arouse your official suspicions."

How irritating it was to have to explain all this with one eye on that corner of the room where Brian was. They must be talking shop; and in ordinary circumstances, this would be interesting in itself. But it had been one of those days in which none of the circumstances was ordinary. Her instinct told her that the two men were reaching some great decision. Yet they were just outside her range and she was tied down by the need to pit her wits against Sam Seagram.

Heathley had been unaware at first of Brian's attempts to corner him. They had gone on talking about the barbed wire, the issue of an elaborate set of new passes, the tapping of telephone conversations and the periodical searches of the non-technical staff. It was all a part of the tightening up of Security. Everybody had recognised the need for it but it was difficult, as a human being, not to resent it. "Bord's a very tactful fellow, of course," said Heathley, "and I don't envy

89

him his job. We'll have to watch, though, that he doesn't press his schemes too far."

"I think he's got his limitations weighed up." Brian spoke a little grudgingly, feeling himself to be under some sort of obligation, and wishing in any case to lead away from that subject.

"Maybe, Brian. But there's always a possibility that he'll carry his investigations a bit far. I hope he hasn't been interfering with you?"

Brian shrugged his shoulders. "Just a few routine questions."

"Too many damned routine questions," Heathley said irritably. "The fewer people who discuss Phase II the better. It's talking shop, I know, but. . . .?" His anger passed. He came to the point. "But, since we're talking it, Brian, I just wanted you to know that I'm not in the least annoyed, but in fact grateful, for the way you spoke up at this morning's conference. I imagine you felt, as I did, that we needed to clear the air, eh?"

It had come more suddenly than Brian expected and now the question was posed in such a way that he could only give the affirmative answer which Heathley demanded. "It did no harm if it cleared the air; and I only hoped that you'd understand that I didn't raise it just to emphasise a divergence of views. Thinking it over, in fact, I've realised that I left quite a lot unsaid."

Heathley laughed. "You must have been thinking very hard since I left you in the office."

"I didn't mention it in the office because I hadn't expected to see you and I was still working over the final details of the test as I see them from my point of view," Brian lied quickly and resolutely.

Heathley seemed to know what he was going to say and to take it for granted. "I suppose you're going to wonder why I didn't suggest anybody going with me on the first test? Is that it, Brian?"

Brian allowed himself to be awed once more by the character of that man to whom he owed so much and with whom his own specialised knowledge over the last twelve months had forced him to disagree. It was this that made him speak the lines as if he had rehearsed them. "It was a little more positive than that, though you'll agree that this morning's conference left the thing pretty indefinite. No, I simply want to say that I would like to come with you myself. I imagine that you had good reasons for not asking for volunteers. Everybody must have tumbled to that, this morning. Well, I'm volunteering."

"But you're sceptical about the whole thing?"

"Nevertheless I'm volunteering. You need another man with you with an all-round knowledge of M.7, and with ability to take over dual control if necessary; and I can say without boasting that I'm the best candidate. If I'm sceptical, it's a personal matter. The department is committed to both methods of air testing and the prototypes are available. It would be mad if disunity is carried to the point of not giving your method fair trial. If you and I go together, sharing some of the work, we shall clearly get the best possible results—even if they turn out to be disappointing."

Heathley smiled and said nothing for a moment. He seemed to gain a few inches in height. "You're quite right, Brian. I had made up my mind to see this thing through by myself. I've that degree of confidence, I'll admit. If you really mean it though, I'll take you like a shot. It couldn't be better. If one of us blacks out, there'll be the other to take control."

He made no pretence about being pleased with the offer; but he was still shrewd enough to examine it warily before coming out of the corner. "You've reached this decision very quickly, Brian, if I may say so."

"Oh, I gave it a lot of thought, as I said, after you left my office this afternoon."

"But weren't you very occupied?" Heathley began edging back toward the others.

"No, I. . . ." Brian fumbled for the truth, for it was, in fact, true that his decision had been reached after he had watched Heathley leave the room. . . . "I wasn't so occupied that I could not give this priority."

"Not with the Security Officer?" Heathley used his bantering voice, but the words fell cold as hail. "Why, if I'm not very much mistaken, Bord must have been with you for a full hour," he said as they joined the others.

In itself the exposure of this small concealment did not matter. There was nothing unusual in the Security Officer spending an hour in any department, particularly when he was holding an investigation to satisfy an outside authority. It was not even uncommon, in that building of glass partitions and long corridors, for one executive to be unaware of visits to other offices. Whatever the trend of their collaboration, whether they were formally in dispute or in agreement, Heathley had never displayed personal emotion. If he had lied to Heathley about the visit of Bord, he could have taken this rebuke. All that he had done was to ignore the interview with Bord because it had no bearing upon his decision to volunteer, though it had actually confirmed it. It was unlike Heathley to show such signs of trifling hostility, trifling distrust, particularly after their talk in the corner. But then was he himself perhaps becoming a little over-sensitive, over-critical, of Heathley? He suddenly felt uncomfortably tense. He indulged in the brief childish wish that the testing flights of Phase II were over. There had been weak moments when he had felt like that about an exam. Then Heathley was reminding him that he was to cure Lydia of slicing the ball. They were all having a drink together, such ordinary decent people.

"What a nice little gathering!" The Memsahib said, as she came in from High Sonding. "And there's Brian Jackson. I want to take you into a corner, young man."

Everybody laughed and Mem, not knowing why, laughed with them. She noticed at the same time that Lydia was not quite herself. Her eyes were anxious, her manner a little over-sociable. Lydia was doing one of her acts and her mother wondered why. That was only a passing thought, however. The Memsahib enjoyed the company much too much to let it bother her. They were quite a presentable lot; and that, in itself, was some consolation for this garrison life which had none of the advantages and most of the drawbacks of a real garrison. Barbed wire now! That was playing at soldiers. Somebody on the bus had mentioned it. The people in the bungalow two doors away had stopped her and pointed it out. She was quite accustomed to living within a stockade or behind ramparts where the whole thing was properly conducted by uniformed people and one had some inkling who the enemy might be. But this ridiculous performance with barbed wire! They had all looked forward to the old lady's reaction and she did not disappoint them. Perhaps her effect was the greater because it enabled them to stop thinking about themselves and each other.

She watched her opportunity and took Brian Jackson aside. "You'll think I'm an interfering old woman, I expect, but I want you to know how much I enjoy my visits to Chestnut Lodge, though I sometimes wish your people had gone on calling it Clumbers. . . ." That was how she began and it was some time before Brian found that there was any purpose behind the polite talk. By that time, he had also lost himself in what she was saying. In spite of the bright room's nervous preoccupations, the chatter of Mrs. Loose drove him back to his own people in the Sondings. He had never cut himself off from those roots. He had never even wished to. He went back regularly to Chestnut Lodge. His affection still steady. He expected little of them; and they nothing of him. It was an easy comfortable step backward into boyhood. He had to make no effort to be himself. He would talk endlessly to Richard and listen to the sharp-tongued reminiscences of his father. He would be forced to eat too much wholesome food at the kitchen table by his mother and his aunt. He had never understood how it was that he gained such strength from these visits. He had never tried to understand.

When the Memsahib started to talk about his father, so characteristically practical, in saving trouble and expense, wanting to go downstairs to meet his coffin on a more convenient level, Brian's heart melted unaccountably. He had not thought about death for a long time. Sometimes, to be sure, he had thought about love, but for most of his waking hours his feelings and his sympathies were tied up in the dynamism of thought and theory which was his life and his ambition.

"I haven't thought of the old man dying," he found himself saying, as if he had known the Memsahib for a very long time.

"I don't suppose he thought of it himself until he knew it was nearly time to go, Brian. Then he mentioned his little problem to me, mostly I think not to hurt anybody's feelings at home. I'm a newcomer, but

I'm used to talking to all sorts of people, particularly people of my own age."

"It's strange, that. The old man has never really talked to anybody."

"It's not so strange, Brian, to want to talk if you know you're going to die." She said it so simply that the whole thing seemed as natural as any High Sonding discussion on the spring crops. She was unaware, perhaps, of the full impact of that sympathy upon the highly organised nature of Brian. The old man was going to die. He took her word for that. He would also do her bidding and see that the old man was moved. He would go tomorrow morning. No: he had this much-talked-of golf match. He would have to go after that. There would be no hope of going upon any of the days when the tests were on. "Do you think it's urgent, this business of moving the old man?"

"Urgent? I hadn't thought of it that way. I should have sought you out and spoken to you about it to-morrow if I hadn't had the good fortune to meet you tonight."

The Memsahib gave him little to assuage that panic which accompanied his first thoughts of death. The Deputy had just died. Was there somebody who had wished to speak to him and look at him while he was still alive, who had thought death to be a terrible and unheard of urgency? Abstract thought hovered insecurely like a silvery girdered structure without any of the comfort of reality. Anybody might die. He himself might die with Heathley in the air test. Old George Jackson, his father, might at this moment die in bed. Was that the end of the whole thing?

"I'm sorry if I've upset you, Brian," said the Memsahib in a gentle even voice. "I know some of you clever people live in the air and it struck me that a word in

95

season. . . ." She patted her black silk dress. It was an elegant hint that there was nothing more to be said. For a desperate moment, Brian wanted to take one of the little old ringed hands and to ask their small authority what happened to people when they were dead.

It was too late for that. Everyone was standing up. The Heathleys' little party was over.

CHAPTER IX

THE M.7 specialists had been working intensively over a long period. They had given up the last two weekends to finish Phase I. The Wednesday had been set aside as an enforced break. It was needed both for physical relaxation and to give the Marine and Engineering Sections a chance to overhaul their equipment before the testing programme began.

It was not surprising, therefore, that the nine-hole golf course at Cresham Strand was crowded. In the little pavilion, the dispirited Mac who acted as Secretary, Professional, Greenkeeper and Bartender, cursed the vagaries of the Research Station which, on days like these, would disgorge, without warning, a host of strangely clad, enthusiastic and, for the most part, erratic golfers. Except when the summer season brought holidaymakers to chafe at the yellowing turf, Mac was able to devote the midweek days to his dreams. Over the hot stove in the office where the steamy windows were rattled by everlasting winds, he could spend long hours planning imaginary golf courses, with evergreen turf, devilish hazards and armies of staff.

It was a cool spring day, that Wednesday, lively with skylarks and the sheen of sunlight upon the gusty grass. The Port Amberley invasion began early and caught Mac just as he was savouring his first brew of tea. Several parties arrived in the official Port Amberley transport. Then came Brian in his car with Alex Leon, Seagram and Baird. The Heathleys were late.

This was not only for the domestic reasons which Lydia gave, though they were convincing enough. The Heathleys had surprised themselves with another domestic wrangle. It had been little more than a tiff, and this time it really had started with the barbed wire.

"I don't see any need to get quite so hysterical about it, Lydia darling. The wire's surely just common-sense protection. After all, there are so many more important things to worry about."

"Then, if it's as unimportant as all that, why did you have to announce to the company at large last night that I was upset about it?"

"You were justifiably upset, Lydia. Why not? Anyone would be. Quite apart from giving one a closed-in feeling, the thing's an aesthetic monstrosity. Anyway, you admitted you were upset."

"If every admission I make to you is to be broadcast as an anecdote, I shall obviously have to be more careful what I say. It seems to me that there are more imprisoning things than barbed wire in the way we're living...."

"Come, come now. It may be a bad idea to live over the shop, so to speak, but it's unavoidable. We're not doing too badly. Surely there are compensations."

"What closes me in even more than the barbed wire," she went on, ignoring him, "is the talk. The everlasting small gossip which makes it necessary to pass on the fact that I'm upset. Then this blasted arrogance of talking shop, going into corners and starting impromptu conferences in whispers. I'm not a fool. I like real talk. But how can I help feeling hedged in by gossip? Do you really suppose that I can ever find it entertaining to spend half my waking life as a lay figure who hears nothing, understands nothing, knows nothing?"

She was unable to stop herself now. The Memsahib had said she had got out of bed the wrong side. It could have been just that, a passing discontent, like indigestion. She had not managed to throw it off, though. She knew that it was deep, not transitory. She knew that she ought to be at her best at a time like this. She ought to be compensating for the strain under which he was working, going more than halfway to meet that reserve of his which lay behind the great stature of his strength and assurance. This should be a time of creative loyalty.

For once it was not. For once, alas, it was the opposite. She had begun with a playful interest in the Red Indian profile of Brian, the graceful turn of a wrist. Then that treacherously innocent image had dissolved into the reality of Alex Leon. After the argument about Alex's invitation to the house, surely Heathley might have noticed her obsession?

She had said not one single word of any consequence to Alex. She could recall nothing of the froth and bubble of that conversation, though its memory was at once blurred and sharp, without beginning or end, like the chorus of the skylarks which soared over the arbitrary patterns of Port Amberley.

If Heathley had shown any capacity for being aware of such an indiscretion, it would be so much easier. If he had not gone off into a corner to talk shop with Brian, with the solemnity of an immortal, she might have had the comfort of being a little abashed by her own recklessness. If he would only be human again, this guilt, which put an edge on her tongue, could have been resolved as a lighthearted frivolity. For was it not—she hastened to assure herself—a flirtatious escapade which had nothing to do with loyalty? Might it not indeed have been confessed without any hurt to that precious understanding which was the very stuff of their life in common?

So she, innocent and perplexed, wove yet another imprisoning strand around herself. Thinking little but feeling much, she tried to justify the homely theory that she had got out of bed on the wrong side. "Suppose I started having secrets of my own?" she finished by saying.

"You're bringing up last night for no particular reason that I can see." Heathley slowed down the car ostentatiously as if she were forcing him to discuss something which might well wait. "All you people could afford to be relaxed last night, but I. . . ."

"I'm a demi-god who can afford nothing, I suppose, and must go into a corner and make a snap decision of the future of the human race?" It was unlike her and she did not know why she said it; but she caused Heathley to stop the car.

"Look here, Lydia, you know as well as I do that we're working on a job which might, in fact, affect the future of the human race. You can sneer at it as much as you like, but that is a sober fact. Sometimes I wish I could get it into a better perspective myself. . . ."

"You don't give yourself time," she snapped. "You'd never *afford* it."

"Let me say this, for heaven's sake, Lydia. Any talk about demi-gods is silly and very nearly obscene."

"So we throw in obscenity as a make-weight?"

"I'm trying to get some sense out of all this, and, for some reason, you seem so obsessed with the trivial that. . . ."

"Drive on, I'm not going to have my game of golf spoilt." She clenched her teeth. At that moment her sense of guilt was a glorious, fabulous, overtone.

Heathley made the great car spurt on. He kept telling himself that this was one of those inconsequential family tiffs. He was angry with himself for being angry. He was doing nearly seventy before he changed into top. In these few seconds of thrusting acceleration, he wondered whether Lydia really hated him. It was an idiotic thought. He was going too fast. Without any finesse at all, he had to brake hard behind a truck full of milk churns.

Her mood changed again. "We seem to be moving by fits and starts, don't we?" she murmured, as if speaking to some clumsy youth who had been trying to show off.

"You said you wanted to get on; and that's what we're doing."

He accelerated again, and the next words which were spoken were her domestic excuses at Cresham Strand. She spoke these looking all the while with a kind of challenging wonder at Alex Leon. She had only half expected to see him there. From the conversation the night before, she knew that he had made no plans about playing golf. Now she believed that he had come because of her, and a silly shock of happiness went through her. Everybody else took his presence for granted. The rest of the party had awaited Heathley's arrival before deciding how they should pair off. The first tee was already crowded with players who had arrived in the official transport.

"I wasn't really thinking of playing," Heathley announced, to everyone's surprise.

Lydia was already on her way to the lockers to fetch her clubs when she heard this. She spun round, suddenly in high spirits. "Don't be silly, Heathley. You must play now that you're here. Such a lovely day for it. And your first opportunity after such a long time!"

Heathley spoke half to her and half to the others.

"I rather thought of going back in the transport later on. There are just a few details I've got to look after. Just a few taps. . . ." He turned to Lydia. "You can have the car, of course."

Lydia walked towards him. "But what about lunch? Mem isn't expecting you."

"I shall manage. There's the canteen. Don't worry. I'm sure that Brian. . . ." He smiled round. He wanted to make sure that nobody would get the impression that he was sulking.

The argument with Lydia had forced him off balance and started a train of doubts. He could not afford to worry. He must check over every certainty, make doubly sure. Ever since he had got up, even during the petulant drive over, he had been telling himself that he could not afford to worry. Yet there was the possibility of the Director telephoning or even returning unexpectedly. There was the business of the police and the Coroner's Officer, with which Bord and Tatham had insisted that they could cope. Bord had been emphatic about not needing any members of the staff. It would be futile, he had said, to break into this one day of leisure. He had only been doing his duty when he questioned Heathley about his own movements after the dance. Nevertheless, Heathley felt that it was taking a chance to be off the Station while enquiries were being brought to a conclusion.

Then there was the routine work of the engineering people. He had no need, and indeed no right, to overlook them. Yet suppose snags developed? Suppose some small unforeseen thing cropped up to delay the tests? His opportunity had been seized. It would be madness to risk a postponement. By going back he would have the place to himself. He would be able to think clearly. There were the larger perspectives to get into focus. He had no illusions about the importance, or the danger, of what he was forcing through. By being alone, he would be able to attune himself to that importance and fortify himself against that danger.

"I'm sure you and Brian will have a hefty lunch after you've beaten him, Lydia," he said lightly, keeping his smile. To himself he added the thought that the change of company would do Lydia good. It might cure these unpredictable moods of hers. It might free her thoughts. It might even dispel that curious persistence, sometimes tender, sometimes querulous, with which she had been probing him.

Brian's response, therefore, surprised him almost as much as it did Lydia. "I'm sorry, Heathley, but I can't stay on for lunch, anyway."

"You don't mean to say that you're going back to the Station as well?" Lydia frowned.

"There's surely no need for both of us to go?" Heathley added.

There was a shadow of embarrassment in Brian's voice which puzzled Lydia and brought suspicion to Heathley's over-active mind. "I might look in the Station. After all, there's no harm in that, is there?" he said, brusquely, to cover the embarrassment. "But I've really got to go over to the Sondings. I've arranged to look in and see my people."

Brian had never had any inhibitions about the kind of family he came from. In any case, he worked in a world where people's reputations were mostly self-made and there was little outlet for social snobbery. His present shyness and hesitancy lay deeper than that. Mem's conversation about his father had aroused a sense of urgency which he could neither throw off nor explain away. He had come to play golf grudgingly because there had been no polite way out. He knew that his brother, Richard, would not be back from the market until after midday. Nevertheless, he would have preferred to have spent the morning at home waiting for him, even undergoing the sly inquisitions of his father.

He recognised the superstition and the thrift in the old man's desire not to die upstairs. He understood that because of his blood. He had telephoned to say that he would be home for the midday meal. That was the traditional time of family conferences. They would wait for Richard before they started. Having had his message, they would wait for him too.

"No trouble at home, I hope?" said Heathley. "The old man's still going strong, I suppose?"

"No crisis of any sort," said Brian calmly. "But, as Mrs. Loose was telling me last night at your house, the old man doesn't seem to be getting any stronger."

"I'm sorry about that." There was warmth in the way he said it. He and old George had always remained close friends. Then he turned to Lydia: "That rather cuts out your escort for lunch. I'm sorry about that, but perhaps if you bring the car back we might. . . ."

There was beginning to be a hint of reluctance in his voice, but Lydia cut him off as if she were unaware of it. "I shall lunch with Alex!"

"That will be terrific!" cried Alex. "And perhaps if the Professor will give me half an hour's tuition before he goes off, that will be better still. . . ."

So it was arranged. Sam Seagram led off with Baird. Lydia and Brian followed them. Heathley, who could never resist giving tuition, took Alex off to the eighth tee, which was surrounded by enough sand-dunes, as Mac always claimed delightedly, "to break a man's heart."

Lydia, of course, did everything except slice the ball.

She played a man's game on the paltry but difficult course where only Heathley had ever beaten her. Brian, excited and exerted to the full, was amazed that anybody could play at once so frivolously and so well. He took his golf seriously and he also regarded it as a social attribute, having a certain prestige value. They were all square by the time they reached the ninth hole, where Alex, pottering about with an iron, announced that Heathley had just gone. "He left in terrific form, singing away to himself. I really believe he enjoyed my bad play. I suppose you two are going round again? If the Professor hadn't exhausted me, I'd come with you."

Intent on their match, delighted with themselves and with each other because they had been playing at the top of their form, Lydia and Brian left him trying to apply the theories of aerodynamics to approach shots.

Lydia was beginning to win at their fifteenth hole when they saw him again. She was delighted that he had strolled over to walk back with them. For the first time since that subtle, delicious treachery in her heart, she felt easy in his presence.

How was she to know that this was the moment when that impressionable heart of his, which sometimes seemed so jaded and which looked out on the world so mockingly from beneath the heavy hoods of his eyelids, found an overwhelming excitement in her presence? Nothing could have been more foreign to his natural taste than the strenuous, fundamentally absurd antics of her skill as she won the game. His desires always surprised him; but never more astonishingly than when he fell in love, with a ferocity which choked him, at the sight of a woman playing golf with wit and verve. He gulped and sighed in an attempt to meet the improbability of the situation.

As for Lydia, she was aware of his admiration, and

played all the better for it, without realising its intensity. It was innocent, it was fatal—that sweet game haunted by the keen salt wind and the choir of skylarks. It meant, when Brian went off, beaten, happy but obsessed with getting home, that his going was unnoticed. It meant, too, that Alex began to woo her; magically, relentlessly, as they sped across the flats toward the ornate, half-empty Grand Hotel at Flimby.

Lydia drove the car expertly, but wide-eyed, because no man had ever spoken to her like that. She entered the draughty palm-court like a queen, and the two weary waiters looked and looked again, unaccustomed to any extravagance of foolish happiness in that place where elderly people wintered for their health.

PART TWO

*L'amour-propre fait plus de
libertins que l'amour.*

JEAN JACQUES ROUSSEAU
Emile

CHAPTER X

THE Director had given only half an hour's notice of
his return. When he landed at the airstrip on the
Thursday, Heathley and Brian Jackson had already
started the Phase II test. Everybody concerned was
either preoccupied with the test or standing by for the
results to come in. Everybody was painstakingly keeping up a pretence of being unaware that anything
unusual was happening.

It was proper enough in the circumstances for the
Security Officer to go to the airstrip to meet the
Director. He was the one senior member of the staff
not tied to immediate departmental routine. It was his
job to keep an eye on arrivals and departures. Moreover, his progress report on the Deputy's death was
likely to be the Director's first concern.

Sir Hereward Cruddock was a figure of international
renown. It was not only his scientific distinction but his
grasp of political and social implications which had
given him such prestige. He had an eye for the public
eye. He had a nose for genius. He had a taste for power.
The few people who did not unquestionably revere
him said that he had his ear to the ground.

Such comments were few and far between. Though

he was not averse to popularity, there was nothing of the charlatan about Hereward Cruddock, even in those nicely calculated expansive moments of his. He knew his stuff. He was a man of justice and integrity, respected, he liked to think, by people who mattered, and feared by those who did not. Even outside the scope of his own work, he was a force to be reckoned with—a force whose full potency only a fool—and there were some—would underestimate. He looked up over Bord's shoulder (for he was uncommonly short) and said testily: "Where's Heathley? I'd hoped to see him straight away."

Bord was just about to explain that Heathley was already testing, when the Director answered himself. "But, of course, Heathley will be busy. I'd overlooked that."

It was his way of finding out immediately but in-directly whether Phase II had started on schedule. He had had to go to Cabinet level to obtain permission to come back at this moment. Nevertheless, he had timed his return so that there could be no question of him being called upon to give the starting signal. He had formerly left such matters in the hands of the Deputy. He had no wish even now to be bogged down by details and so lose sight of the larger implications. While keeping himself informed, he liked his sanction to be remote and to delegate all operational authority.

"You might ask Flying Control why they've not attended to that obstruction on No. 2 Runway, Bord," he said, indulging in his favourite sleight of mind in introducing several subjects simultaneously and keep-ing his subordinates on their toes. "I hope this lament-able business about the Deputy has not been allowed to upset people and take their minds off their work? You realise, of course, that I would have returned instantly if it had been possible. I gather it was heart failure. I'm not entirely surprised. I'd like to talk to the Medical Officer about it, if you'll be good enough to arrange it. You will realise, of course, that I'm particularly anxious not to have the Press nosing about at a time like this. I hope you've taken extra precautions. I shall go straight to the Control Room now. We can have our conference about the Deputy afterwards."

"The Coroner's Officer is still on the Station, sir. I thought perhaps you ought to know the course the enquiries are taking. . . ." Bord began when at last there was a pause.

"Later, Bord, later. . . . We've got too much on our hands just at the moment. I'm sure, meanwhile, I can leave the police side of it in your hands. You might get someone to call my wife, too, and say I'm back. Warn her that we may have a visit from the Minister."

Then the Director was gone and Bord wondered how he had failed to make the best of the meeting. He had wanted to demonstrate to the Director how tactfully the event had been handled. He had wanted to announce that the inquest would be held in Tollbury that afternoon, that there would be no jury and that the Coroner's Officer had made up his mind that the cause of death had been heart failure and that the mishap upon the slipway had been accidental. He had hoped to take credit for this, though in fact the Coroner's Officer had seemed to be only too ready to accept these conclusions. Instead he had had to listen while all the obvious steps were pointed out to him, had been accorded no priority and had been treated as if he were just an administrative cog.

This was all wrong. Cruddock might well be obsessed with Phase II, but this was a wonderful opportunity to stand higher in his confidence. If he were ever going to plant effectively his suspicions about the Deputy's accident, he would need a more leisurely, less formal approach. Yet Cruddock, who was always advocating "get-togethers" among the staff and improvements in social amenities, was the least accessible of executives. Like Queen Victoria, he insisted that his entourage should communicate in writing before asking for interviews. By such means he maintained that he could "keep everything in broad perspective." For similar reasons, and to avoid giving the staff the feeling that he was "living on the top of them," he had taken an ample Georgian house in Little Sonding to which his higher executives were invited as need arose—or, as Felix Tatham had put it, "in the same deadly rotation as any headmaster's tea-parties."

Such men as the late Deputy, Heathley or Baird had rarely gone outside their specialist or academic environments. They were widely known among those in the know. This did not mean that their capacities were limited. Both in research and in administration, they had wide experience and were respected wherever their names were known. Sir Hereward Cruddock's peculiar talent was in being universally recognised not only as a specialist and an administrator but also as an interpreter, as one who understood all the implications. He might joke with the up-and-coming juniors of the laboratory staff, but he could make a lasting impression upon a commander-in-chief. He could speak half a dozen languages. He photographed well. He held a D.S.O. for combat in the string-bag aircraft of the First World War. He was mentioned by name in the memoirs of former Prime Ministers and American Generals. He stood five foot four in his socks, wore pince-nez spectacles with a black ribbon, piloted himself when he travelled by air, had four sons, and was generally voted young for his age. The only people who were not in some way awed by him were his wife, who was an eminent historian, and the Memsahib. Lady Cruddock said: "I have civilised him by regular meals." The Memsahib said: "He would have done so well in India, when India was India. What a pity he's all run to facts and figures."

The suspicions in Bord's mind were not such as could be put in writing. To be expressed with any effect, they needed just the right timing and the correct inflection. That was why he was disappointed by the Director's preoccupied mood. "Sir Hereward Cruddock asks me to say that he is most sorry not to be able to talk to you," he said to the Coroner's Officer when he returned to his office. "Sir Hereward has just flown in from an international conference and he's expecting the Minister of Research and Development. It's a routine visit, of course, but naturally it has to have first call upon the Director's time."

It was his duty to play down Port Amberley to the outside world, but not to underplay its importance—or his own. He would even take certain risks in the course of duty, and the Coroner's Officer was one of them. After his partial failure with Cruddock, it did him good to hear the man say: "I quite understand, Colonel. I'm more than satisfied with all the help you've given me." The details of the funeral and the inquest were discussed. Felix Tatham was called in, for it was now becoming a "personnel" matter. Bord prepared to edge out.

He was making for the Control Room. There were a dozen reasons why he should be there. Apart from the overwhelming interest of the test itself, there was the necessity of capturing Cruddock's attention and confidence, if only for a few minutes. How significant those minutes might be! His eyes misted over, and his dreamy look might well have been simply an inheritance of his Irish blood, were it not for that keen focus which showed him the two men in his office, as it were from the wrong end of a telescope. He still recognised those pigmy replicas of the men he spoke to—one his colleague, the other the acquiescent stranger who had come to bring a legal formula for the wretched Deputy's death. Indeed, he saw them both, friend and stranger, with searching clarity.

For this dreaminess of his was not just an amiable Irish trait: nor was it merely a defence thrown up by a creature who could never come to terms with his fellows; nor was it only a trick of camouflage to cover an aching adolescence for ever seeking maturity. It owed something to all these; but most of all it was the expression of a nihilistic attachment. As he stood by the door taking his leave of the two men, with a genial military nod of his head, with his eyes half closed, he became almost giddy with this exaltation. He saw his present actions and decisions as being of paramount importance in themselves. They rode high over all allegiances. They derided the accepted codes of behaviour.

From his preoccupied gracious exit, nobody could have guessed his tumult. It was a fire damped down beneath the keen exterior of the Security Officer who had so much on his hands that morning. All the way to the Control Room, though, he had to let himself go. He had to let his fancy rip with the urgency of a blasphemer, with the intensity of a fanatic. He exulted in being alone in that place as a blasphemer might have done in a church.

He had to do it. He had to have those moments, however rare, when he saw himself as other men would see their Maker. For that he needed no mirror. The mask of his neat dog-like officer face did not change except for the eyes. And they were those of a man transfigured; a saint or a devil in agony or ecstasy.

Now only that nihilistic power of his was real. His detachment was a trance out of which he could walk at will, the ever successful accomplice to his own grand designs, with the easy military bearing of one whose education, background, war record and integrity stood up to every test. To indulge in such moments too often would have shown a lack of self-discipline. While constant awareness of his inner purposes was essential, even its secret revelation was risky in that it tended to leave him weakened and subdued. After parking outside the Control Room, he closed his eyes for a few seconds and relaxed like a boxer in the corner of the ring, throwing back his head. There was nothing visionary about his eyes as he glanced at the Security Guard on the door and pointed to where a button was missing from the man's tunic.

The Control Room was divided into three main parts. There was the "Floor," which was a spacious galleried room, at a first glance not unlike one of the larger Air Force Operations Rooms in World War II. There were situation boards, plotting tables, operational charts and radar equipment, with side-rooms for signalling, meteorological, navigation, air-control and clerical staffs. The walls were regular on three sides. The fourth, opposite the Entrance Lobbies, was of reinforced glass, built out over the water like a huge bay window and commanding a view of the Experimental Marine Section.

The next level was known as the "Upper Deck." It consisted of a half-moon-shaped room built over the bay, connected by the galleries to a square room built

113

over the Entrance Lobbies. The Upper Deck was reserved for the higher executives and specialists concerned with directional control, navigation and assessment. Above this was a sanctum known as the "Dome." It was shaped not unlike a spacious umbrella, fitted with sliding panels to ensure good visibility in all directions. Batteries of television and radar screens, microphones and amplifiers and statistical and other devices were installed by means of which the detail of any current experiment could be analysed at a glance. There was a horseshoe-shaped table to enable a number of people to sit there to confer and, if necessary, to assume supreme control.

Only the Director and the Deputy possessed passkeys to the Dome, which was not an essential unit in routine experiments. The presence of the Director in the Dome, in fact, came as something of a surprise to the Control Room staff that morning. But when Cruddock tuned in to the communication circuits and asked two or three departments for reports in his most casual reassuring voice, he managed to sound as if he had been there for hours. Everybody heard him say: "I'm leaving everything to you, of course, Duty Controller; but I'm naturally available for consultation in the much regretted absence of our Deputy. For the time being, I should like a personal report from the Met. people and from Intelligence." Then he pressed the switch which cut across everything and enabled him to speak direct to the Duty Controller. "You must be particularly cautious about the scope of this operation, Kennedy. Get the Navigational people to give a thirty instead of a forty second check-plot. We must avoid any large incidence of unfriendly interception of plots. When they pass the supersonic barrier, there is also the danger that they may overrun into proscribed territory." Then he had his little joke which always instilled confidence in the most overwrought of subordinates to whom he had pointed out the obvious: "The earth hardly provides enough room for these projects, Kennedy. The damn place is getting so confined. But we must do the best we can." Everybody smiled. The Old Man was on form.

The Security Officer had been conscientious in working out a Control Room procedure for himself. He would report in to the Floor to indicate that he was available if required. He would be admitted to the Upper Deck afterwards partly as a courtesy and partly as a gesture toward the practical necessity of keeping him in the picture. For special consultations, he was on rare occasions summoned to the Dome, but only fleetingly and with humiliating indifference to the fact that he might be intelligent enough to take an interest in the unique methods of assessment which were used there.

As Bord passed in, therefore, he noted who was on duty on the Upper Deck. Kennedy was an efficient, meek man. One who excelled at technique and whose loyalty would stand up to torture—Bord's imagination applied such tests—but who had overstepped the mark politically from time to time by writing obtuse and irascible letters to obscure journals about the economics of the Mediterranean. This weakness had suggested to some people that Kennedy was "a political." To Bord's discovery that he had once believed in Social Credit he owed his rescue from suspicion.

So Kennedy said at once: "Ask Colonel Bord to come up here," when the message from the Floor was relayed to him. He was very much occupied, but he smiled in a friendly way, for he regarded Bord as an ally. "What's the trouble, now, Colonel?" he asked cheerfully. "Spy-hunt?"

Everyone joked with the Security Officer about spies. Bord liked it. He smiled back "Game's all shot to rags, Kennedy. This is only a minor check-up, but it's one of those little things which won't wait. I realize that you're all very preoccupied." He glanced round. Most of the instruments on the recording panel were in action. He heard Heathley's voice on a small amplifier, then Jackson's. "Everything going all right?"

"Just about running to form and reasonable results so far, though they're using the unmodified prototype. Of course, the real fun will come later when they reach the high-speed tests. Now what can I do for you, Colonel?"

"Answer me one question. Did the Deputy ever hand you over any keys?"

"I should naturally have reported it by now if he had," Kennedy said primly. "Why? Are there some missing?"

Bord shrugged his shoulders. "That's just a point I have to settle. You've given me your answer and I don't need to trouble you any further. Sorry to have interrupted you. I'm just sticking around here for the time being. I know the Director wants to see me. He told me to come along when I met him on his arrival at the airstrip."

"Was he very cut up about losing the Deputy?" Kennedy had a nose for Port Amberley gossip.

"I'd say it was impossible for Cruddock to be cut up by anything happening to one of his juniors," Bord said, with just the right amount of spite to appeal to the ill-humoured rhetorician in Kennedy. Then, like a teacher passing through a playground, he began to move around tactfully, unobtrusively, observing the preliminary results as they were assessed, controlled and checked by the Upper Deck staff.

The proceedings were strangely dominated by Heathley at the controls of the prototype machine. He was amplifying the data which poured in on the recording instruments which automatically and instantaneously plotted the position and behaviour of the craft under test. Sometimes Heathley discussed some point raised by one of the specialists as gravely and as unhurriedly as if he were in the next room instead of making this unique cruise already several hundred miles distant. He answered queries from the Control Room. He held discussions with Brian Jackson and they carried out several special tests together, taking it in turns to report back. It was clear already that M.7 was at least a partial success. Bord was conscious of the tremor which passed through those privileged ones on the Upper Deck who were sharing these significant hours with Heathley and Jackson. From time to time, somebody would turn and grin at him spontaneously, glad that he was there to witness at least a part of the vital secrets which he, above all, was responsible for guarding. The Director only intervened once on these busy craft-to-base communication circuits, which were shared perhaps in all by two dozen people and which were scrambled so efficiently as to be unintelligible to the rest of the world.

"It's Cruddock speaking," he said over the circuit. "I just want Heathley and Jackson to know that I'm following their efforts with intense interest. I congratulate you both upon the results so far. The only point I have at the moment is navigational. I think you'll have to increase the rate of your navigational check. What do you say, Jackson?"

"I don't think it's going to be at all easy to check at

this end, sir," came the country burr of Brian's voice. "I think we must rely on instruments for that. Don't you agree, Heathley?"

"Most certainly I agree, sir. When we increase speed, I see no hope whatever of increasing the navigational check rate."

"I see, thank you," said the Director.

Then there was a moment's pause which, though it was not intended as such, contrived to register annoyance and doubt in Cruddock's mind. It only lasted as he switched from one circuit to another, this pause. Bord noticed, though, that Baird and Kennedy exchanged glances which could only mean "I told you so." Then the Director was asking for the head of the Navigation Department and the Duty Navigation Officer to report for a conference in the Dome. Did this mean that there was a weak spot? Bord almost overlooked the urgency of his own need to see the Director in his preoccupation with this.

His turn came sooner than he expected. Cruddock still wished to emphasise that the operational responsibility was in the hands of his subordinates and that he had other things to think of, both with the organisation of Port Amberley and in the higher spheres of influence outside. "I shall be receiving a visit from the Minister within the next hour," he announced, so that everybody could hear him. "It goes without saying that no special acknowledgment of the Minister's presence is needed from anybody. He fully realises that concentrated work is in progress and will not expect any personal attention from anybody but myself. Now, I'm ready to see the Security Officer."

CHAPTER XI

"IT's not that I don't trust you, Colonel Bord. It's an automatic precaution. I've let myself get into the habit of it," laughed Sir Hereward Cruddock as he pressed the various buttons on his desk operating the security blinds which covered the more important situation board, charts and statistical summaries in the Dome.

"Quite proper, sir, I'm sure." Bord stood to attention, underlining the formality of his entrance. By such means he supposed, rightly, he was most likely to persuade the Director to relax. His purpose could not be served if the interview were to remain upon a strict official footing.

"You will realise, Bord, that I have returned to singularly exacting tasks. The death of the Deputy could not have come at a more awkward moment—just when we need an unbroken pattern. So I want you to understand that this is a matter for decisive action rather than talk, whatever one's personal feelings may be. I'm relying on you to summarise the situation as you see it. It should be quite possible for us to have everything cut and dried by the time the Minister arrives."

Bord liked the use of the word "us" in that sentence. It encouraged him as much as the cigarette which the Director thrust toward him across the horseshoe table.

"I think, sir," he began, with a gloss of self-respecting humility in his voice, "that we shall be able to write off the whole of the official proceedings by this afternoon. Our Personnel Officer, Tatham, is of course handling the details with the Medical Officer, the police and the Coroner's Officer. It would not be proper for me to anticipate the views of the Coroner himself, but I think I can add that the cause of death will be found to be heart failure. The verdict of the inquest will be death from natural causes. I hope I was right in seeing that the investigations here were not prolonged. In fact, sir, from the moment I took over, which was within a few minutes of the Deputy being found in a coma, I've done everything in my power to limit the impact of the affair and to damp down anything which would lend itself to publicity. It seemed to me from the start that undue publicity might invalidate or even postpone operational work."

It came as a slight shock to Cruddock to realise how intensely he had been staring into the milky-blue eyes of his Security Officer. He had encountered visionary eyes like that before, but only rarely. He considered himself to be well equipped as a judge of men. His individual judgments were vital in holding together the complex organisation he controlled, and indeed they often had far-reaching effects outside it. He had often found clues to character by scrutinising his man in a seemingly offhand manner like this. There was something odd, however, about this fellow Bord. Those eyes of his contrasted in a disturbing manner with the efficiency of the report which the precise voice was reciting.

Even before he had spoken to members of the Cabinet about the sudden death of the Deputy, Cruddock had been aware of the far-reaching importance of the appointment of his successor. He had welcomed the suggestion of an immediate visit from the

Minister, not because he intended to rely upon the shrewd but amateurish judgments of that able young politician; he was autocratically self-reliant in his choice of men. The Minister's presence, however, would facilitate that knack of his for shifting the apparent responsibility on to others. While there was every reason for the new appointment to be made at once, it must not look as if it had been made hurriedly. The choice he had in mind might not be generally popular. That was why he wished to make certain of all his facts and to let it be known that he had weighed up every possibility which might have a bearing upon them. It was his second nature now to behave with such detachment, but a dash of cunning went with it.

He was particularly pleased with the Security Officer's report because it took off his hands all necessity for making investigations personally. He tilted himself back in his chair with that pretence of sleepy preoccupation which he adopted when his mind was working at high pressure.

"That seems very satisfactory as far as it goes, Bord," he murmured. He waited just long enough for Bord to look pleased and to hesitate. Then he needled: "But what really happened, man? I need a little more from you than just an efficient report."

The pale eyes were flecked with shadow, and Cruddock knew that he was right to pursue this. The Security Officer's manner was elaborately reticent when he said: "I don't quite understand what you mean, sir. There are, of course, certain small details of the case which would seem . . . how shall I say . . . would seem as if they might need a little elucidation. . . . But I propose to let them lie."

"So you regard the whole affair as being completely covered and explained? Is that it, Bord?"

It was obvious that the man was unable entirely to conceal the doubts in his mind, though his training or his professional tact made him hesitant. It might all have a bearing, Cruddock told himself. He had had to make many far-reaching decisions in his time. Perhaps the reason why he had never made a fundamental mistake either in science or in human relationships was that he never forgot the nursery adage to leave no stone unturned.

"Come on, Bord," he said. "I need more than just a correct attitude. Our work here is much too important to be left to the mercy of a group of watertight minds. That's why I've always stressed the importance of human relationships. Now smoke that cigarette and tell me what is at the back of your mind. Remember I'm quite accustomed to talk with complete frankness off the record with a great many people here simply because I can trust them and they can trust me." He rapped out the word *trust* with his ring on the horse-shoe table.

As Bord sat down, excitement flickered and then blazed in the pale eyes. "It's very nice of you to put it that way, Sir Hereward. I'm sure you appreciate that it's the nature of my job as your Security Officer to work on suspicion. Naturally it's a side of my job which I have to keep to myself. I'm only responsible to you for hard and fast conclusions and matters of fact." He cleared his throat portentously and the Director began to fidget with the set of sharp pencils which, out of habit, he had taken from a drawer.

"I quite realise, Bord, that it's no part of your task to keep me posted with the Station gossip, though from time to time Tatham seems to think that I should like to hear it. But there! Young Tatham is something of a wit, and he very rarely tells me anything that isn't amusing. It helps me to keep in touch with people. Now, in security matters, I can quite see that you've to keep yourself a little to yourself. You need your finger on the pulse. You have to know what is going on without appearing to be nosey. For that reason, I have, I hope, always seen to it that you've been kept in the picture. You've reasonable access to the Control Room, for instance. I have always insisted on that. Without going so far as to take any operational responsibility, you've always been entitled to a fair degree of operational knowledge." Cruddock slipped back into his old vice of pointing out the obvious, but he believed he was putting this keen but somewhat inhibited officer at his ease, or at least to bring him to some point where those latent forces in his eyes could be expressed, if not explained. "I take it, Bord, that the Deputy did, in fact, die from heart failure?"

"He died in hospital and the doctors think it was heart failure. One of my own men was present at the bedside from the time the Deputy reached Tollbury Hospital till the end."

"That was a sensible precaution, Colonel."

"One tries to take whatever precautions are necessary, Sir Hereward. The Deputy only spoke once. We had no idea at the time, of course, that they were his last words. His sudden death, I imagine, came as a surprise even to the hospital staff."

"And what did he say, Bord? That's surely a matter of great importance." The Director began to doodle formulae with one of the pencils.

"It's of importance to the verdict, of course. The only words he said, sir, were *entirely my own fault.* Just that and nothing more. Of course, it suggests that the whole thing was an accident. In fact, it appears to be almost conclusive."

"But to your mind it was not conclusive?"

"I am trained not to accept every conclusion at its face value, if you'll forgive me for saying so, sir. I'd already begun a routine investigation before these words were said. In view of some odds and ends which hardly amounted to circumstantial fact, it seemed to me that these words could be interpreted in two ways. The obvious one is that the whole thing was an accident. The less obvious interpretation I felt was that the Deputy was trying to excuse somebody else—mentioning that it was his fault and not that other person's."

"That's very subtle of you, Bord. In fact, it verges upon the far-fetched. Had the Deputy been drinking more than usual?"

"The doctor gave the opinion that he'd been drinking rather heavily." He stopped. "But, as you know, it was the night of the dance. . . ."

"Surely there's not what you call heavy drinking at these get-togethers of ours, Bord? That's not what we meant when we initiated them."

"I don't think the drink necessarily had a lot to do with it, Sir Hereward. And in any case there's no drink to speak of at these social functions. Mrs. Heathley and other members of the committee provide some sort of wine cup."

"I remember that from the dance before," said the Director, permitting himself a humorous shudder. "So you think it was not just a few too many drinks which caused this admirable Deputy of mine to stumble into the slipway."

"I've no proof of anything, sir. I merely have some vague surmises of my own that rather point to the fact that the Deputy might not have been alone at the time."

"Aha! Where were you yourself when this was happening?"

"I was with several other people at Professor Heathley's quarters."

"So you heard the news there? That must have been something of a shock to Heathley, wasn't it?"

"Professor Heathley wasn't there, Sir Hereward." Bord's right hand went out to the ashtray and he slowly, deliberately, ground out his cigarette, so that the pause took on a significance without a word being said.

Cruddock glanced across the table quickly, hoping to catch sight of those revealing eyes, but they were lowered. Then he tilted his chair again, acted the stifling of a yawn, and said: "And Jackson? Was he with you?"

"No, Ilse Leon, Jackson and Heathley were all in or about the Experimental Block that evening. It's clear enough that Jackson was on his way to the Aerodynamics Department to check up on the wind-tunnel work. I'm not clear about the other two."

"That's where your suspicions and surmises begin. Yet it was Heathley who spoke to me."

"Professor Heathley was not in his office when our people first telephoned to notify him of the accident. He got to hear of it immediately afterwards because he rang up his wife before I'd left his house. Then we met in the Sick Bay and afterwards he insisted on speaking to you on the telephone from his own office."

"That was proper enough in the circumstances. There were operational issues involved," said the Director thoughtfully. "You wouldn't like to tell me your surmises, I suppose, Bord?"

"I don't think I should, Sir Hereward. But I will just add that Heathley himself seemed to have a curiously sudden desire for a check-up on Ilse Leon that evening. He telephoned to my office soon after he had spoken to you."

"So you and Heathley felt that there might have been something odd in the behaviour of Ilse à *propos* the Deputy?" He tapped his teeth with the pencil which had already covered a sheet of paper with hiero-glyphics. "She's a steady worker, though I sometimes notice that there's a funny sort of intensity about her. You checked up, naturally?"

"Checked and cross-checked, sir. She had certainly had a number of dances with the Deputy, but you will recollect how he tended to come out of his skin at these functions and Ilse Leon is nothing if not skittish. I'm fairly satisfied in my own mind that she went to the Experimental Block, as she said she did, after the dance." There was a long pause. This time it was not contrived. One or other of them had to say it, and after a time the Director realised that his Security Officer would never say it. So he himself was forced to break the silence: "That really only leaves Heathley out of all the people were were at all likely to have been with the Deputy by the slipway after the other people had gone home?"

"It seems too ridiculous for me to suggest it, Sir Hereward, but that's what I have in mind. And I felt that it was something which I couldn't even hint at—at least not to anybody but yourself. . . ."

The Director threw down the pencil. "It's really too far-fetched. But you're right to mention it. You're perfectly right, too, to close these particular investiga-tions. Now tell me one thing, have you any reason to suspect that Heathley. . . . No, it's too ridiculous. There would be no possible motive for Heathley. . . ."

The Director, who had bent down his head over a

fresh sheet of paper, surprised Bord with a searching look. The excitement still lingered in those strange pale eyes. That startlingly hypnotic shadow-play had not died down.

Once again, Bord's behaviour seemed to contrast with those eyes of his. He spoke steadily, thoughtfully. "It's none of my business to understand more than the general trend of the work here, Sir Hereward. But I think it's common knowledge among those in the know that there's been a certain amount of conflict between Professor Heathley and the late Deputy."

"Conflict?" Cruddock seemed taken aback at such a forceful word, and Bord was quick to notice it.

"Perhaps I should say a certain measure of professional disagreement, Sir Hereward. A disagreement, perhaps about means rather than ends. In any case, I don't stress this—er—conflict. I've noticed—and again I must emphasise it's part of my duty—that Professor Heathley has been working under something of a strain. He seems very conscious that he is the foremost among those working on the M.7 project."

"Not necessarily."

Bord wavered. "Naturally you're the best judge of that, sir. I've always taken it for granted that he is the one indispensable individual. . . ." His voice took on a questioning, almost a pleading, tone. "With such great responsibility on his shoulders, it seems only natural— at least that's how I see it—that the Professor should not be quite his normal self." Bord's eyes flickered, but the Director was doodling again and did not see them. "Now, sir, one's not here to make a study of normality. On the contrary, and with due respect, I don't think such an organisation as this, working under pressure upon matters of such vast importance, can lend itself to the normality which one expects in the armed forces or

127

in commercial life. Therefore I feel myself bound to make allowances but also to be on the look-out for abnormalities which are potentially dangerous. That's all I have to say at the moment, sir. You'll forgive me if I've said too much."

When Cruddock looked up, blinds, like the security shutters, had been drawn down over the eyes of Bord. "I'm glad you've been frank, Bord. I shall not ask you any more."

He pressed the button which brought to life the amplifier carrying the craft-to-base circuit. Heathley was talking calmly and deliberately to the Duty Navigation Officer. His voice came into the room so suddenly that Bord started as he turned to go. Cruddock, tilting back his chair again, wondered if the Security Officer himself suffered from nervous strain. He stopped Bord near the door and said: "You might ask Major Seagram to stand by. I met him in Washington during the war, and I think I ought to have a word with him as he has just joined us."

He timed his remark well. Nevertheless, it caused Bord to make a quick reorientation of his attitude toward Sam Seagram. For Sam, though he had spoken of having a nodding acquaintance with the Director, had neglected to be specific about any former meeting in Washington. Bord never overlooked a trifle like that.

CHAPTER XII

LYDIA listening to the story of old George Jackson which Mem told in a matter-of-fact voice which she might have used for any everyday occurrence, envied her mother's talent for becoming involved, always creatively, in other people's lives. A spirit like that could never be pent up behind the barbed wire of Port Amberley.

Talk of old George revealed much that was in Brian. Incidentally, it also explained his anxiety to rush home from the golf course. Heathley's urge to return to the Station instead of playing golf had also been explained subsequently by his decision to participate in the Thursday air test. Yet, in spite of these two good reasons for her being thrown into the company of Alex, she still believed that there was something magical, fatal, about what had happened. It was as if an all-seeing tempter had been reading the secrets of her very blood, and, because of them, had contrived that incredible but so readily explicable turn of events at Cresham Strand. No sooner had she begun to suffer a shallow fancy for Brian Jackson which had developed into a deep passion for Alex Leon, than the most ordinary circumstances had shaped that devastating encounter.

After the small talk of the evening before, when she had exchanged banter with Alex at the little gathering which must have seemed such an ordinary occasion to everyone else, she had told herself that this frenzy of hers was safe. A quixotic safety, perhaps, for it depended on Alex's airy disregard for her, except as the wife of a colleague, and, she hoped, as an amusing companion.

Her heart had leapt innocently, therefore, when she turned the nose of the car toward Flimby. This chance of having Alex all to herself was a windfall. She could be happy, so her innocence told her, in his presence without the least danger of revealing herself. His able chatter, his sophistication, his almost comic politeness, could never land her into indiscreet confidences. What was wrong with it as a gay interlude? Even if it were weighted on her side by an extravagant joy mingling with a disturbing guilt and the innocence of a daffodil day.

That Alex could have changed overnight never occurred to her. Even when he confessed that he had never really been moved by her beauty until it was revealed as she played golf so joyously and recklessly, she dismissed the idea as some playful extravagance. It was inconceivable that a woman could look her best in that way on a golf course. It was quite bizarre that a man of Alex's maturity should declare that he had developed a passion for her while she was swinging a golf club. As the Memsahib's daughter, Lydia was well founded in the conventions. So Lydia supposed that it could only be an Englishman, and the wearer of an old school tie, to boot, who could possibly fall in love with a person playing a game—and then it should surely be lawn tennis.

She had been then quite unprepared for the potency of Alex's wooing. That would have been formidable at any time. It had been (as she suspected, and as he was at no pains to conceal) just as forceful many other times before. Coming as it did at the very moment when she

130

could have resisted anything in the world but the desire of this one man, she had been defenceless. With all her guilt, and the hysteria of her imprisoned spirit, she could only throw herself at his mercy.

Alex Leon, of course, lacked any sort of mercy. There were none of the code tactics of the old school tie about him. After lunch, they motored inconsequentially out along the high ground between Flimby and Ruxtable. At the highest point, he made her stop the car. "We're just two people who have been waiting for each other all our lives, Lydia. It doesn't surprise me in the least that we happened to be unaware of it. It was something predestined. So many things have happened to me that way. Look at the sky over the sea, Lydia. Doesn't it convince you that at this moment we are the only two people in the whole wide world?"

She looked at the sky and felt giddy. He was watching her raised profile, the petal-delicacy of her colouring in that unearthly light. Then she turned to look at him in the loneliness of their sudden love. It might be a moment of illusion, but it had reality for her as a pinnacle above the world. The imprisoning barbed wire lay far below, a pinpoint of sunlight upon some buried valley lake. Their kiss lasted long, until this vision formed a sheen of sky and water, without horizon, with a multitude of specks dancing.

"You see, Lydia, this had to happen and it found its own time. It had to break out and declare itself. Though you and I were meeting, as we shall go on meeting to-morrow and the next day, as chance acquaintances. . . . Though you and I were merely brought together by work, little units in that portentous fortress of reason which may change the face of the world. . . ."

131

"Please Alex! I'm so weary of being made to feel insignificant, of being only human in the midst of some great ugly calculation. All this talk of abstractions and loyalties. . . ."

"Damn the abstractions; but the loyalties, they're important, but terrifically important . . ." he lingered over his rolling r's, and she savoured them with delight. "Not one, mind you, but several. Loyalty first to yourself. Every human being demands fulfilment, to be let out of its cage of personality and environment. Have you ever thought of that? Have you ever considered such a thing as loyalty to your own character?"

He was putting into words the madness which possessed her. He was not attempting to justify anything. He was one to whom everything had happened. Love and joy, sorrow and danger. He was not jaded. He had long since thrown away his pert sophistication, the easy flippancy with which he addressed the day-to-day world. It caused him no effort to put such things into words. His values were established. They were hard and mature and, in their own way, realistic. They were founded upon loyalties other than hers. She leaned her head on his shoulder and said: "Don't let's talk about loyalties. Let's have a rest from all talk. I'm terrified of waking up out of this . . ." Then she broke off, raised her head so that he could see the sparkle of laughter in her eyes as she imitated him and rolled her r's, "But terrified, Alex . . . terrifically terrified."

He took her hand. "Don't be terrified of waking up, Lydia. Have that much loyalty to yourself. Don't live in a prison."

"Not if you. . . ." She could not go on, and say in so many words that it was he alone who had let her out of prison, that, without him, she would still be enmeshed within the barbed wire. The thought was too extravagant. Even as it passed through her mind, she could not tell if it were really true. To give herself some reassurance, she said, with a catch in her voice, "I suppose you'll treat this as just an incident. One of many. You'll want us to forget all about it?" The sentence ended unexpectedly with a sob.

"Why do you talk about it already as something which has happened?" He made no conventional effort to comfort her. "Suppose it is closed, as incidents are, sooner or later? What's wrong with that? Isn't the rest of life just work and dreams?"

"It isn't that I want it to end. It's. . . ."

"Drive on, for heaven's sake, Lydia. Drive anywhere. Drive to the pier at Flimby. On a day like this we'll probably have it to ourselves."

They had it to themselves for most of the afternoon. They paced about, watching the sea, dodging the wind, working slot machines and telling each other their life stories. These were tales without beginning or end, fabulous, romantic, embroidered with half-truths and fantasies. They behaved so ridiculously and childishly that three Flimby boys who had cut school to come there to fish, had a solemn and vituperative argument among themselves as to whether they were a "spooning couple" or "honeymooners."

Alex boldly approached these miniature cynics, born and bred to the high life of the seaside resort, to ask what time the pier closed. When they told him that there was half an hour to go, he led Lydia along to the last shelter nearest to the turnstiles. They sat on the wooden seat and she leant against him as she had done in the car. They listened to the sea and sat there, without needing to speak, until somebody rang a bell and shouted "All off."

Then he kissed her lingeringly, as if settling some

133

argument, or even sealing some vow, as he lifted her to her feet. The evening was still and grey, the sunset a hazy frieze of amber and green in the direction of Port Amberley. He took her arm and squeezed it as they walked towards the turnstiles. "Remember that I've given you the courage to come back out of this dream," he said. "As for you, you've given me the courage to return to Port Amberley as if it were heaven."

"I suppose so," she whispered. "I hope so, Alex. . . ." They separated because there were figures silhouetted against the turnstiles. A man in a raincoat broke away from the Assistant Piermaster. He walked off to buy on evening newspaper from the vendor as the street lights came on. The Assistant Piermaster said: "Good evening, sir," rather pointedly as if to make amends for having seemed to be obviously discussing them. Then he turned and roared at the boys: "Hurry along there, you youngsters. I'm not staying here all night." Lydia walked on blithely, mischievously toward the car. As she crossed the road toward the parking place, however, she faltered and held her hand out to Alex. "We've been mad, Alex. What have we been doing?"

"We've been happy, that's all."

"But look! Over there! That car at the far end of the car park."

"You mean that Port Amberley vehicle? What about it?"

"It's one of the Security vehicles. I went home in it the other night. That was Dennis Bord talking to the man at the turnstiles."

"But that's ridiculous. Why didn't he wait and speak to us? He must have seen us."

"Because he's Dennis Bord, that's why. It had to be him of all people. Oh, Alex. Why that man?" She was shivering as they got into the car.

134

"That's what they call the long arm of Security," Alex said lightly. "But I fancy he'd have made a much better job of it if he were really shadowing us."

"In any case, why should he shadow us? Why should he be here at all? I don't understand it, Alex. It scares me all the more because there seems so little reason for it."

"There isn't any reason for it. If Bord came to the pier, he came to take the fresh air, or to meet somebody, or to carry out one of his mysterious investigations. He couldn't know what happened to us, Lydia, between last night and now. Nobody could know that. We were not ourselves, not Mrs. Heathley and Dr. Leon. We were just wonderful human beings. When we get back to Port Amberley in half an hour's time, we can tell anyone who's interested that we went for a walk on the pier. They won't know how wonderful we were."

All the way to Port Amberley, Alex had talked and Lydia, driving fast, had attempted to quell the rising fear and the sense of guilt which encompassed her.

Heathley had seemed particularly relaxed and forthcoming when she returned. She could tell instantly that he was to carry out the air test the next day. He mixed her a drink but would touch none himself. Then he explained with careful elaboration that this would be much like any other test, and that he felt particularly confident because Brian Jackson would be with him. He said how sensible she had been to have spent the afternoon with Alex Leon. "I don't believe either Brian or I would have been very good company, but Alex is always good company." He seemed relieved, as if she had been on his conscience, when she told him that she and Alex had been on the pier at Flimby.

Paradoxically, she felt happy and assured. She might have been on an infinitely long, infinitely stimulating journey which at last had brought her home, windswept, full of the echoes of strange tongues, guilty, but slightly defiantly so, at having been away so long. Why didn't Heathley notice this languor? Why didn't he perceive that she was distraught and wearied by some other happiness? Why, because it was a routine necessity of his own resolution, did he make demands? She was drowned with tiredness. Her voice slipped back into its monotone.

Had Heathley been disappointed with her? It was impossible to tell. He showed no sign in the morning of being conscious of anything but the ordeal before him. He had kissed her lovingly and a great pang of guilt had made her quake, so that he murmured: "Don't worry, old girl," as he went.

When the Memsahib had finished the tale of old George Jackson, she said: "I expect Brian's gone off to-day feeling all the happier for having put the old man's mind at rest. I don't blame myself for that in the least. Anything that brings about tranquillity between people is worth the effort. And, speaking of that, Lydia, I think you've got to give up worrying the whole time about Heathley. I know these are anxious days. Even I can see how much depends at this moment on what Heathley and Brian Jackson can do between them. Everything that we say and do should give them confidence. I don't mean that one should necessarily say or do anything. Men need to be brought home. You're entitled to your ups and downs just like anybody else. As soon as Heathley's through his present ordeal, I've a feeling that you and he. . . ."

"I won't! I can't!" Lydia jumped to her feet, her voice absurdly shrill in the quiet house. But she was

protesting to herself. Her mother was the one person
in the world who could have helped her—and the one
person to whom she dare not speak. Mem would understand everything. She would measure everything
against that tranquillity which she saw as the ultimate
virtue in people, which might even condone disloyalty
as a weakness, but which was blind to the grosser
disloyalty which was treason among loved ones. It was
inconceivable to talk to Mem about the escapade with
Alex, this reckless glorious lapse of principles, this
wanton challenging happiness. *"You and he!"* Mem's
conclusion was that all that was wanted was a change
of air, a break from Port Amberley routine, a holiday
outside the barbed wire, with Heathley calculating
that he could afford it.

No: telling Mem was out of the question. This was
not a shame to be shared. Her guilt was growing every
moment more defiant. She was no longer afraid of the
presence of Bord on the pier. Let him spy if he dared.
Hers was a necessary sin, too wonderful, too urgent, to
be reduced to a mere tittle-tattle for a nosey Security
Officer. Very soon this exultant mood would leave her.
It would give way to the necessity of confessing to
Heathley himself. It would become a symbol of what
loyalty really was, that old matured, experienced
loyalty which Alex had spoken of. Hers would be a
sacrificial act of loyalty.

But was this need to shock and to confess just a salve
to the conscience? It might be flamboyant and over-
heroic but it would be cleaner than that self-conscious
reorientation of the *you-and-he* business, the reinforce-
ment, by means of a sort of school-treat, of the bars of
the cage.

"Lydia, darling, I know only too well what these
constant stresses of anxiety are like," the Memsahib

said quietly. "You and Heathley need one another, but it wouldn't be human nature if things didn't sometimes go wrong."

"What do you mean about things going wrong, Mem?" Lydia was quiet again now, steeling herself against the anxiety for Heathley which hour by hour as the test went on would add its force to her guilt.

"I just had a feeling about you two," her mother said. "I've never, I hope, been fool enough to interfere with you. If I did, I ought not to go on living here. . . ."

"Of course you don't, Mem," said Lydia, tenderly, her reassuring laughter, nevertheless, a little out of control. "Even with your appetite for interfering with people for their own good. . . ."

"All the more reason why I'd be happier if I didn't feel that I had to say this now. It happens to all of us, particularly when a man is so absorbed in his work, and that work important. A woman is cooped up in a home which is not her own, in an environment which isn't hers—and the atmosphere of this place, believe me, Lydia, is not of this world. Not of this world at all, my dear, and I've been on garrison duty in every corner of it."

Lydia sat down at a side-table in front of some sewing, but instinctively she chose a position, Mem noticed, within reach of the telephones. "The trouble about this place is that everything is standardised, Mem, and I'm not. It's all too easy to forget that we're human beings not just pieces in some beastly puzzle. Things haven't been right. It's partly my fault, but it's also partly his; but please don't go on rubbing it in by talking about us needing a holiday. I think that if anyone mentions that again—either you or. . . ."

The Mem shrugged her shoulders. She neither helped Lydia to finish nor said more herself. Her silences were full and effortless; yet she could not restrain herself upon this occasion from glancing often at the clock.

These involuntary glances became, for Lydia, as portentous as the swinging of the pendulum between her own anxiety and her sense of guilt. When the children came in, she let her mother go into the kitchen to give them their milk. The afternoon outside was a replica of yesterday. Not a mile away, in the Control Room probably, Alex would be engrossed in his part of the work on this most significant of tests. Hundreds of miles away, with his life in his hands, and the whole experiment balanced upon his judgment, was Heathley, with Brian Jackson to help him. Her mind went from one to the other of them. Brian, with his deeply rooted strength, his Red Indian profile, his eager competence. Brian, who had been a single ripple of disturbing beauty upon the surface tension of her being. Brian, whose father was being brought down a crooked staircase to die, in the old farmhouse at High Sonding. Brian, who still drew character from the dark people who lived and died like that.

The ripple had gone and there was the contrasting turbulence of Alex. Alex, whose past was everywhere, who had no roots; who spoke so glibly of loyalty. Alex, who said that incidents such as these were life and that the rest was work and dreams. Alex, with his respect for Heathley, but with his values which allowed him to say that faithlessness was something predestined and that it was best left at that.

Suppose Heathley did not come back? Lydia's hand went out like a child's toward one of the telephones. She checked herself and was frozen into silence again. To Heathley she owed all that had been good in life, love and happiness and children. Had been? Dare she use such a thought? Heathley, posed in the midst of his abstractions, might be exultantly happy at this moment. She could allow him that. But he would come back for her to complete his happiness. He must come back. For a long time, her heart seemed to stop, while she was listening for him.

If only she could whisper to him at this moment, to explain. What was there to explain? To confess? What was there to confess? Surely he must be told of her wanton urgency, her mad readjustment of loyalties? He must understand that it was only by saying it that she would ever shock him out of that state of mind which made him say he could not afford to worry.

When the telephone went, she could not lift the hand which had reached for it. A cold heaviness fixed everything in the room except the jangling bell. When the bell stopped, it was dark. Light only began to come back as the Memsahib gently patted her cheek and called to the children to run and fetch a glass of water. The light came floating back while her mother spoke on the telephone. Then she was drinking the water and the Mem was saying: "It's all right, Lydia darling. It's Richard Jackson."

"Richard Jackson?"

"Brian's brother. He wants us to break the news that old George has passed away, as soon as they made him comfortable downstairs. . . ."

They went into the kitchen to have tea. Lydia had never known old Jackson, but his death moved her more than the curiously mysterious death of the Deputy a few hours after she had danced with him. She made no protest when the Memsahib said, in her most matter-of-fact voice, "I should like you to go and break the news, Lydia. Brian's expecting it. In fact, it's a burden on his mind. I think you ought to telephone somebody in the Control Room and make some arrangement to go across to the slipways when they return. It may seem odd to you but you can take it from me that I know what I'm doing. And, of course, on a special occasion like this, it would be rather nice for you to be on the spot when Heathley's coming back. I'm sure the Director will see the point of that."

"But surely Cruddock's still away."

"On the contrary, I had a little chat with Sir Here ward before lunch, when I was posting a letter, and he had just come from the Control Room. I even mentioned that you might go along to see Heathley."

"Why did you do that, Mem? I don't see. . . ."

"In the circumstances, we both thought it was a sensible idea. As you know, Sir Hereward, under the crust, is a very discerning man. Anyway, Lydia, be practical. The change of scene will do you the world of good. It just bore out everything I had been trying to say when I saw you slumped in that chair by the telephone. You're caring too much about Heathley, in spite of yourself."

CHAPTER XIII

"WELL, Sam!" The Director jumped up from the horse-shoe table and strode across to the door to shake hands.

"It's good to see you, Hereward. It sure is good. But I seem to have brought an awful load of trouble along. I wish there'd been a chance for you to brief me about this outfit."

"I'd no intention of doing that, Sam. I calculated you'd arrive while I was away so that you'd make your own observations and jump to your own conclusions."

"You didn't make allowances for a corpse on my second evening. Even you couldn't have fixed that, Hereward."

"No, when I suggested this particular moment, I was thinking only of the start of Phase II. Just the time for a double check on Security. Just the right moment for somebody like yourself to take an objective look at our set-up. We've always agreed that there's a danger in watertight compartments, in over-specialisation, in too stable a pattern. That favours the cell system; I've always noticed that."

"If you weren't such an old ally, Hereward, and if I were not used to it, I'd point out respectfully that you're up to your old tricks of teaching your grand-mother to suck eggs. But there, I'm glad to see you and I'm impressed with the organisation. This sad business of the Deputy did give me an insight into the people too. I'm not going to pretend for a moment that everything's been plain sailing, except, as far as I see, on the operations side."

"I'm not so sure about that, Sam. But go on."

"Well, this mishap at least established my own status much more quickly than anything else could have done. The rather vague appointment of Personnel Liaison Officer with Security duties seems to have been accepted by everybody. It meant, too, that I was right in the picture. Mind you, there's been a good deal of curiosity about me, almost amounting to suspicion, in some quarters, but that's to be expected. I suppose I ought to mention, sooner or later, that you and I once met in Washington? Otherwise I imagined it's your wish that we keep to the purely formal relationship we agreed?"

"Yes, Major," Cruddock said with a grin. "None of your old buddy stuff, and forget those fishing trips we used to make in the States. I shall send for you quite formally whenever there's a chance of having a chat. It will be a good thing, though, for you to meet the Minister. Only mind he doesn't lecture you on the impact of popular science upon the masses. It's a tiresome, rather amateurish trait of his. Anyway, as to routine, your cross-check on this organisation, both from your point of view and mine, can only be of full value if we regard each other in public almost as strangers."

A red light flickered on the horse-shoe table. Cruddock switched in to a circuit. Kennedy's voice said: "You asked me to let you know, sir, when they begin the preparations for the high-speed tests. According to schedule, they should start now, and in twenty minutes they will be ready. I've just had this time confirmed from the prototype craft."

Cruddock said: "Thank you, Kennedy. You've

tested the take-over procedure, of course, in case we need to help them out?"

"Tested, sir. We took over control from base for a short test about ten minutes ago."

"It's essential that you're ready to take over at a moment's notice during the high-speed tests."

He switched off and turned to Seagram. "If anything does go wrong and they have time to throw over the switch to base control, we can get them back. The orthodox method of testing, of course, would have been run entirely on ground control and automatic assessment. But there, this test of Heathley's must take its course, though I'm not convinced it's the right approach. In fact, between ourselves, I'm extremely concerned both about the navigational risks and the actual danger those two will be running after they reach supersonic speeds. It seems to me to be an altogether unwarranted strain on the physical as well as the nervous system. It would be wrong for me to intervene, but I've a lurking suspicion that Heathley has been forcing the pace."

"Which, of course, was all too easy once the Deputy was out of the way."

Cruddock looked startled. "You've spotted that point? It struck me as almost too far-fetched. But I'm worried about Heathley. His balance is usually above criticism and his judgment in most things is as solid as a rock. Mind you, he's never been entirely balanced or judicious about the M.7 project perhaps because he has done so much to build it up. That was the trouble which the Deputy himself frequently pointed out."

"He kind of thinks of it as his baby, eh?"

"That's just the sort of possessive complex we can't do with. We don't want people having babies." Cruddock grinned again and would have made one of his more ponderous jokes if Sam had not been such an old friend. "The next thing is to appoint the Deputy's successor. I'm not asking you to advise me on that. I'm the only person who can weigh everything up and make that decision, but there are a hundred and one little points that can have a bearing. . . ."

"The last thing I want to do is to choose your Deputy for you, Hereward. All I can offer is the result of a few hours' observation, but there are one or two of those hundred and one points which I could make now."

The Director threw down a pencil. "So long as they're relevant, Sam. . . ."

"You can't leave me to decide that—out of a hundred and one points."

Cruddock hunched his shoulders and said nothing.

Seagram had been walking round to the other side of the horse-shoe table. He sat down opposite the Director.

"All your people here, Hereward, are working under pressure, not the pressure you exert from above, but that which is the sheer momentum of what they're doing. Things might be easier, really, if they were working in some inaccessible spot in a country where there was a lot of room. Their detachment and isolation would then seem at least dramatic. But here they're living and working in a synthetic cell in the very midst of an old, steady civilisation with a hard-and-fast set of values which some of them have assimilated and which some haven't. This in itself places a strain on them—and I'm talking, I know, as if they were a whole lot of cattle instead of a highly individualistic bunch of human beings. There's that dear old lady, Mrs. Loose, Heathley's mother-in-law. She believes the wildest things about the United States, but she's taught me more about this place than all of the rest of the inhabitants put together."

145

"She frightens me to death," said Cruddock, "with that eccentric outspokenness of hers. . . ."

"Right then!" Seagram went on relentlessly, "your people naturally get stewed up at a time when you have this important project on your hands. They are also made over-sensitive by all the stuff that's written about Security and such-like. There's been the vogue in treachery and it's not surprising that these people have become a bit self-conscious about that too. It's not your fault, Hereward."

"Thanks!" grumbled Cruddock.

"Don't think, though, that I'm taking some heavy psychological line. I'm not trying to make out that your specialists are a bunch of crazies, each riding some personal neurosis. They didn't look at all like that at the dance. They didn't look like that on the golf course —though, mark you, Hereward, they play some pretty treacherous golf. No, we're dealing with ordinary and, for the most part, unimaginative people who happen to have a flair or a mental development in a certain direction. They're no more remarkable than people with flairs for medicine, cost accountancy or industrial insurance. Colonel Bord, your Security Officer, goes about saying that he's dealing with abnormality. That scares me a bit, Hereward. Point one—what about Bord?"

"A bit slimy beneath it all, I should say. A most efficient officer, mind you, but, when I was speaking to him just now, I noticed a certain sliminess."

"The way you cling to schoolboy jargon, Hereward. What you really mean is that you're not all that impressed with the fundamental integrity of that very efficient Security Officer of yours. Well, let me say at once, nor am I."

"I've nothing to go on, Sam. Bord's background is

everything that it should be, though, of course, he's a post-war intake. Then, his war record was splendid. He got an M.C. before he went to the Security side and eventually the Control Commission people were very sorry to give him up when he came across to us."

"And before the war?"

"Police service in the Middle East. The right schools and, I believe, an Irish country house upbringing."

"No Irish political background?"

"Couldn't have been, or we'd have heard about it."

"You've checked up on the Control Commission period?"

"If there'd been any funny business, Sam, they wouldn't have been so anxious to keep him. No, there's nothing actually wrong with Bord except that he strikes me sometimes as being almost too efficient. Then from time to time there's that feeling which I call sliminess. Don't let me mislead you, though. There's no harm in your asking me the questions, since you can't very well ask the fellow himself. I don't want you to have the impression that I'm really uneasy about Bord, because I'm not."

"You got a full report from him about the Deputy?"

"Of course. He seems to have made a good job of that."

"He mentioned, I suppose, that the Deputy seemed to have had more than enough to drink?"

"He said something about it, Sam, but he didn't seem to feel that it had much to do with subsequent events. As a matter of fact, I examined him rather closely on the point as it seemed all wrong to me if these get-togethers of ours were tending to become orgies, which is not my idea at all. . . ."

"And he satisfied you?"

"He said there had only been some sort of claret-cup

made by Lydia Heathley, so presumably the Deputy must have had something of a bout elsewhere. It was not really like him to do that, not at least when he knew he was going to be mixing with subordinates. I knew, of course, that there were times when he liked to put it away on the quiet, but he was always discreet. I never had occasion to be worried about it . . . so I accepted Bord's view that there might have been something of a private orgy but that it was of no fundamental importance to the case—and we left it at that."

"He didn't drop any hint about who the Deputy had been drinking with?"

"I didn't ask him. I suppose I might have done; but we can easily find out."

"There's no need. I happen to know. The Deputy had had a long session in his own quarters with Bord himself."

"Now that's strange, isn't it, Sam. I think that's a point you might care to follow up. It can't have any effect on the inquest. In any case that's probably over now. But it might be interesting to have some idea of what went on during that session, why it took place and why Bord has not thought it necessary to mention it to anybody."

"I'll do that, Hereward. Meanwhile I'm going to take a look at the Deputy's quarters as soon as I can slip along. I don't want to appear to be meddling. It's obviously expedient to have let these enquiries go through quietly and smoothly. The man's dead and no amount of scandal is going to bring him to life. But I'm still not sure whether that Deputy of yours fell or whether he was pushed. It seems more than likely, for instance, that there was somebody with him in his car on the slipway. Bord must have thought so, too, from the questions he's been asking. And, of course, it struck me as elementary police work to think about finger-prints. Yet, by the time I got round to it, there weren't any finger-prints. The car had been moved and there were just the marks of the men who had moved it. Not even the Deputy's finger-prints when I saw it. Yet Bord told me that the finger-print tests had been negative, at least except for the Deputy's. Then surely somebody had taken the trouble to wipe out the Deputy's marks before the car was moved? I'm not trying to perplex you with details, Hereward. I can only suggest that here again you leave this with me to follow up, if there's any following up to be done. Meanwhile there's just one last point, and that's the Heathleys. They're a fine couple, but something, probably his state of mind, has put them both on edge. Lydia Heathley seems to me like a woman who's baffled. She's perplexed by her husband but doesn't realise herself how wholeheartedly bored she is. That may be why I got the impression yesterday that she was just flinging herself at Alex Leon. I don't think her escapades matter in themselves, but I don't like the idea of what might happen to Heathley, who has taken on such a lot already. . . ."

"Too much, that's the trouble," Cruddock murmured thoughtfully. "This test he's doing to-day is going to be just about the last straw. It's unnecessary anxiety to force on his wife. It's a murderous risk in which to involve Jackson, particularly when Jackson himself is against the whole thing. I met the old Memsahib just now and I told her we wouldn't mind a bit if Lydia came along to the Control Room as soon as Heathley's on his way back. The old lady told me how worked up Lydia was getting and I know how it eases a person's mind to be there on the spot when things are going on, though it's not very regular and you

149

mustn't think that it's the sort of thing we encourage as a general rule. The Memsahib told me about Jackson's father being on his deathbed, too. That's a bad thing for a man to have on his mind when he's working on a job like this. Still, there is nothing we can do about it." He glanced at the clock. "In a few minutes we shall be able to cut in on the circuit and know what is really going to happen. But let me just explain the situation as it stands."

Cruddock's gift for lucid exposition was at its best at such moments as these. He took Sam by the arm and led him from one point to another in the Dome. He drew out his own assessment of current results on his pad on the table. Sam whistled and said: "Gee!" many times over. Then, while they stood face to face, Cruddock switched in to the craft-to-base circuit.

Heathley's voice came over, saying: "We're nearly ready now. Approaching the supersonic barrier quite smoothly. I'm at the controls. For some time now we've been using our pressurised hoods, by the way. They seem to be working very nicely since I made that last modification, don't they Brian?"

"Mine's completely efficient."

"This is Cruddock speaking. I just want to say good luck to you both."

The next moment they were launched on the high-speed part of the test, their voices more high pitched than before because of the excitement and the increasing strain of speed.

Throughout the Control Room, people stood and moved on tiptoe. Their preoccupied voices whispered against the gentle whirr and flutter of the mechanical equipment. When he had to speak, Kennedy's voice was abrupt and thick. Like many of the others, he was sweating, though the Control Room was air-conditioned and a little cool. For Sam Seagram, the minutes dragged. It was difficult to grasp that these people were working against time while ten months of closely-guarded concentrated work was being put on its first critical trial. Because he had no active part, his restlessness was the more acute. He had to make a continual effort not to look at Cruddock's face, which, he knew, would reveal an anxiety so much more complex than his own.

After what seemed hours, he fancied that Heathley's voice was becoming slurred and that Jackson's was coming through slower but more staccato. Then Heathley's voice began to go wrong altogether. Instead of the steady flow of facts and figures, Heathley was saying: "I'm sorry . . . I can't see properly . . . I'm not able to register this . . . It's no good . . . I'm afraid I'm blacking-out."

"Take over, Jackson, take over at once," came Kennedy's voice thickly.

"I'm taking over, but . . . but I don't know if I can. . . . For God's sake give me a fix. . . ."

Cruddock moved about the room like a panther. Then his voice bit into the circuit. "Let her go, Jackson. Switch her over to base control. We're taking over. Assuming full operational control from base. Cancel the test from this point, Kennedy, and bring them back."

Seagram tiptoed out of the Dome. From long experience, he knew when to leave his old friend alone. He went out into the grey afternoon and the Security Guard on the door duly reported his departure, by telephone, to Bord.

Lydia had just driven into the car park. She said with a heartbreaking attempt at casualness: "Everything going all right, Major?"

Seagram said "He's been doing a whale of a job, that husband of yours. A really wonderful job, lady."

"He's all right, is he?"

"I think he's been having a tough time, but he will be all right."

"And Brian?"

"Why, he's all right too. Don't fret yourself about him."

"I don't as a rule get into a state about these things, Major Seagram," she began, trying to explain the tears that stood in her eyes. "This time it's partly my mother. She seemed to think I ought to come along here. You see, Brian's father died this afternoon and Mem wants me to break the news. Brian made her promise to let him know about his father wherever he was and whatever he was doing. He wanted the old man to die peacefully downstairs. It sounds odd, perhaps, but he particularly wanted to be moved downstairs to die, and that apparently has been on Brian's mind."

"That sounds human enough, Mrs. Heathley. You'd better come back in with me," Seagram said. "I think there was a kind of understanding that you might be along."

By the time Lydia and Sam had been passed through to the Upper Deck, the atmosphere in the Control Room had eased. The prototype was on its way back and both Heathley and Jackson had recovered and were talking again on the circuit. Cruddock came down and spoke to her. "I'm afraid he's had a tough time, too. By the way, I heard him asking just now if there'd been any news about his father sent through from his home. I believe your mother knows his people very well, and I was wondering if. . . ."

"That's why I came, Sir Hereward. Mem was

particularly keen that I should break the news to him. How soon will they . . . ?"

"They won't be back just yet. But in these rather special circumstances, I think it won't do any harm if I get Kennedy to let you speak on the circuit. I'm thinking of Heathley rather than Jackson, but I don't think it will do either of them any harm to hear an unofficial voice. It may help them to relax." He glanced at Seagram. "I hope you won't regard this as a customary procedure over here, Major. This is rather an exceptional operation, and, since Mrs. Heathley happens to be here, I believe that anything which tends to relieve the human anxiety is justified, whatever the rules may be."

"From the personnel point of view, sir, I agree with you entirely," murmured Seagram, with due formality and an encouraging smile at Lydia.

So Kennedy said: "We've got a surprise for you, Professor," and then Lydia said: "Hello, darling, I just happened to be here. The Director told me to say that everybody was very pleased. . . ."

It was like a long-distance telephone call between people who had been parted for a long time. They spoke briefly and said nothing of any significance at all. She could not keep the catch out of her voice and he spoke with a terseness which was not really like him. She also spoke to Brian, dreading the possibility that he might ask for news from home, but when she said she would be there to meet them, Brian already understood her message.

By the time she had finished, the Director had vanished, and Seagram, who she knew least of anybody there, stood beside her, friendly, comforting and sympathetic. It was only when she had let him escort her half-way to the exit, that she was able to look about her clearly, and then she saw that Alex had been there too, his back to the window, watching her with an intentness which nobody else could notice. She sent him a vague, proud, wonderfully defiant salute. She wanted him to see that she had courage enough to live through an incident which had no beginning or end. She would be different when she welcomed Heathley back. She would be able to speak to Heathley now with forthrightness. The texture of her blood was stronger. Her nature had deepened. For those few moments of her relief at Heathley's homecoming, she was no longer afraid of herself. Her gratitude to Alex demanded that he should know it.

CHAPTER XIV

THE news of his father's death downstairs in the parlour at Chestnut Lodge unexpectedly brought a sense of peace to Brian. When Lydia told him what he knew already, she could see that he was in no need of comfort. He had already answered the last summons of his father, like the dutiful stranger he was. The mystery of death loomed up in the midst of all his orderly patterns of abstract thought. He was reconciled to it not by thought but by those characteristics of the dark people to whom he belonged.

A man might struggle with sparse unyielding obstinacy for a return from his own acres. He might live closely and have a keen eye for city markets. He might use his church seldom and drive life's bargains hard. Nevertheless, drunk or sober, prosperous or beggared, he accepted the confines of his close world and, without so much as a grudging prayer or a plea for pity, he acknowledged the presence of the Almighty, as it were, by default. Both cynicism and fatalism could have become easy habits of mind in Brian's chosen vocation of research. They had been kept under, however, by this strain in his blood. Never had they been so drastically subdued as when the Memsahib made her intervention.

"I hope you'll tell your mother that I shall never forget what she has done for me, Lydia. It's wonderfully kind of you, too, to have taken the trouble to have come to tell me personally."

"I'm sorry to have been the bearer of news like this at such a moment of triumph, and after all that you and Heathley have gone through."

"Forget about the triumph, Lydia. We were just doing a job of work and I don't think any of us can pretend that it was a triumph. Whatever credit there is, goes to Heathley, anyway. I only went along, so to speak, at the last moment."

She was looking at him as if she were seeing him for the first time. She was wondering how it was that that other Lydia of a few days ago could have been panicked by this image. Neither he nor Heathley was looking the worse for the ordeal. They were receiving congratulations as if it had been tacitly agreed by all concerned to ignore that brief flirtation with death, the long dragging seconds in which Sam Seagram had stood in front of Cruddock and tried to avoid looking into his face.

It was all over now. Those like Lydia on the outside of things would never know what risks had been taken. It was as if some great machine was gradually cooling down. The collation of facts was already beginning and would continue for some hours. Meanwhile there were the congratulations on the one side and a self-deprecatory reserve on the other.

"Is there anything I can do?" Lydia said to Brian. "Is there anybody to be fetched? Or would they like Mem or I to go to your home and offer to lend a hand?"

"It won't be necessary, thank you very much. The family was expecting this. My people always like to see your mother. She means so much to them, but. . . ." They were interrupted by the arrival of the Minister of Research and Development, who had walked across with Cruddock from the Control Room to the slipway outside the Experimental Block

One of the burdens which the Minister had to bear was a film star's good looks: one of his persistent aberrations was that his face was his fortune. He was recognised as one of the ablest politicians and administrators of his time, in spite of the sultry preening in which he indulged, not always in private. The Memsahib had once remarked, after an official reception, that if his mother had taught him not to carry a comb in his pocket, he might well have become one of Britain's youngest Prime Ministers, "instead of waiting," she added prophetically, "until he is bald."

So Latin himself, both in colouring and temperament, the Minister was instantly put on his mettle by the lanky, trim Anglo-Saxon stance of Lydia. Such things brought out his sense of rhetoric. Before anybody could head him off, he had made rather a silly speech, addressed to Cruddock but within the hearing of nearly a score of people and in medium close-up to the newsreel camera, about the devotees of Science, the Heroes of Research, and, of course, the March of Progress. His eye was on Lydia the whole time and, when he had finished, the operator said: "Now would the lady mind leading a round of applause? Thank you!"

Lydia was in a mood to accept any inane challenge. She began to clap her hands. Everybody joined in sheepishly. Then the Minister shook hands with Lydia and explained that such film shots as these were records of historic occasions and would, of course, only be released at some future date. It was part of the programme to interpret and popularise research and development achievements.

Heathley winked rudely as all this was being said. While he had always revered the Director, nobody could persuade him to take the Minister with any

157

seriousness. His prejudices against politicians were well known and were sometimes the subject of respect- ful baiting. During the General Election, the whole staff had been spoofed by an announcement that Heathley intended to stand for Parliament as an Independent Pragmatist. The author of this practical joke had never been unmasked, though Felix Tatham, aided by the late Deputy, had always been suspected. "I've been through it all," Heathley had once ex- plained to Lydia. "From whichever angle you look at politics, it's the pursuit of the expedient by the vain and self-assertive. The blind leading the blind is a better risk any day."

Sir Hereward Cruddock could not conceal his dis- comfort when the Minister started up the cameras again by launching into a vague but enthusiastic acclamation of Heathley. It included such phrases as "this great mind," and "this idealistic pioneering spirit." No doubt it was another speech which would have particular value in the future in enshrining the policies of one who, formerly a scientific journalist, liked to go on record as a Patron of Science. It was, of course, premature, and Cruddock cursed himself for not having been able to give more time to briefing the man. The Minister's arrival had originally been timed to coincide with the latter part of the air test. Without committing himself to any very positive judgment of the issues arising out of Phase II, Cruddock had in- tended to give the Minister a leisurely hour in the Dome during which the simpler forms of assessment could be explained, the simplification of his own views expressed and the necessary details of the Deputy's death and successor discussed. The calling off of the test had spoilt his timing. There had only just been the opportunity to outline the pattern of Phase II and to give a few elementary details of the results. The Minister, with his flair for present and future publicity, had been anxious to press on to greet the returning men. He was conscious of the potential of M.7 as a social and political force. He had assimilated, more shrewdly than many, the world-wide implications of M.7. For all his good looks, he was no fool.

He had been articulate enough in Cabinet and top-level international circles to have aroused just the right measure of interest in the project. Though in the eyes of a man of such deep and varied influence as Cruddock, his efforts had been somewhat superficial: these were also useful and necessary. That was why Cruddock blamed his own carelessness when the Minister allowed his own dramatic over-simplification of events to carry him away. Perhaps because of the presence of Lydia Heathley, the Minister was savouring his own oratory with particular relish. The huge empty phrases went up into the wind like bubble balloons as Cruddock became more and more fidgety.

It was Heathley himself who saved Cruddock the trouble of intervention. His resonant voice cut effortlessly across both the wind and the bubble balloons. "I'm always grateful to hear my work well spoken of, Mr. Minister," he said, "but it hardly does justice to single-minded concentration of effort by a number of distinguished specialists working as a team to hear you mount your political soap-box and address me as if I were a head-teacher here on a sports day in your constituency."

Heathley had spoken with deliberation and, as he paused to choose his words, most of his audience went limp, fluttering in the wind as if they were clothes hung out on a line to dry.

"Heathley, dear. . . ." Lydia's protest ended in a

gurgle which might well have been distress, but was, in fact, outraged laughter.

The Director cleared his throat, as he turned to glare first at Heathley then at the camera, then at the darkening handsome face of the Minister. But Heathley thrust his hands deeper into his pockets and went on. "This is the kind of daft patronage which has been served out by the political boys for much too long. If you people would really come to grips with what is being created and pioneered and thought of in the world, I could take in some of your well-meant poppycock with a grain of respect. Yet you, sir, stand there blithely going on record for posterity, with what you call an historic occasion. What is the use of our creating an occasion for history if you come down almost before we have started, to gum it up with your banalities? I once read an article of yours, Mr. Minister, dealing, in pseudo-scientific terms, with the progress of human thought arising from what you called 'Man's inherently rhythmical conquest of natural forces.' I thought of it just now and was sorry for you." His voice had taken on a laughing, robust stridency rising above the fluttering of consternation, protest, rage and suppressed laughter. He raised his right hand in a dignified gesture, brushing aside all interruptions, and then added, in a lower voice, "I realise that you're only doing your job, Mr. Minister. There's nothing personal about this protest, though I realise that it's against good manners, and, for all I know, a breach of discipline. But we're concerned here with clear—and yes, dangerous—thinking. Let's clear the air. Thanks largely to Brian Jackson, we've got back. Now, for heaven's sake, let's go on"—his voice now had a tremor in it—"thinking and acting like mature people."

160

The flutter became a babble. Several people were trying to apologise at once. Others were arguing. Others were so shaken with indignation, shock or laughter that they did not know what they were saying. In a stunned way, the Minister behaved well. He interrupted the apologies by murmuring something about believing in free speech, and something else about realising only too well how people easily got worked up under conditions of strain. The Director, his small figure bobbing up and down, emphasising each soothing remark as he made it, led the Minister away toward the Control Room. For a few moments, a group, some inarticulate, some garrulous, surrounded Heathley. Brian stood before him grinning, both puzzled and awed. He was wishing he had the courage to walk up and shake Heathley publicly by the hand, less for the substance of the protest which he thought foolish and fanatical than for the performance of a devil-may-care act of debunking. Lydia, frowning anxiously, but laughing at the same time, pushed her way through to Heathley. "You've surely done enough harm for one day, darling. I think you'd better come home and have a very, very calm cup of tea."

"I daresay it's all been a bit exciting. . . ." Baird put in.

"On the contrary," said Heathley, "I never felt better in my life. But I'll have that very, very calm cup of tea." He took Lydia's arm. They had almost reached their car parked by the Experimental Block before she noticed the unsteadiness of the hand which closed and unclosed over hers.

CHAPTER XV

BRIAN felt isolated and ill at ease as he stood there near the head of the slipway. Lydia had caught his eye and smiled understandingly before she went off with Heathley. Most of the others knew about his family loss and would have liked to have offered condolences, had it not seemed that anything of this sort would have been such an embarrassing anticlimax.

Everyone realised now that the test could only be regarded as a partial success. Such a result, followed by the incredible behaviour of Heathley, would already begin to resharpen those differences which had been buried deliberately, albeit with a certain effort, after Heathley's conference and Brian's decision to support Heathley personally in the test. Some people, such as Baird, would obviously decide that the time had come to take sides.

Had it not been for that amazing oration which had persuaded Baird that Heathley was not himself, and had therefore aroused his sympathy, Baird would have told Brian bluntly that this was the moment to punch home his own views. There were several men in that audience who had been moved by what Heathley had said. In any case, they had all witnessed one of those bold, mad acts which would be instantly whispered round the scientific world and, perhaps, hilariously, recalled at Port Amberley for years to come. Heathley, the born leader, the opponent to humbug, the freethinker, the baiter of politicians, had done

162

one of those acts by which a man is remembered.

Heaven only knew what repercussions there would be upon the higher levels. The Minister had kept his dignity and his good temper but such control was unlikely to last. There would be a complicated chain of apology and explanation. No doubt the outburst would be ascribed to the stress of operational conditions and long, concentrated, mental overwork. By some such means, the vanity of the Minister might be assuaged and the flouting of the dignity of Sir Hereward Cruddock might be smoothed over and even explained away. Whether they were angry or amused, whether they agreed with him or not, most of his audience felt some measure of loyalty toward Heathley, enough, at least, to look for excuses.

As Brian, in his semi-heroic isolation in their midst, walked toward the Experimental Block, he found it difficult to hold the small talk which those few minutes demanded. He was conscious of the advantages which the near-failure of the flight, together with Heathley's outburst, had put into his hands. His reputation had grown by having taken the risk of going with Heathley. His own ends had been served. His knowledge was equal to that of Heathley. Yet, unlike Heathley, his reputation was undiminished. He recognised, and could not help but admire, the challenge of Heathley's insult to the Minister.

It was in keeping with the great size of the man's make-up. Where his work demanded it, he could be perspicacious. In relationships with his colleagues, he was shrewd and arbitrary. With him there was not even talk of principle. The most prolonged scrutiny was unlikely to unravel his ambitions from his beliefs. The moments when his principles were touched were unpredictable. When they came, he roared like a lion.

Brian had studied and admired Heathley long enough to recognise that the insult might have been simply an expression of the man's sincerity, though it could be interpreted as plain arrogance.

Alone in his office, he began a cool assessment of his own situation. But his thoughts wandered with a curious reverence to old George, his father, with whom he had had so little in common; to whom, since he had been a schoolboy, he had been almost a stranger. He sat, gathering strength, alone there at his desk. Then he deliberately drove his thoughts back to the theories and criticisms of M.7 which flooded in from the experience of the test. Though the Control Room system ensured that the whole experiment was automatically recorded, there were certain points he must get down on paper in preliminary form while they were fresh in his mind.

Ilse telephoned just as he was finishing. "I expect I'm disturbing you, Brian, but I wanted to say how sorry I am to hear about your loss and to congratulate you on everything. I've also got something rather important to ask you about—something personal."

"Can it wait? I've still got a few notes to finish." He frequently met Ilse in the course of a day's work in the Experimental Block; but when he saw her off duty he liked to feel at his best. Every encounter put him on his mettle. Everything that was feminine about her was desirable. Yet her over-alertness, her smartness, and of course her unquestioned ability combined to keep those womanly qualities at a distance. There was something more than her sophistication, too, which gave her character a perplexing instability. Brian might dance with her, take her out to dinner, talk for hours and even make a pass at her, without their relationship breaking through the good-humoured, bantering camaraderie upon which she insisted. Her appetite for enjoyment demanded a strenuous response from him. This was pleasant enough so long as his vanity assured him that he was feeling up to it. He made the vague excuse about his notes now because of that. It was becoming increasingly, enchantingly, more difficult to resist storming into that instability of hers to find the real Ilse.

"Finish your notes, of course, Brian. But what I want to say can't wait. It can't be said on the telephone either. I've got to talk to you. . . . I'm in my office, by the way."

The note of pleading in her voice was quite new, and, of course, impossible to ignore. "I'll look in for a moment on my way out, Ilse."

"Thank you so much. I know you must be going to your own family. The Memsahib has told me about your father. I hate to worry you at a time like this."

It was difficult to finish the notes. There had been an urgency about her voice which kept breaking in upon his concentration. He had noticed Ilse's devotion to the Heathleys. Had she some notion of rescuing Heathley from the embarrassment which would obviously follow his attack on the Minister? Something would have to be done about that. It would be good to talk it over with Ilse to get some idea of what attitude people were going to take. There might have to be some general movement of support for Heathley, perhaps an organised intercession deploring what had happened but stressing the great strain to which Heathley had been subjected. Brian sighed. This fantastic event might have strengthened his own position in relation to Phase II, but it would complicate his attitude toward Heathley. His opposition to Heathley would inevitably toughen-up in the sphere of work just when his personal loyalty ought to be most active. Ilse would be helpful. She would understand the pull both ways. He would have no hesitation in being frank about that.

She took off her glasses and slipped out of her white laboratory jacket when he went in. She made no attempt at her usual brightness but apologised again. Her perfume was just noticeable in the sparse practical room. The light shining upward from the illuminated table-top, used for examination of negatives, caught her hair and flecked it with amber.

"I suppose you want to talk about Heathley?" he said.

"No, Brian. About myself, if you don't mind—and Bord."

He had forgotten about that. It was part of his efficiency—and his youth—to dismiss irrelevancies even if they were unpleasant. He judged everything by its degree of relevance. It was at once a strength and a weakness; and now her reference to Bord proved it to be a weakness. He had allowed the importance of his own decisions and the significance of events to thrust into the background that talk with Bord which had been so disturbingly full of double meaning.

Ilse's eyes were singularly dark in colour, a fiery darkness which he had never noticed before. "Brian! I've promised not to waste your time. You know that I was in the Deputy's car. You saw me when you came down to say good night."

"I saw that somebody was there," he said truthfully. "I had no idea who it was," he added, half convinced of the truth of what he was saying, recollecting with a pang how Bord had talked round this point.

"Brian, I'm frightened." She folded her hands. There was no hysteria about her. She was weighing her words. "I was with the Deputy when you looked into

166

the car. I was perhaps behaving foolishly. When I'm off duty, I sometimes do. I was prepared to explain why I was with the Deputy, and even to mention how he was drinking out of a flask. . . ."

The sophisticated Ilse had vanished indeed. Brian reached out and placed his hand over hers. "Why don't you, Ilse? Surely there wasn't any point in not being frank with a character like Bord?"

"But he seemed to take it all for granted. He just warned me that it was wiser to ignore the whole thing, and to keep quiet about it."

"Why are you telling me this, then?"

"Because you're the one person, apart from Bord, who might know that I was there. You might even think it very odd that I hadn't come forward with evidence." She shuddered.

"What are you frightened about, Ilse?"

"I've a horrible feeling of getting into the power of that man Bord. I'm not being reasonable, I know. I'm giving way to my instincts; but I've been in the hands of Secret Police in my time and something tells me that Bord is going to make use of that power."

Brian's hand tightened over hers. His instinct about Bord had been the same, though it had not developed beyond a passing uneasiness and even now it did not approach fear. "Perhaps the very fact that you've had experience of the Secret Police has made you a bit over-sensitive?" he suggested. "I grant you that Bord's handling of this case is rather extraordinary. It might be put down to a policy of hushing things up, but . . . It's funny, I thought it might be you in the Deputy's car and hoped it wasn't. I wasn't going to tell Bord that, so don't worry."

"What did you tell him, Brian?"

"All he insisted on from me was silence. It does

167

rather look as if he's cooking the evidence." He felt her shudder again. "I suppose you'd better tell me what the evidence is, hadn't you? At the moment I don't really see anything to be frightened about."

It was her turn to speak. He stared down to his own hand and hers on the desk. He felt her warmth; but he went on looking at the two hands as if they belonged to two other people. He found himself murmuring encouragingly: "After all, two heads are better than one." Then he looked up and saw that she was smiling. Not this time the brittle smile of easy camaraderie. There was a tenderness which touched his heart; but he was unsure of himself and wanted to lift his hand. Before he could do so, she raised it quickly to her lips, then held it against her cheek with a strength that surprised him.

"Forgive me, Brian."

"What is there to forgive?" He drew his hand and her cheek towards him and kissed her on the lips. It was quickly done, as if they had both intended that and no more, but they both let out a sigh which was a kind of gasp, for neither was, in fact, prepared for it. They had kissed before, in fun, on the dance floor and at parties; but this was singular, burdened with a meaning which neither of them was ready to express.

Ilse sat on the desk and said: "I'd better tell you about the Deputy. He made a specialty, as you know, of hating women, and I suppose I first got to know him well because, in my silly way, I looked upon that as a kind of challenge. He had been unhappily married twice, I found out, and I began to be sorry for him. That, of course, was just what he wanted. He liked to feel that he was all alone in the world. It added to his sense of achievement. He needed somebody, though, to whom he could express this complacent isolation.

168

It made him quite fond of me in a discreet and temperate way—everything about him was discreetly self-centred. Even before I stopped being sorry for him, it dawned on me that he was such a bore that the tedium alone could have been grounds enough for any marriage to go wrong. Any man so completely lacking in curiosity would obviously be impossible, and I said so."

"You told him what a bore he was, eh?" said Brian with some relish. "There must have been so many people who would have liked to do that."

"We never talked shop until that time," Ilse went on. "But then he became pathetic and sometimes talked shop madly. I noticed that he'd begun to drink more heavily—that was only about a couple of weeks ago when we were collating the results of Phase I and there was a certain amount of conflict between him and Heathley. It was as if we were coming to the end of Phase I, and while these private drinking bouts were going on, that he really started on me. He talked about our going off together and promised to prove once and for all that he was not a bore. But it was also typical of him that he said that I would be the one person who would be able to stop him drinking altogether and to protect him."

"Protect him from what, the demon whisky?" Brian made an effort to laugh it off.

"It wasn't whisky. It was some special brandy he was drinking. He never offered me any, and in any case I wouldn't have liked it. No, Brian, I fancy the talk of protection meant a little more than that. It didn't appeal to me in the least to be anybody's protector and I never did find out quite what he meant, even at the end. You see, we were talking about that in the car on the slipway."

169

"Pity I didn't know that. I might have joined in."

"You wouldn't have enjoyed it. I'd never seen him the worse for liquor and, if I'd known what he was really like, I'd never have agreed to him taking me in the car and having one of his cosy chats on the way. But, when I went across to the car, he seemed to have suddenly become silly and incoherent and I'm sure he had a flask."

"You didn't go with him?"

"I had to call in here to turn over some negatives. He had already reached the car when I joined him."

"And what happened in the end after I'd gone?"

"Well, as I say, he was rambling a little. He admitted that he was in liquor and appealed to me once again to become his wife or his mistress to save him and protect him. Not exactly an attractive offer. I told him not to be a fool and to give up drink before it became notice-able to the staff. It cheered him up no end when I assured him that nobody had noticed it yet. Then he fell into a state of gloom and said that Heathley had noticed it already and that I must protect him from Heathley at all costs."

"My God! Why Heathley?" Brian exclaimed.

"That's what I said. But he only rambled on about various unspecified dangers which he had to face, coming round, of course, to a frontal attack on me which looked as if it would very quickly develop into a rough house."

"I do wish I'd not driven off."

"Not as much as I wished it, I can assure you. Well, the long and the short of it was that I left him and came back here to cool down. I had a few odd jobs to do and I did them. I didn't want to walk back by myself as he had talked of overtaking me in the car, so I had the silly notion that the odd jobs would justify me using official transport. I remember I sat here trying to piece together some of the things he had said. He had talked about his keys, for instance, and wishing to hand them over to me for protective custody. He talked of Heathley wishing to undermine him. He spoke of the American, Major Seagram, as being a special agent. I was upset. I was also genuinely sorry for him if he were really going to give way to drink. I thought perhaps I ought to have a word with Heathley, though it obviously might cause a lot of trouble if I did. When I had worked all this out, I telephoned for a transport and it was then that they told me that he had been found in the slipway. . . ." Her voice broke and Brian stood in front of her, holding her two hands.

"Why, in the name of God, didn't you tell me all this before, Ilse?"

"I didn't feel quite so sure of you as I do now. You do believe me, don't you, Brian?"

"I believe you, of course. I shall always believe you."

She was no longer catching up with time. "You believe me. . . ."

He said: "It must have been terrible when you heard about the accident. But you've nothing to blame yourself about."

"After they told me the news, they asked if I knew where Heathley was, and of course I couldn't tell them. They said I'd have to wait for a transport because of the accident. So I said that I'd walk back. I felt weak and miserable. I went into the laboratory next door and made a cup of coffee. I wondered whom I should talk to. I decided I'd put a bold face on it and say nothing. I've been through enough troubles in my life to have learnt a little caution, to shut up and say nothing until somebody starts asking questions and even then sometimes to say nothing."

171

"You certainly put a bold face on it. Nobody could possibly have known. . . ."

"Nobody but Bord and perhaps you. But what else could I do? After Bord had asked me those questions and told me to keep quiet about the whole thing, there was only you. And, well, here we are." She smiled again and rose from the table. "There's only one other person I very nearly did tell and that's Heathley. When I'd finished my coffee, and pulled myself together, I noticed that there was a light in his room. He was sitting there alone, looking just as rattled as I felt. In fact, he more or less turned me out. It was not really like Heathley, but I suppose he had some excuse."

"I wish I knew what excuse he had. I wish I knew what all that talk of protection meant. Anyway, Ilse, the inquest is over by now and I can't see any point in our trying to tell this story to anybody, though I'm glad you've told me."

"Bord may say something. Then there's this Major Seagram who seems so very curious."

"I don't understand where Seagram comes in; but I've an idea that Bord will be only too glad to let the whole thing drop."

Ilse took his hand and pressed it. "I'm so grateful, Brian. You've given me so much strength and now I'm not going to keep you an instant longer. I know you've got to go home. I suppose you'll have some leave? We'll talk again when you come back."

"I'm going home now, certainly. But, apart from seeing my family, there won't be a lot for me to do. I shan't take special leave except, of course, for the funeral. I belong there and, in a way, I don't. I'm a stranger and yet it's my home."

"I'm always a stranger," said Ilse, coolly. "But without any home."

172

For a foolish moment, it was on the tip of his tongue to ask her then and there to go back to the house of mourning at High Sonding. He made a movement toward her, but she said:

"No, Brian, go home to your people. They need you. Go now."

The loudspeaker system in the Experimental Block interrupted them with a message that Brian was wanted on the telephone. Brian went back to Ilse's desk and picked up the receiver. He was put through to the Director, who said: "I imagine that you'll be taking some compassionate leave, Jackson. But I'm afraid I must trouble you to come and see me for a few minutes before you leave the Station."

CHAPTER XVI

The Heathleys had talked about the children, about old George Jackson, and even about golf and the weather, on their way back from the slipway. When Lydia brought in the tea, they were simultaneously overcome with laughter.

"It really was preposterously funny," Lydia said with cup poised. "It was one of those moments which nobody will ever forget. It will become legendary. I never felt so ashamed of you and so proud of you at one and the same time. Of course your only hope now is to go straight to the Director and ask if you can apologise personally to the Minister." She put down his cup thoughtfully as she stopped laughing. "I suppose you do realise what a complete outrage it was, darling? If you weren't so important, it would be quite enough to ruin a career."

"You're quite right, of course, Lydia—about it being funny, I mean. Now I come to think of it, the looks on their faces alone were worth a year's pay. But I meant every word of it. If I thought this career of mine entailed the surrender of the rights of free speech, as well as living in a guarded and screened cage, I should go out and find myself another one in a bicycle works where the secrets are few and the hours of work more regular. As it is, I don't consider it's an essential part of a project which may well alter the shape of the civilised world for me to be obsequious to visiting politicians, least of all to a jumped-up little jack-in-

174

office whom I first knew as a pseudo-scientific journalist."

"You made that abundantly clear," murmured Lydia.

"Why not, Lydia, for God's sake? I simply can't afford to be worried by ballyhoo. . . ."

There it was again, that word *afford*. Lydia bit her lip, for it summed up the very arrogance in his nature against which she was protesting. "Aren't you being a little bit arrogant about all this?" she said.

' Arrogant?" He gulped some tea and glared at her. "In spite of the fact that you're in such a privileged position here that you're allowed into the Control Room—in spite of the fact that anyone would have to be a complete idiot not to have some inkling of the significance of what we're doing—you seem quite determined, Lydia, to treat it all as if this were indeed just a bicycle works and you'd married one of the foremen."

"Arthur, we agreed that this was to be a very, very calm cup of tea. I want to talk some sense into you, darling. If you won't let me, I'm equally determined not to let this develop into a silly wrangle."

He smiled then. "That's a very neat new set of rules, my sweet. You're proposing to call me names and, if I make any comment, you declare it to be a wrangle and automatically win the match."

Lydia smiled, too. At all costs, she must play to his exultant mood. "It's not quite like that, darling," she said softly, "but it did seem as if there were a touch of arrogance about it all, it really did. You know very well you don't have to tell me, of all people, how significant this work is. I know that only too well." She sighed. "I've had to live with it for a very long time."

He blustered again. "If you're not content. . . ."

"I'm not content just to live with a man's work. I want you to be a human being, not an abstraction. Can't you understand that?"

He looked at her in astonishment, then he began to say: "Today I realised that M.7 is really going to succeed. Just as soon as this job is done, then we. . . ."

"If you say a word about our taking that holiday together, I shall throw this tea in your face."

"A very, very calm cup of tea, isn't it, Lydia?"

"I just want you to think and talk like a human being. I'm happy about your success, but all it seems to have done so far is to make you preach to a man who was trying to pay you a compliment."

"For all you know, he might have been paying you a compliment—after carefully combing his hair. No, Lydia, what is needed at the moment is a little clear thinking and plain speaking. We had, I admit, only indifferent success during today's air test, but we did well enough to prove that my methods are completely justified. I imagine we did well enough to put a stop to the Deputy's favourite gambit about orthodoxy. I want you to realise that, Lydia. And I think I can claim, without boasting, to have brought this thing right through from its inception on the drawing-board to this partial realisation. After another test or two, I can guarantee that it will be realised. Complete realisation of one of the most potent forces in the world! I've believed in it long before even I met you, ever since I was a youngster. Am I now going to let it be watered down and whittled away by red tape and ballyhoo? Am I simply going to hand it over to versatile nincompoops like that young man who is so busy recording himself for posterity as a patron of research? Who am I to work for a patron? Why should I devote my talent and risk my life for an idea which has absolute value in the orientation of human affairs only to find that the hangers-on, the greedy predatory second-raters, the men without quality in their minds, come thieving, battening. . . ." He banged his fist on the table. "Is that an abstraction, Lydia, or the sound reasoning of an intelligent man?"

She astonished him again by saying boldly, as if another woman's courage and perception had taken hold of her. "It's the talk of a demi-god, and I, for one, am sick to death of demi-gods."

His lips moved as he repeated these amazing words over to himself. "You talk as if you were unaware of such things as loyalty or ideals or faith."

When she made no attempt to answer, he went on more calmly: "Don't you see that this is the actual moment of achievement, the moment I have looked forward to. I wanted to share it with you. You've had a lot to put up with, I know. This, it seemed to me, might be one of the compensations. But no, you refuse to recognise it. You talk a lot of clap-trap about demi-gods. Well, what do you expect me to do?"

Lydia felt at least that she was holding her own. She had even gained by making him listen to her. She was penetrating for the first time for months into that redoubt of his. But she knew that he would always win in any contest of ideas, for he could be so articulate while she would be forced to go on repeating herself within the limits of her own powers of self-expression. So she answered the rhetorical question by simply saying: "The first thing you've got to do is to go to the Director and apologise for that sermon."

"You seriously mean, Lydia, that you expect me to go and beg permission from Cruddock to grovel in front of that Minister? When I have nearly killed myself to achieve this measure of success, when this huge vista of ideas has become a practical possibility, am I supposed to indulge in petty politics and niggling party manners?"

"I'm only asking you to behave like a human being. You're surely too big to go out of your way to insult a man because you think he's a lesser being when he has not offered even a shadow of an insult to you. Suppose, after all, that the test was not such an unqualified success as you make out, surely you can see that your behaviour has been ridiculous?"

"I've never made out that this test was an unqualified success. We were unable to complete it. You know that as well as I do. I only claim to have had enough success to justify any action I took. I've made what they call the orthodox methods look silly. I may have taken a risk or two. There was, in fact, a considerable navigational risk and there was a chance of our running into proscribed territory, as they insist on calling it. . . ."

She saw that it was becoming a soliloquy. He was justifying himself in his own eyes. He was reassuring himself of that higher god-like level of his. "I expected a degree of failure. I had even calculated it just as I'd assessed the risks. And do the means justify the ends? Of course they do. Within the course of another test, I shall have achieved everything. I shall not just say 'test complete' and . . . ." With a fluttering sigh, he drew himself up and stood looking across the garden toward the barbed wire. His spirits were rising again. His achievement assembled with visionary clarity over the barbed wire skyline. He was withdrawing from her. She thought of Alex quite deliberately, boosting her courage.

"You talk as if Brian Jackson did not exist. Yet I

gather he shared the controls," she said desperately, too carefully.

"If he hadn't volunteered to go at the last moment, I should have done it by myself. But Brian had enough common sense to be open to conviction. You see if he's not convinced, too. I shall go straight on with this, Lydia. Personalities mean nothing. The quibbles and dissensions of politics mean even less. You ask me to be big enough to apologise for speaking my mind. I hope I'm big enough to rise above such paltry . . ."

"And what about me, Heathley? Where am I supposed to come in?" she asked, standing beside him in the waning light.

He sighed again, but his voice became more natural, even tender. "You come in everywhere, Lydia. That's why I talk to you like this. We share. That's why it's worth arguing. I came back here with you because I wanted us to share this beginning of my achievement. I wanted you to understand what it really stands for."

She warmed to the tenderness. It left her in no doubt that she still wanted him. No doubt, too, that to hesitate and drift back into her old acquiescence would be to pare herself down, to accept a lower temperature of living, to acknowledge the reality of the barbed wire and with it her sense of guilt.

"What are we sharing, Arthur? Tell me that. Not the life of a superman, I can promise you. You'd have to find someone with far greater talents than mine to do that."

"I'm not looking for anybody with any other qualifications. I'm not looking for anybody at all. We have our own shared happiness. That's enough for me."

"And how is it shared, when you withdraw into some

other reality where such creatures as I simply don't belong."

Heathley drew her towards him, as they stood in front of the long window still looking out across the garden which was their pride toward the barbed wire which meant nothing to him and which had become such a symbol for her.

"You're talking, Lydia, as if you'd suddenly decided that everything we most treasure wasn't worth while. As if you'd shut your mind to everything I'm driving at. In fact, you almost talk as if you thought somebody else could make you happier, or somebody else could make me happier."

"Suppose that's just what I meant?" she said as steadily as she could. "Suppose I'd found out that my happiness didn't depend upon you? Suppose I told you that I'd lost the modest wifely loyalty which you always take for granted?"

His hand dropped away from her. He leant his forehead against the window. He sagged. She wanted to throw her arms round him, to restore him. It could be done still, even after that first impact. She could still say that she hadn't meant it. He had crumpled so suddenly, so pathetically. She needed all her courage to go on. But only by doing so could she purge that which had come between them.

He spoke now from some inner darkness, in a voice she had never heard before. "There's only one loyalty which matters in the end. Perhaps I've been a fool to assume that it would always be there. I suppose I couldn't really afford to do anything but take it for granted. There are some things, Lydia, which a man like me, trained by science to take nothing for granted, must nevertheless accept."

"But why, why?"

180

"There's a point where a man stops proving and begins believing. It's a point beyond which I couldn't just afford. . . ."

The repetition of the token word hit her. It stood for the bleak atrophy in him. It obstinately pointed the contrast between this and the reckless humanity of Alex.

"It's that word alone which kills something in me, Heathley. You could not *afford* to worry. You could not *afford* to live almost. Now you cannot *afford* to do anything but accept my loyalty. You call this sharing, this living behind this barbed wire? And my share, I suppose, is to keep my loyalty for a man who might turn round at any moment and say that he couldn't afford that?"

The image of him leaning against the grey window was swimming before her eyes. It had not occurred to her that he might make her angry, that this would be less a declaration of guilt than a furious self-justification still tender, perhaps, because of the pitiful way he had sagged at the first impact.

"So you've chosen this moment, Lydia, to give me a lesson in loyalty! A moment which might have been one of triumph, when I have spoken up to establish my integrity." His voice was still dark with despair and bewilderment. "I suppose I've earned this. I suppose this is part of the sacrifice I'm supposed to make?"

"It's nothing to do with sacrifice or with your work. Don't you see that? For once it concerns me. It's just plain talking, Arthur, so that we can be fair to each other, so that we can really share."

"Then, for God's sake, talk plainly," he thundered.

"I've begun to think about other people." She wavered, urging herself on toward the hysterical but

181

essential confession. "First, and only for a short while, it was . . ."

"I don't want to hear," he shouted. "I don't want to be broken by a hundred stones. Just say who it is."

"Nothing has *happened*. It's only me."

"I don't want to hear what's happened. I just want to know who . . . or should I know that already?" He was measuring himself against the host of her lovers, which this faltering ill-managed confession threw like lightning into the confusion of his mind. "Who is it?" he repeated.

"You're not going to do anything to anybody?"

"Do anything? No, I shall do nothing," he was whispering now.

"It's silly of me. And it's not his fault. Indeed, he hardly realises. . . . I'm telling you because I've got to." She could not explain her compulsion. "It's Alex Leon. I can't help myself. I want to tell you this not because anything has happened but just to put things right between us."

He licked his lips: "So it's all wrong between us, is it?" He stumbled away, out of the room, out of the front door.

"Not wrong, Arthur, not really wrong. Listen," she called after him in an agony of tenderness and fear and wonder.

Mem tried to restrain the children, but they called out too. The only answer that came out of the grey evening was the sound of the starter of the great car. Then it moved off at speed.

PART THREE

I could not love thee, dear so much,
Loved I not honour more.

RICHARD LOVELACE

CHAPTER XVII

OUTSIDE the Experimental Block, Brian hesitated beside his car. Because of Ilse, he had not thought of enquiring where the Director had spoken from. Then he saw Heathley's car streaking across between the Control Room and the Main Gate and he concluded that Heathley had been with Cruddock in the Dome, where preliminary operational reports were sometimes made.

He was glad that he and Heathley were not apparently being called upon to report together. It was too soon to come into open conflict with Heathley, however inevitable it might be in the end. Even before the outburst in front of the Minister, he had been appalled by Heathley's over-sanguine, almost truculent mood. Not only his own opposition, but the Control Room evaluation of the test would put an end to that eventually. He had hoped that there would be no cause for open disagreement, however, until the effects of the outburst had blown over. He did not want to seem to take advantage of that. Without Heathley, he could be non-committal and discreet in making his report to Cruddock, leaving no doubt that he had strong views of his own. He would be particularly guarded if the Minister were still there.

He drove slowly across to the Control Room and glanced up from the Floor to the Upper Deck where there was only a skeleton staff on duty. There was no sign of the Director, and he assumed that he was expected to go directly to the Dome. He went to the small elevator in the inner lobby which was used by higher executives to reach the Upper Deck and the Dome, and pressed the top button. He travelled upward silently, so silently that just before he arrived he heard the heavy door of the Dome clump to, and wondered who else beside Heathley had been summoned by the Director. He was sufficiently nervous about the interview to pause to study himself in the mirror as he opened the elevator gate. Because of that half-backward glance, he stumbled right across the path of the Director's last visitor who had closed the door and was making for the stairs. It was Bord.

"Ah, the very man I want to see." Bord fended him off, frowning and smiling at the same time.

"Sorry, I've been summoned to the Director and afterwards I've got to push off home."

"I heard about your father. I'm sorry, Brian." His arm fell across Brian's shoulder, expressing his sympathy, but there was nothing but wariness in his pale eyes when he added: "By the way, the Director isn't here. You know that?"

"Not in the Dome? Then why are you . . .?"

"Just my routine duty to prowl and prowl around, old boy. Got to make sure the place is properly locked with operations like this going on."

"But surely he was seeing Heathley here just now?"

"Most likely he was seeing Heathley," Bord shrugged his shoulders meaningly, "but not here." He thumped on the closed door. "He's in his office over in the Admin. Block, I expect."

184

Brian looked at the door as if he still half expected an angry Cruddock to respond to the thumping. "You may cover a lot of ground, Bord, but I didn't realise that you ever extended to the inside of the Dome," he said, and, if he emphasised the name, it was because he was determined not to call the man Dennis.

"My dear Brian, who do you suppose I am? I've only been once or twice inside the Dome for top level Security conferences." He in turn emphasised the name and gave it a curiously patronising twist.

"Then who went in just now?"

"Nobody went in and nobody came out."

"I heard the door slam as I was coming up in the elevator."

Bord's arm reached over his shoulder again. The man's eyes flickered hypnotically. "Don't tell me you're going round the bend with Heathley after this test flight of yours. It seems that he's saying things and you're hearing things. Let me assure you that all you could possibly have heard was this Security stooge thumping on his master's door. Come on now; if you've got to find the Director, we'll go down together. I've finished in here for today." He propelled Brian into the elevator and nothing more was said as they stood there, going down.

By inclining his head slightly, Brian could see his companion through the mirror. None of the hail-fellow-well-met spirit lingered in this unguarded view of his face. He was licking his lips, and his right hand was fidgeting nervously with something in his waistcoat pocket. For no good reason at all, Brian, whose mind was trained to work only by reason, became obsessed with the thought of there being a key in that waistcoat pocket. With the same unpremeditated directness with which he had questioned Heathley at his conference, he found himself asking: "By the way, Colonel, where do you generally carry your keys?"

Bord managed to turn what seemed like a gasp into a snort of mirthless laughter. "Good God, man, what extraordinary things you scientific brains manage to think up." As they left the elevator, he lugged out his key chain from his trouser pocket. "I think you'll find that anybody who's been accustomed to wearing uniform keeps his keys where I do. What makes you ask?"

"Oh, I've been dabbling in a little mass psychology on my own account since our last meeting. An awful lot depends, I'm told, on where a man keeps his keys. You ought to pass on that hint to Major Seagram. He's the latest thing in psychologists, isn't he, or is that too hush-hush to be mentioned?"

"I can't really tell you much about Sam Seagram myself," Bord said, in a steady conversational tone. "Of course it's a great asset to have somebody from America with us, though I daresay some of our methods may seem rather outlandish to him. Did you ever know him before, by any chance?"

"Never," said Brian, opening the door of his car.

Bord came closer so that the door would not shut. "You can set your mind at rest over one matter, Brian —and that's something which Seagram doesn't know all about, however hush-hush he may be. They brought in a verdict of death from heart failure, accelerated by accident. That means we can forget, once and for all, everything about that little investigation of ours."

Brian looked up slowly. The pale eyes, admonitory and threatening, were boring down into him from outside the car. He recollected Ilse's fear. There was nothing palpable to be afraid of and yet the man's goodwill made one uneasy. Because of those eyes, it was difficult to drag words out of himself. "Perhaps it's best forgotten, unless there's any occasion to remember it."

"Take it how you like, Brian. The verdict's going to be a great relief to a number of people, not least to Heathley. As I told you the other evening, I thought Heathley was running into difficulties. You were very wise in holding your hand. But after what's happened now . . ." he shrugged his shoulders and smiled again, and now there seemed to be no focus to his eyes. "You'd better get weaving," he said airily, beginning to close the door. "I shall have to have a little conference with the Director myself as soon as you've finished." The door slammed and Brian drove at speed toward the Administration Block.

When he went to the Dome, he had prepared himself for any course which the interview might take. The encounter with Bord, casual though it had appeared to be, had broken his train of thought. He tried to put out of his mind the unreasonable, but instinctive, suspicion that the Security Officer had carried a key to the Dome in his waistcoat pocket and that he had, in fact, slammed the door after letting himself out. It matched the equally vague instinctive suspicions of Ilse.

There was nothing surely to be done with such thoughts but to suppress them, at any rate for the moment. Far too much had happened already during that one day. The brief revelation of happiness with Ilse had altered the perspective of even the most ordinary events. She herself had recognised that when she had urged him to leave her and go home.

It all came back now to Heathley and the problems of Phase II. They must take precedence over family and personal relationships, over happiness, too, and the vague uneasiness which the presence of Bord induced.

Cruddock was sitting at his desk. The Minister,

smoking a cigar, was ranging about the room. The presence of Sam Seagram, sitting with a notebook in the attitude of a secretary, surprised Brian, but he had never fully understood the American's exact status.

"This is the last of all moments when I feel I have any right to ask you to come here," Sir Hereward began, "but as the Minister will be moving on, and you yourself will obviously need a few days' compassionate leave. . . ."

He paused for the Minister to take up his cue, and the Minister duly spoke the few eloquently sympathetic phrases which he had prepared as he jotted down a note to send a wreath to the Jackson family. He had, he believed, a long and distinguished career in front of him. Such personal touches as these, taking up only a few minutes of the time of one of his several secretaries, had their value in building up that cumulative goodwill which even the ablest of politicians could not afford to be without. Brian, thinking of old George, contentedly laid out in the front parlour of Chestnut Lodge, found it impossible to explain that there was nothing tragic about this loss, which would be mourned, but not sorrowed over, among his own people. He said a few embarrassed words and added that compassionate leave was not necessary. "It's very kind of you, sir, but we've a lot on our hands here and there's little enough that I can do at home."

"Right! Now I propose," cut in Cruddock, as if he were working to an agenda, "to say nothing whatever about that idiotic outburst of Heathley's. The Minister has taken a generous attitude." Once more, he offered the Minister a cue, which was neatly taken.

"I realise," said he, "that this incident may well be an even greater embarrassment to the Director and the staff here than it was to myself. I admit I found it distressing. After all, like yourselves, I was only attempting to carry out my sometimes rather complex duties in an agreeable way."

Cruddock frowned. It looked as if it might develop into a political speech, but as a veteran of years of conferences, he was adept in polite suppression. "Anyway, as far as you're concerned, Jackson," he said quickly, "we're ignoring the whole thing. The Minister, as you see, is being most understanding. We're here to assess facts. Personalities must come second. Though I never pretend to go into detail, I must confess that I'm a little in the dark about the final stages of Phase I, and the beginning of Phase II. If the Deputy had been here, it would have been different. The Minister realises the unfortunate accident—and I gather the verdict is accidental death—coming at a time like this has slightly confused the issue. Now, Jackson, before I arrived today I had no opportunity of speaking to anybody on the telephone except Heathley, and naturally I have his slant on things. Let me emphasise again, that I'm not being influenced by Heathley's conduct after the air test. It just happens that between the time I last spoke to the Deputy and my return today, I spoke to nobody at Port Amberley except to Heathley. I mention this to encourage you to . . ."

Brian had let his mind swiftly range over the sequence of events. It was not, he knew, good policy to interrupt the Director, but the recent impact of Bord made him pinpoint that inconclusive conversation with the Security Officer which had been so full of meaning on the evening he had volunteered to go with Heathley. He could not let that pass. He said: "Excuse my interrupting you, sir, on a very small point, but surely you spoke to Colonel Bord, the Security Officer?" The

Director and Sam Seagram exchanged glances. Cruddock said: "I certainly did not."

"I'm sorry, sir. The thought just flashed through my mind. I understood you had." Brian was a little cowed for having blurted it out.

"And if the Director had been speaking to the Security Officer, what would he have been speaking about? Do you mind telling us that?" It was the first time that Sam Seagram had spoken. His voice was so peremptory that Cruddock turned to the Minister and said: "I'm sorry, sir, but this is quite an important little domestic issue."

"He said you'd spoken to him about the investigations following the Deputy's death. He implied that you'd wanted the business played down. It was natural enough, I suppose, as he said, not to want the attention focused on Port Amberley at a time like this."

"That's reasonable enough," said the Minister. "I can endorse that. A little publicity after the event, by all means. . . ." He suddenly seemed to notice the intensity of interest which was passing between the other three. "But it was peculiar, wasn't it, that he should have said that he had spoken on the telephone to Sir Hereward when in fact he didn't? It's worth bearing in mind, though, that our Security people have to be a bit cunning at times. It may have been that it was just a white lie to strengthen his own policy."

Cruddock said coolly: "I think we'll leave it at that, sir. It's really a matter of detail which concerns certain aspects of Major Seagram's special work." Then he astonished Brian by dropping a bland and comprehensive wink in the direction of both Seagram and himself.

"If I may return to the point, Jackson," he went back to his semi-official tone of voice, "I should like to make it clear here and now before the Minister leaves, that the Minister and I are fully conscious that there is a division of opinion on the methods used in Phase II. The Deputy told me about them in a very frank and balanced way. In the short space of time in which I had to rely solely upon Professor Heathley's report, it seemed to me to be just practical for today's test to be carried out—but only just. Heathley and you have obtained interesting, but not conclusive, results. I gather that you were against the whole thing. May I ask why, at some risk to yourself, you participated in an experiment in which you didn't really believe?"

"I owed a certain measure of loyalty to Professor Heathley," Brian made the well-prepared statement.

"Such loyalties are admirable," Cruddock said, "but I think you must face the fact that they can easily come into conflict with larger, more important ones."

It was the spot which Brian had dreaded. It was not only premature to come out against Heathley, it would amount to an act of hostility to express the full extent of his conflict. How could he explain to the three of them that he had taken the risk of going on the test not through any confidence in its results but from a complexity of reasons, including a genuine belief that he could help Heathley and an ambitious reluctance not to let the opportunity slip by?

The Minister unexpectedly came to his rescue with the jargon of popular science. He said: "You wanted to keep an open mind?"

Brian nodded gratefully. "I had doubts about Heathley's theories all along. But as they were going to be put on trial, it seemed illogical not to participate."

"You intend to oppose these particular theories in the future, Jackson?" the Minister asked.

Brian looked at them steadily. "I don't intend to take advantage of Professor Heathley, whom I respect and who has meant more to me personally than any other man."

"Come, come, Jackson. We're talking about facts, not personalities, as I said before," said Cruddock, getting up and walking round the desk with the cigarette box. "I'm most reluctant to force such an issue on you, but we haven't time to mince words. We want to find out where you stand—and individual loyalties mustn't come into it."

"I shall stand with Professor Heathley as long as I can," said Brian, with more frankness than he intended, "after that I shall have no alternative but to . . ." Cruddock turned round to the Minister and said: "Since you're here, sir, you'd better tell him."

This seemed to be a prepared speech, too: "We've weighed up the pros and cons very carefully, Jackson. As the Director said, personalities don't enter into this, though we realise that there may be personal problems to be faced. Your Director has recommended your appointment as Deputy Director, and I've accepted the recommendation."

"But, sir . . ."

Cruddock shook hands and said warmly: "This is a case which has gone entirely on merit. I want you to understand that, Jackson. The appointment may not be popular and indeed I can well imagine that you may have initial difficulties. In order that you and I can have some chance of assimilating these difficulties, no public announcement will be made until tomorrow at least. For that reason, I wanted to catch you before you left the Station. You can go home feeling that you can take your time. Time, as it happens, is quite precious. You can come back to me tomorrow and say that you're ready for the announcement to be made. Meanwhile Major Seagram is in my confidence. Nothing will go beyond these four walls, and I'm sure the Minister will hold the release of the announcement . . ."

Then Brian was shaking hands all round, and it seemed very odd indeed that he was shaking Sam Seagram by the hand, for he still regarded the American as one who belonged to the inscrutable world of Dennis Bord.

CHAPTER XVIII

BORD was not in his own eyes a traitor. In order to betray, a man must have allegiances, and he lacked them all. Not only the conventional loyalties to king and country, to kith and kin, but the deeper adherences to God, to people, to a way of life. Dennis Bord, at first perhaps unconsciously, then deliberately, had stripped himself of all these.

For him, freedom and maturity could only be achieved by the perfection of nihilism to which he had devoted his life. He could never feel himself to be adult until this had been realised. He could only grow up and become whole by rising above the smallest allegiances of love and loyalty to which even traitors clung.

Throughout his life, he had submitted to every convention. He had even taken the trouble—and there was much exhilaration in this—to excel within the ordinary pattern. Without first savouring, he could not despise.

While he had excelled at games and jealously held his own in life, his boyhood had taught him to despise his Irish blood sullied by English marriages. From the very soil which nurtured the leisurely country house life of his people, he managed to absorb at once hatred of the English and shame for the Irish. He saw the aimless unhappiness which neither quite divided his parents yet kept them apart. He learnt his first lessons in self-control as a younger son by bottling up his jealousy of the other members of the family. Because of this reserve, he was considered to be too young for his age at home; but at school, where he was savagely competitive, turbulent and vicious, they complained that he was old for his age.

It was at school, however, that he first learnt to mock at the easy-going, religious teaching of his upbringing. And in all things that mattered materially, he attained success. They were satisfied in the end, both at home and at school, for he told them nothing. He acted with well-bred decorum, learning to despise the orderly structure of society. Others might take their momentum from books, but the violence of his protest grew from conformity and the promise of some future maturity.

Police service in the Middle East had taught him the arts of self-discipline, of cynicism, of intrigue. War service had tempered his courage, educated his sense of violence and affirmed his nihilistic detachment from people and situations. Love never touched him—only lust. His tastes in personal relationships when they were not conventional were coarse and a little dangerous, but that heart of his was always safe in its callous disregarding immaturity.

Bord's cover was his apparent happiness and success. He was not content with the negative efficiency of the well-organised system of treachery which he had already achieved. It was perhaps a means to an end. But the end must be glorious. Meanwhile he despised the small traffic of traitors who danced on the strings of inducement and idealistic pedantry. As a Security Officer, he waged war against such people with genuine fervour. It was his single-minded keenness as well as his skill which had earned him so many good marks before he came to Port Amberley. His good-humoured and tactful zeal since his arrival had satisfied everybody. The case of the Deputy was not, of course, wholly a Security matter, and Felix Tatham had done most of the donkey work. Nevertheless, its satisfactory conclusion had already been flashed through in the form of a neat report to all the right quarters where it would represent yet another good mark.

To compensate perhaps for the Heathley incident, and for the rather indecisive start of Phase II, the Minister declared himself to be most impressed with the Port Amberley Security arrangements. He said this pointedly, while Seagram was still in the room, adding, with a propagandist emphasis, that he dared to believe that nothing could be done better on the other side of the Atlantic. Sam's Texan good manners guessed that this was so; and it was Bord's good fortune to ask if he could make a personal report before the Minister left.

"I always like to keep in touch with the Security side of things, Sir Hereward," the Minister said. "I'd be grateful if you'd ask him to come in."

Cruddock nodded toward a side door and said to Seagram: "I don't think we'll need your help any further, Major," explaining, as soon as Sam had gone, that it was policy that it not be known generally that the American enjoyed any special confidences. Cruddock was careful not to own up to his own personal friendship with Sam, however. It was part of his broad perspective which he preferred to keep to himself.

Bord, as usual, made a good impression. He was brief and to the point. He reported the inquest and, in hinting that it had been tactfully handled, effortlessly took the personal credit for the result. After the Minister had congratulated him, he turned to Cruddock and said, with just the right degree of deferential concern:

196

"The Deputy's personal effects are, of course, being dealt with by Tatham. There's one small detail, however, which made me venture to ask for this interview straight away, if the Minister will forgive me mentioning it"—his hand went to his waistcoat pocket—"the late Deputy's pass key to the Dome. I thought that it ought to be handed to you personally with the least possible delay. I sent in a man specially to fetch it from the police. I've left Tatham's people to deal with the rest of his things, of course. Meanwhile, until I had your instructions, I've sealed the deceased's private quarters and put a guard on his office in case he's left any confidential papers about."

He placed the key on the desk as intently as if it were a chalice. Not by the flicker of an eyelid or the tremor of a finger did he betray the triumphant mockery which surged up inside him like wild music.

"A model of efficiency," the Minister exclaimed when he had left the room.

Cruddock picked up the key with a complacent smile. "At Port Amberley we take no chances. Of course, when Jackson's appointment is announced, I shall hand it over to him. It doesn't do for only one of us to have access to the Dome." He wondered if his uneasiness about Bord had been justified. The Security Officer had, after all, given them a gratifying demonstration of efficiency, most appropriately timed. He could not have done better even if he had organised it himself.

As for Bord, he indulged himself to the extent of laughing aloud as he drove off. He was strong. He was reaching a climax when his strength would be manifest. For years he had developed the photographic sphere of his brain. The scientists among whom he worked had never achieved such a proficiency as his for memorising and forgetting at will great blocks of information which he did not even need to understand. He liked to think sometimes that they worked for him. He was their master.

A mere traitor needed to shuffle and duck through life. Bord merely unlocked a door and took his treasure. It was as easy as that. He laughed aloud because of it. He fell into one of those spasms of exultation which were the buttresses of his normality. He was a man of the devil; he was also a man of luck. His achievement now was assured. The gist of the M.7 project was photographed in his mind and would be transmitted with his usual efficiency. As a perfectionist, however, he made far greater demands of himself. The potency of his work was negative until he found the positive accomplice, the corrupted loyalty of another. It was only by such means that his creative genius could be fulfilled, his ultimate grandeur assured.

Whose loyalty was he to steal? It was a deliriously challenging thought, this. A lesser man would have been content with what he had got. The small fry of treachery would have been satisfied with much less.

He would be revenged against the God who had tormented his youth; against the Nature which had lavished lust upon him but denied him love; against the preposterous English blood which had sullied his Irish nobility; against the education and status which had so ruthlessly forced their conformity upon him. He returned the salute of the man at the main gate and he headed for Flimby.

"The Colonel's off to his billiards," said one of the gatekeepers. "I don't know what he sees in it. But they say he's a regular wizard. I suppose it makes a break for him." The man yawned as a protest against the

198

whole idea of Security. "Makes a break, eh? That's good enough for the B.B.C., I reckon."

"Takes more than your puns and the B.B.C. to make anybody laugh in this Godforsaken hole," said the man on the other side of the gate. "I don't wonder they all rush off in their cars. I'd do the same myself, but I wouldn't have fancied a ride with Professor Heathley just now. Looked as though he was all set to break his neck."

"It's the old trouble, that's what biting him. That was who rang up just now. Mrs. Heathley, in a fine old state, to know if he'd gone through the gates. Of course he had, and I said so. You should have heard the way she was carrying on."

They looked out over the twilight wastes towards Flimby. They had received new instructions for tightening up the Security at Port Amberley. Such things meant harder work, though they were patient men and brave in any emergency. They were glad that the barbed wire had gone up. Anything which simplified their turn of duty was to be applauded. They were simple, slightly underpaid, family men of great integrity. They might have served as sentries at Agincourt, at Bannockburn, at Waterloo or at Caen. They looked for a recognised enemy, or an overt act. History was on their side after all.

"I'm sorry for the women," said the man who had spoken to Lydia on the telephone, "in a place like this where the men have so much on their hands they don't know whether they're coming or going."

"I'm sorry for the Colonel, come to that," said the man who had saluted Bord. "I don't wonder he wants a game of billiards as a change from his barbed wire."

Bord's prowess at billiards was well known, not only in the Recreation Centre at Port Amberley, but also in the Constitutional Club at Flimby. The Club was not without its Colonels. There was a nucleus of all-the-year-round retired military officers who discreetly let out the surplus accommodation in their spacious homes to summer visitors. There was even a General, who was Director of the Brewery in Tollbury, and a wealthy Major who had something to do with insurance. Such names adorned the seldom-used headed notepaper of the Flimby Constitutional Club and would sometimes foregather in person there in the mornings to add to the bar revenue. The presence of a colonel still holding an important position in Government service, mixing with the chaps and playing billiards like a wizard, had become a matter of pride to the Club as soon as the novelty had worn off. Dennis Bord knew how to get on with the rank and file without ever becoming vulgar or familiar. He was not merely a Vice-President, he was an active member who could beat Lupin, the fish-monger, at his own very crooked game. He kept his distance but he was never aloof. He was known to be much preoccupied with Port Amberley, but it was a pleasure to watch him at the table with his favourite partner Lessing, the Assistant Piermaster, who had knocked about the world a bit and stood up so well to the ruthless chaffing with which the Colonel delighted to amuse himself.

As he entered the Club, Bord looked at Lessing and said: "I'm surprised that you dare show your head here again."

Lessing went through the movements of leaving, and said: "Come to that, Colonel, I don't think I'll bother, not if you're not on better form than you were last time." Lupin, the fishmonger, found this exchange stimulating and witty. Colonel Bates, who, as a Vice-President, had "looked in to show the flag," found it stimulating and in bad taste, for it was a principle of the Flimby Constitutional Club that all members were equal in the sight of God, but that God Himself had found it convenient to work through a conventional chain of command.

While the cues were being chalked, Lessing quietly told Bord what he wished to know about Lydia and Alex Leon on the pier. In the course of the game which Lupin and his partner just failed to win, Bord put over a restrained but optimistic preliminary report on the M.7 project, saying that the full details would follow as soon as transcribed. The game helped him. The discipline of playing kept him steady. Lessing's cryptic, almost grudging acceptance of all that he said was in the same style as his acceptance of their famous banter which so delighted the members of the Club. The only sign of his being in the least impressed with the interim report was his brusque departure, saying: "I've got a home and a missus with a rolling-pin, even if you haven't, Colonel—and tonight it's bath-night."

The members greeted the code phrase "bath-night" with roars of applause. When Bord capped it by calling out that he always had his bath on the first day of the month, but that he didn't have the same opportunities of keeping himself clean by swabbing Flimby pier, they were equally delighted.

Bord had seen something like awe and admiration in Lessing's cynical eyes. He had been gratified by Lessing's swift response to the preliminary report—for the talk of "bath-night," of course, meant important transmission. He was gratified, as usual, by the alacrity of agents like Lessing to attend to his every need and to every word he reported. These were but small manifestations of his powers. A smaller man might well have rested and done no more. Even a man of his character could have called it a day and resisted all pressure to go on. A man of assured courage as he was could have stood firm even at the risk of his life for a month or two after achieving so much. Bord's conceptions, however, were of an even grander scale. He needed no set campaign for his groundwork had been completed long since and he was now in a position to behave with the utmost flexibility. They knew better than to give him directives from above. He knew the rules of the game, and they knew that he knew them.

When Lessing had gone to carry out his orders and to transmit his reports, he drank a pint of beer with the fishmonger. It was a principle of his not to order ostentatious double whiskies in the Constitutional Club. Some ostentation was necessary and he had been at some pains to avoid any reputation for being furtive or standoffish. A slight emphasis on modesty, however, was essential, and the ordering of pints of beer gave just the right touch. He patted the fishmonger on the shoulder and drank the stuff with so little relish that he shivered. His business at the Constitutional Club was finished for the day, for there was no likelihood of Lessing coming back and incoming messages would reach him by another channel. Always careful to avoid the impression of haste, he announced that he would step along to the Oceanic Bar at the Grand Hotel, which, he had let it be known, was a favourite haunt of his. He did not add, of course, that he would treat himself to a large whisky to get rid of the taste of the Club beer, much less that Jose, one of the Oceanic bartenders, under the impression that he was working for the British Secret Service, was in the habit of passing on to him messages by means of boxes of matches. It was Jose's day off, and so there was no need for Bord to visit the Grand Hotel, but he liked to give the impression that he did not go there specially to see the bar-tender. He felt also he had earned a strong drink to toast his own success. So it was partly by instinct but mainly by the devil's own luck that he found himself, in those unlikely surroundings, in the company of Heathley.

"Just the man I want to see," his clipped voice spoke the set phrase automatically. He met a steady look which failed to hide the fact that he was the last person whom Heathley wanted to see.

"I came in for some cigarettes. This is one of your haunts, is it?" Finishing his drink, Heathley rose from the chair and put down a pound note upon the illuminated glass bar top. Jose's second-in-command politely ignored the note and greeted Bord effusively with: "The usual, Colonel?"

Heathley scowled. "Just give me my change, barman, if you will. I should be getting along."

"But Professor, you're just the man I wanted to see," Bord said, taking his drink and walking away from the counter toward the centre of the nearly deserted bar, as if to lead the way to a confidence.

"For God's sake, don't let's talk shop. That can wait for another time." As he spoke, he held out his hand impatiently for the change, but the bar-tender obsequiously destroyed the gesture by murmuring: "It'll be another two shillings, sir, if you don't mind."

Even in the Oceanic Bar, which was Flimby's tribute to the opulent, this figure represented several drinks or at least four times the number of cigarettes contained in the unopened packet which Heathley was holding. This elementary arithmetic gave the Security Officer his first advantage. "There are plenty of important things besides shop, Professor," he said easily, heading

Heathley off from the bar. "Though I suppose you're afraid I'm going to congratulate you on that very timely speech you made today." He winked as he said this, indicating that he might have said more but for the presence of the bar-tender. "Let me get you another drink, Heathley. I'm sure you need one," and before he had finished speaking he sent another wink to the bar-tender ordering the drink before any protest could be made.

Heathley had a strong head for drink; but it was years since he had drunk like this by himself. The shock of Lydia's confession had driven him in a stupor of misery and fury across the marshes to stand looking at the pier at Flimby. When the first numbness had gone off, appetites had reappeared, but quite out of focus. He would drink by himself deliberately, but it was not just the thought of Lydia which made him drink. He was too strong for that. He was strong enough, too, to realise that he would have to bear company. He could have insulted Bord and driven him away. An hour earlier he would have done so. But he had to find himself again, to come out of the vacuum into which her words had pitched him. He could not stand alone listening to the sea for ever. He was entitled to go on living. Yes, that was the first thing to be learnt, to go on living—in spite of his heart's inertia, in spite of the frustration looming over his work. And why merely go on living? Why not rediscover the zest of his boyhood, now in the prime of life? The initiative, surely, was his for the taking.

He accepted the drink from Bord, and forced some graciousness into his formal smile. A sensation of understanding, kindliness and even admiration in the pale eyes of the other man surprised him. His thoughts, still lingering with M.7, he was hardly aware of what commonplaces were being exchanged as they raised their glasses.

Commonplaces continued while they had had another drink, and the pale eyes were soothing as deep water after the desert heat. The drinks had no effect on Heathley except to generate a small warmth in the pit of his stomach. Then he noticed how the second one loosened Bord's tongue. For some strange reason, the Security Officer seemed to realise this, for he began to explain in somewhat tedious detail how many whiskies he had needed to win at billiards.

"Anyway, Heathley, I've promised not to talk shop, but I'm going to say, now that we can't be overheard, that your performance with the Minister today was historic. It's not even shop to say this. It's something bigger. It takes a really big man like yourself to say what you said."

"It was just on the spur of the moment . . ."

"For Pete's sake, don't try to be modest about it." The eyes focused with prophetic fervour. "There are very few men in the world and those who bear the certainty of greatness must never be tampered with. A man like yourself bears responsibility for millions of human beings. Your power rises above such things. You create a project—we won't discuss it here in the bar"— Bord smiled and licked his lips. "It may be a project of war or of peace. It's certainly one which is a dominating factor in either. The civilisation which you and I love, whether it's cricket on a village green or listening to Beethoven"—Bord's mental filing system could evoke at a moment's notice the most appropriate detail— "may be enhanced or destroyed by that genius which you keep in your head. Are you to be regarded as a mere technician? Cog? Of course not. That's why you spoke up today, and though most people will not dare to say so, they will recognise your genius, because you spoke and, if they don't . . ." He shrugged his shoulders.

"One has one's loyalties, I suppose," Heathley sighed, unaccountably moved and determined not to show it.

The other's voice, for all its softness, swooped like an eagle. "Loyalties to whom? To the Director? To the Minister? To the Administration which may prevent civilisation from making proper use of your work, which, but for your own courage, might even prevent the fulfilment of your work. What do you really mean, Heathley?"

"I mean just simply king and country," Heathley said, "and everything that goes with them. It's a cliché, I know. But you, as a Security Officer, understand perfectly well what I mean."

"I may be a Security Officer, and they tell me I'm a very good one; but I'm a human being also, and my loyalties are also to the human race. Don't think that this is just political jargon, Heathley. I may have had a few drinks, but I want to tell you that I, as a small man, can recognise that overwhelming loyalty which is the basis of a man's integrity. For a man of genius, whose talents and perceptions are head and shoulders above his fellows, that integrity is multiplied a hundred times. You and I serve our king and country. That goes without saying, but it is the duty of a man like you to think of yourself, to consider your potential not just in the terms of a petty administration which is going to frustrate you, of a country which is too small for your ideas, of a single race which is just one of many in the world. . . . Forgive me if I'm talking too much, Heathley. It all arose simply from my admiration for what they are already describing as your 'outburst' today.

I didn't mean to talk to you about this at all but about something quite different."

He paused and Heathley said: "It does no harm to talk." He admitted to himself that it had done nothing but good at a moment when the numbness was leaving him and he needed the wide horizon of thought to readjust himself before he began to dare to think about Lydia. "Loyalties are funny things," he heard himself saying, as he made a gesture refusing another drink, more for Bord's sake than for his own. He would drink no more now. He despised the idea of drowning his sorrows. He might perhaps spend the night unostentatiously at Flimby to prepare himself to be reasonable, gaining sufficient strength to talk to Lydia again. In the morning he would go on with his work just as if nothing had happened. He had already made up his mind that he would insist upon another test immediately, alone if Brian Jackson was set against it. He might even boldly offer the opportunity to some other member of the research team to go alone, even as a passenger. What better token of his renewed confidence than that?

Bord's company had stimulated him in a curious way. That persuasive voice had enabled him to see his destiny reflected in the compelling pallor of the man's eyes. It was almost as if some part of himself had used the lips of another man to form the words which he had never dared to speak. Perhaps he could lose himself in this destiny. He might even forget Lydia's confession. He could perhaps for the moment dismiss it as hysteria, born of the tension which had been growing between them. He almost forgot the presence of Bord as this optimism brought him to his feet. He would have to be alone now to think. Even Flimby Esplanade was inviting.

"Before you go, Heathley, I must just mention a personal matter—which is something I really wanted to say just as soon as I could manage to find you in your office."

"Then let it wait, if it's shop," Heathley said flippantly, with all his new-found courage.

"In some ways it all fits in with what I was saying just now," the Security Officer went on, ignoring him. "I don't believe I'd say it to any man of lesser stature than yourself. I wouldn't say it to any man unless I knew it to be of supreme importance. Everything about you is important, Heathley, and, though it's slightly outside my official duty, I think I've made it abundantly clear that I'll do anything I can to protect a person of creative genius."

Heathley sat down again, on the arm of the chair. He frowned slightly. He did not want any more talk. When Bord said, after a moment's hesitation, bluntly, "It's about Lydia," his big frame slid back into the chair with a whistling sigh as if he had been bayoneted. His optimism came crashing down. He broke into premonitory sweat. Bord, looking apologetic and serious, let him take his time. Heathley's voice cried unwillingly: "What about Lydia?"

"If it were just Port Amberley gossip, rest assured that I should say nothing. If it were just hearsay or some little incident at one of the dances, or something like that, I wouldn't dare to mention it to you. Do you want me to go on or are you going to hit me?"

"This time last week, I'd have hit you. You'd better go on."

Heathley lowered his head so that his black straight hair fell forward, but it was an attitude of strength now rather than dejection.

"Security work tends to sharpen one's senses of

observation. It becomes a habit, and I can't pretend that one switches it off when one goes off duty. You'll forgive me, therefore, if I mention that it seemed to me that you and Lydia have been getting more and more on edge with each other."

"I shouldn't have thought it was noticeable even if it were true."

"Be that as it may. It's true even if you're not aware of it yourself. . . ." Bord was acting the part of a man who wished to avoid giving offence at all costs. The flat of Heathley's hand came down on the table so that the glasses jumped. "Go on, man! Say what you've got to say and get it over," he stormed.

Bord was undeterred. He did not even blink at the show of violence. "You've been so preoccupied that I think you've let things go a little far. It's not your fault. It's simply that other people don't always realise the full significance of your work and the essential depth of your preoccupation. Perhaps Lydia is a little vulnerable, or, shall we say, innocently impatient. I mention no names, but it's been obvious to a fairly keen observer like myself that she's been attracted to other people. After all, there are a number of quite present-able unattached men in the research team. . . ."

He paused again, and this time Heathley could not stand it. He got up and pushed back his chair. He was losing control of himself again. "Just give me this evidence of yours in so many words, or I'll . . ."

Bord made no move except to raise the fingers of his right hand as if to catch something rolling off the table. "I want you to promise not to do anything. My job is to make the peace, not to break it. I want you to swear that you'll do nothing rash or immediate."

"I know who it is, and I'm doing nothing rash or immediate. Is that good enough?"

Bord nodded and spoke in an even voice as if he were making an official report. "When I left this hotel on Wednesday to go to the Constitutional Club for my usual game, I had occasion to call on Lessing, the Assistant Piermaster, who very often partners me. I knew that the pier was just about closing. I wanted him to come along for a knock-up game. Your wife and Leon were on the pier. They must have imagined that they were quite alone and unobserved. In fact, they were alone but for some kids who were fishing, and for Lessing, who would not have been in their line of vision had I not come to look for him. So, to all intents and purposes they were alone and quite by mistake I saw them just before they left the shelter. . . ."

Heathley made a choking sound as he turned and stumbled away. Dennis Bord glanced round and saw with some satisfaction that nobody had paid any attention to this strange exit. Then he went to the bar and treated himself once more to a drink he felt he had earned.

CHAPTER XIX

AFTER she had telephoned to the man on the main gate, Lydia went to the window where Heathley had stood. She cried. Did ties break in this muddled, half-baked way? Was this clumsily expressed, half-understood confession really the end of her life with him? Had it been, after all, some preposterous whim which had built up her discontent into such a major issue?

There were several Lydias in this. Her sense of frustration yearned for the shock which would renew the shared reality of life between Heathley and herself. Her guilt demanded a sacrificial confession. Her passion for Alex cried out for atonement or for fulfilment. It was a matter of life and death to escape from the prison of which Heathley seemed still so unaware, to trample down the barbed wire before it enmeshed her spirit.

The affair with Alex was more than a mere means of escape. It had been a liberation in itself, but it still obsessed her. She might rid herself of it by degrees; but she would never be quite the same. As she stood at the window, she wanted Heathley back. She had meant to penetrate his heart and make him understand what had happened. All that she had managed was to blunder toward his heart. Was it possible that any human being, least of all a dutiful, conscientious house-wife, mother of two children, could be so inconsistent and confused? She suffered because Heathley's going had left the room unbearably empty: then she suffered because the thought of Alex still crowded her heart.

"It's happened before, and it will happen again," said the Memsahib, switching on the table light and standing beside her with a cup of tea, two aspirins and the bottle of smelling salts which had attended so many crises, large and small, in many countries. "Your father once walked out on me in Malta. It was a garrison which had rather more tone about it than this place, but naturally it put me in a social dilemma. Mind you, I had the advantage that the place was an island and your father couldn't really get far. . . ."

"Can't you see that it's not just a social dilemma, Mem?" sobbed Lydia. "I don't care tuppence about what people think. They all know too damned much already, with their gossip and their Security, which is just another word for spying."

"Sniff hard up each nostril between taking the aspirins, darling. That's the secret of it. I'm just putting first things first, Lydia. One can't offer an immediate cure for the trouble between you and Heathley, but one can at least put a good face on it, such as not blubbing in front of the other ranks. I only hope that gatekeeper on the other end of the telephone didn't get the impression that you'd taken to the bottle. I must remember to speak to him and put it right. That's better, dear. Now the other aspirin and just one more sniff."

The merit of the little green bottle was that it caused such convulsions that mental distress had to take second place to sheer physical discomfort. Her mother imperturbably patted Lydia as she choked. "The first thing to do is for us to get some sort of sense of proportion. It might even turn out to be partly Heathley's fault."

"There you are!" wailed Lydia. "You say it might be partly Heathley's fault, as if your son-in-law were some mythical creature to whom ordinary things can't happen."

"On the contrary," the Memsahib answered smoothly. "It's all too evident that much too much is happening to Heathley, enough to break a man's spirit, and I've seen some good men broken in my time. When your father left me in Malta—you'd hardly remember, you weren't much more than eight—I gather he spent a suicidal night alone in that very fusty hotel which was considered the best place in those days. The next day I found him playing polo as usual. There wasn't much else he could do, poor man. If there'd been anything more important, he'd have been doing it. My guess is that it will be the same with Heathley, though he's a younger man than your father was and he's got much more important work on hand. I suspect that you'll find him at work tomorrow."

Lydia was accustomed to reminiscences from her mother, but this anecdote took her by surprise. As she had stood crying by the window, she had been convinced that nothing like this had ever happened before, except to remote people one sometimes read about in newspapers. In spite of herself, the telling of the Maltese incident comforted her. "But that's all so very different, Mem. It was so much simpler for you. Just an ordinary quarrel in a nice safe conventional world."

"A more conventional world, my dear; and people were not doing quite such dangerous things—though polo had its hazards—but not a simple one. There was a Maltese. . . . I suppose the trouble was that he was so little and dark and exquisite. . . . Its neither here nor there, but he belonged to one of those noble families

213

who consider even the Normans slightly *parvenu*. . . . It was just a wanton passing fancy of mine. I suppose your father had become just a teeny bit too engrossed in garrison life. Of course he was furiously jealous. . . ."

Lydia put down her tea and took her mother into her arms. The small neat figure of the Memsahib was almost dragged off her balance, but she was cunning enough to see that she had made her point, and was able to be deprecating. She murmured: "Of course it was a long time ago and after a time one forgets such things, though when they happen it sometimes seems as if the world has come to an end." She made no attempt to question Lydia. For her part, Lydia was at a loss to try to explain, despite the fact that her mother so calmed her.

Instead, she described in some detail the incident with the Minister, which caused Mem to chuckle with satisfaction. "It's just like Heathley to do that," she said. "No doubt it was a bad breach of discipline, but Sir Hereward is much too sensible a man not to see that somebody like Heathley must have good reason for doing such a thing."

"I don't think anyone'll ever understand Heathley's outburst," Lydia said. "I'm sure I can't. It seemed to me quite unforgivable and unwarranted. We should probably never have had words if there hadn't been that . . . and now, on top of that, if he rushes off because of me. . . ." A new intensity of fear swept through her. Was it conceivable that Heathley, dragged one way by his unrepentant exultation, and another way by the dark dumb fury which she had engendered, would be driven to some madness?—to suicide even? She recalled how he had appeared to shrink as he stood by the window. She was still startled by his going. It was so unlike Heathley to run away, even from a scene like that. She blamed herself for bungling it all.

Though such things happened to others, and indeed to such stable people as her own mother, she could not believe that her own circumstances were not unique. Heathley was massive. He had so much on his mind. By her own miscalculation, she had struck him so cruelly as to make him run away. Was she to sit there with the Memsahib and the children helplessly waiting for news of him? To whom should she turn? She could drive her sense of guilt to its cruellest absolute by finding Alex and telling him that he had been the victim of a mean adventure of hers. Perhaps he was enough of an adventurer himself to accept that without realising that it was an act of atonement. But what was the good? It wouldn't bring Heathley back. No: Heathley must be found. At this very moment, he might be doing himself some injury. In her heart of hearts, she feared some excess to which the outburst in front of the Minister might have been a pointer.

For all the consolation which she had offered, the Memsahib was restless, too. She was wondering aloud whether it would not be a good plan if she had one of her little frank private talks with the Cruddocks, when the muffled squeal of brakes sounded outside, and both she and Lydia hurried to the hall window.

"I think this is the very best person for us to talk to," the Memsahib said quietly, when she saw that it was Sam Seagram coming up the garden path.

"I'm not going to talk to anybody connected with Bord—not about Heathley," Lydia said. "They're spying on us. They don't need to know this. . . ."

"The Major's a gentleman," said the Memsahib in the same voice which she used for responses in church. "He comes from a country where values still count."

She opened the front door. "Good evening, Major. Do come in. We don't stand on etiquette in these days. . . ."

"I wanted a word with the Professor." Seagram stopped on the threshold."

"You know as well as I do that my son-in-law's gone off somewhere," the Memsahib said, pulling him in and closing the door.

"Since you put it that way, M'am, I just wondered if he'd gone to any particular place. I did just wonder that," Sam Seagram said, looking this way and that, as if he expected Heathley to be hiding in some cupboard.

"What does Cruddock say about it all?" Mem said, taking Seagram's raincoat and propelling him toward the living-room.

"The Director is a little puzzled by what happened. Good evening, Mrs. Heathley. I hope I'm not intruding?"

"It's very nice to see you, Major Seagram. . . ." Lydias lips somehow formed the words.

Sam accepted her bleak look and savoured the distress in the room. He came straight to the point. "I'm paying you ladies a visit because Professor Heathley behaved rather strangely this afternoon. Let me say at once that I want you to regard me as a friend."

"Can friendship and Security mix?" Lydia said defiantly.

"I'm one of the people who believe that Security is not an end in itself, Mrs. Heathley. Its very nature is to be negative, like barbed wire. That's why it's so easy to bust, if you have wire-cutters or a little determination or, what is most effective of all, some fatal illusion."

Lydia was still keeping him at arm's length. "If I had any wire-cutters, I should certainly have used them, Major Seagram."

The Memsahib came between them with a smile. "Personally, I intend to grow runner beans over the beastly stuff," she said with resolute cheerfulness. "The wire's there for some purpose even if it is rather old-fashioned like me. No, the whole thing really depends, as I see it, on people believing in the good of the cause. I don't know what you mean, Major Seagram, by fatal illusions. I was brought up in a world in which you sacked a man who was a cad, but you put a traitor up against a wall and shot him, whether he had any illusions or not. And what was the result? I can recollect precious few traitors. I don't think treachery on a grand scale really came in until this century. Everyone in your country clings to a traditional belief in progress, and I suppose you'll explain away this treachery business as just a neurotic by-product of the pressure of the civilisation."

Seagram held up his hands in mock supplication. "You'll forgive me, Mrs. Adderley-Loose, but I guess you've been reading the American glossies."

"When I've read my Bible and the advertisements in *The Times*, I usually do, Major Seagram. I find them so solid and soothing. They take me right out of this rather hectic day-to-day world."

Lydia had left them. She was standing by the window again. Her fingers travelled along the glass. She was listening, but not to them. Sam noticed this even before her mother became aware of it. He kept going with the cross-talk long enough to enable him to return to the point.

"I've been given to understand, Mrs. Heathley," he began again, "that the Professor left Port Amberley rather precipitously a short while ago. . . ."

"So you're shadowing him, are you?" Lydia did not look round. "I suppose your friend Bord is actually pursuing him while you come here to cross-examine the family?"

"You seem to rate Colonel Bord as a kind of super-spy, Mrs. Heathley."

"Lydia hasn't quite forgiven him the barbed wire," Mem said, "though she did give him a cup of tea."

"Can't you see I want to forget the barbed wire?" blazed Lydia, facing them, letting her head fall back with a bump against the window-pane. "Just remind me that you're doing your duty, Major Seagram, and ask your questions. Don't tell me that Heathley has been over-working. Bord loses no opportunity of rubbing that in."

' I want you to forget about Bord and the barbed wire, Mrs. Heathley. I'm going to lay my cards on the table and tell you here and in confidence that I'm an old friend of Sir Hereward Cruddock's and I'm in his confidence. I'm saying this because I want you to understand that I m acting with his authority and that I'm rather more than just another of the Security people you dislike so much. This is a critical time on this Research Station, as you know—and you know more than most people, which, in the circumstances, is fair enough. I expect you could see for yourself that your husband's handling of the air test, brilliant and courageous though it was, was not quite the unqualified success which he seems to claim. At least it didn't seem to justify the speech he made when he got back. I'm not going to ask you why he made it. I suspect that nobody knows except himself."

"He made it out of arrogance," Lydia whispered, coming away from the window. "I told him so. I wanted to save him."

"I think I understand, Mrs. Heathley," Sam began to say; then the door clicked. The Memsahib had left them. Her common sense had told her that Lydia would have to be alone with him to speak about Heathley.

Despite his reverence for the old lady's capacities, Sam was relieved. "Let me tell you, then, Mrs. Heathley, that Sir Hereward was hoping that your husband would make some little gesture, shall we say of appeasement, after he had calmed down. It's the wrong time for personal quarrels or for men to stand on dignity. As a sort of delegate from my old friend Hereward, I wanted to say this to Heathley. The Director has always respected him, and always will. He realises that Heathley has perhaps too closely identified himself with M.7. He realises that the job must come first. It was my mission to express this when I set out on this visit to your husband. Then I heard that he had gone. You can see now that it's not just a case of shadowing him. Bord is off the Station; he knows nothing about this."

"And you want to know why Arthur went out?" Lydia said quietly.

Sam nodded. He patted her hand encouragingly, as if he had known her for years.

"It's my fault that he went away. I don't know where he's gone. I want him to come back. It's all my fault, but I thought I was doing it for the best." She bit her lip.

"You mean there was some domestic crisis which had nothing to do with the air test?"

"There are other things in life beside research and development," her heart cried.

"But of course there are. You don't have to tell me that, lady."

"I had to tell Arthur, though. I just had to tell him. I called it arrogance just now. It may be just that. But it's really something far deeper and more corrupting. It's made him behave like a fool, but it doesn't end there. It forced me to tell him, to confess what kind of fool I'd been, to shock him. I thought I'd make him become his old self. That's why I did it. And now it seems that all I've managed to do is to drive him away."

"I'll find out where he is, don't you worry," Sam said crisply.

"Mem thinks he might stay out all night, but she feels sure that he'll turn up in his office tomorrow as usual."

"She's probably right. That old lady knows most everything about everybody. But I think we'll just keep an eye on things, and I don't want you to think that by that I mean spying. You've been frank with me, Mrs. Heathley. Now you must let me do anything I can to help you."

"I haven't told you much. I'd have liked to have told you more, but there are things which are much too intimate and complicated; things I can't talk to my mother about."

"I'm not pressing you to explain more; but we don't want any further eccentric gestures from Heathley. I'd feel happier if I knew where he was, or what he was up to. Are there friends of his, or favourite haunts around here where we might make a few discreet enquiries?"

It gave Lydia a pang to think of the places they had discovered together since they had set up their home at Port Amberley. "Where have we been together?" she said. "The Mitre at Tollbury, the usual places in Huxtable, sometimes the Grand in Flimby." Seagram noted down the names and she added: "We've never known many people in the neighbourhood apart from the staff who live out. I don't suppose my husband has kept up with anybody in the Sondings except possibly the Jackson family and, as you know, the old father's just died. I expect Brian's at home there now."

She thought of Brian and immediately afterwards of Alex. "I'm particularly anxious that Alex Leon gets no hint of what I've just told you," she blurted out helplessly.

Sam Seagram had stopped writing. He was methodically putting together patterns in his mind. He was aware of the innocent childish tragedy in those words, though he was now convinced that the whole atmosphere surrounding the life of this graceful seemingly imperturbable woman was, in fact, tinged with hysteria. He had intended to take advantage of Bord's absence to visit the late Deputy's quarters, but though Heathley's behaviour might be easily attributed to a domestic fracas, he still felt uneasy. Both because of this uneasiness and because of the overwhelming pity in his heart for Lydia's distress, he decided to go back to his office to try to work out Heathley's whereabouts.

When the Memsahib forced upon him a large drink, he did his best not to show reluctance or haste, but Lydia said: "I'm sure you'd like to drink that down and go," and, noticing the way her voice trembled, he went.

CHAPTER XX

On a private line from the Director's office in the Administration Block, Sam made a brief telephone report to Cruddock at his home. "I'm worried that Heathley has not been in touch with you, Hereward. I'm concerned about the whole Heathley set-up. There is, as I suspected, some domestic trouble, but that doesn't explain everything. I gather he's a man who has never shown temperament. You regard him as a steady—perhaps a little obsessed, as men are apt to be, with the significance of the work he is doing?"

"Too obsessed, that's the trouble," Cruddock said. "I look at it this way, Sam. He's now had plenty of opportunity to offer some explanation or apology. If he'd done so, it would have given me a chance to dissociate the new appointment in his mind and in the thoughts of the staff from anything which savoured of personal animosity. If he chooses to ignore me, it means that the announcement of Jackson's appointment tomorrow will be just a bit more complicated. I can't help it. The Minister is pressing us to go ahead with Phase II, and we can't make any real progress with that post unfilled."

"You wouldn't let me try to sort things out for twenty-four hours, Hereward?"

"But why? Is there anything wrong?"

"There are certain things which don't seem to be quite right."

"Then, my dear Sam, you must do what you came

here to do. You must work out the root of the trouble so that we can put it right. Meanwhile I've got my own job to do...."

Sam Seagram smiled into the telephone mouthpiece. Hereward was up to his old trick of delegating authority. "You see, Sam, I have to keep an eye on all the larger implications, both political and strategic. It's out of the question to stall even for twenty-four hours. After all, I'm dealing with matters of hard fact on a high level. You, quite rightly, are concerning yourself with surmise, and some pretty intricate human relationships. You do see that point, Sam?"

It was one of his characteristic recitals of the obvious. Sam saw the point only too well. "It would be all the same if I didn't," he bantered, before hanging up.

For all his methodical thinking, he had to admit that much of his uneasiness rested upon surmise. There was the death of the Deputy, which was still not wholly explained, except in the eyes of the law. There had been a breath of suspicion that Heathley, who was at loggerheads with the Deputy, had something to do with it. There was the fact that this suspicion had been publicly suppressed but privately fostered, by Bord. There was the implication, also suppressed, that Ilse Leon knew more than she should. There was thin, but not perceptible evidence that Bord had not only been manipulating the truth but also lying. Finally, there was what looked ominously like a crack-up on the part of Heathley.

That could be explained by Lydia Heathley's seemingly tragic, but innocent affair with Alex. But not entirely. Sam recalled the phrase he had used, half in jest, to the Memsahib. Was it possible that Heathley was indeed suffering from some fatal illusion? Clearly it was now a case of starting from this and finding out

223

if there were indeed anything in Heathley's present activities to support the thought. The difficulty was to check up on Heathley without arousing suspicion generally, or interest on the part of Bord who had so many means of keeping himself well informed. The list of places mentioned by Lydia were far from adequate, particularly to one who was a stranger in the country. He rang up the Mitre at Tollbury and learnt that the manager knew the Professor well, but had not seen him or his wife for ten days or so. Making the best of his Texan accent, Sam said that he was an old friend who wanted to get hold of Heathley before going back to the States and pumped the manager for other likely places in Tollbury, Flimby and Ruxtable.

He worked over the Tollbury telephone numbers without result. Then he suddenly recollected Lydia's mention of the Jackson family at High Sonding. It would not be easy to ring up a man in that bereaved house without offering some sense of urgency as his excuse, but in spite of the inherent delicacy of Brian's own situation with regard to Heathley, he decided to take the risk.

He apologised to Brian on the telephone, but he was coldly received. In spite of the fact that he assured him that he was using one of the new telephones which was proofed against tapping, Brian still spoke to him with some degree of suspicion. "If Heathley's not in his own quarters, I don't quite see how I can be expected to know where he is. As I'm sure you appreciate, this is hardly a moment at which I can be expected to seek him out."

"I understand that, of course, Jackson, but perhaps you'll allow me to add that we're a little concerned with the precipitous way he left and we're wondering. . . ."

"Lydia's worried, is she. But then Heathley always moves quickly in that great car of his. Come to think of it, I saw him myself driving toward the main gate. I took it for granted that he'd just seen the Director."

"He hadn't seen the Director. He didn't tell Lydia where he was going and, as you know, he hasn't been quite himself."

"That's the sort of line that Dennis Bord has been taking lately." There was a strong hint of distrust in Brian's voice and Sam realised that this was the moment to come into the open and share his own doubts. He said: "Bord knows nothing about this. I'm acting for the Director himself. He was expecting to see Heathley this evening. In view of to-morrow's announcement, you can well understand yourself that Heathley really ought to see Cruddock either to-night or first thing to-morrow. Let me be frank with you, Jackson. I'm getting into quite a flap about Heathley. What do you think yourself?"

"He may talk a little wildly if he feels that people aren't agreeing with him, but I'd back him against any other scientist I've ever known not to go off the rails. I say that quite deliberately after what happened today. He may have come round to the fact that things after all were a little disappointing. He's probably gone off somewhere to have a drink in a pub and worry it all out. I should have thought he'd have told Lydia; or have they been having another tiff like they did on Wednesday on their way to Cresham Strand?"

"I guess they had a tiff." Sam weighed up what Brian had said. It was clear enough that Brian was erring, if anything, on the side of loyalty toward Heathley. "I've taken you into my confidence, Jackson, and I've interrupted you at a most unwelcome time. I've only done so because I know of the respect you have for

Heathley. For everybody's sake, including Lydia's, it would be better if we knew, at this moment, just where the Professor is and what he's doing."

"The only places in the neighbourhood that I've known him to use from time to time are the Golf Club and the Grand Hotel at Flimby, where we were all to have lunched last Wednesday. In fact, I believe Lydia and Alex did have lunch there. I'm sorry I can't be more helpful, Seagram. I can quite see that Heathley going off into the blue might be disturbing just now. Surely you could have a discreet word with the police if you feel really rattled, though I suppose that would be going a bit far. . . . Heathley would be furious if he ever got to hear about it."

It was the kind of sensible suggestion which anybody might have made, but Sam took it as a hint that Brian was rather more disturbed than he pretended to be. It would, in fact, be taking a grave responsibility to institute police enquiries, particularly if Heathley were, as Brian suggested, merely sulking in some local bar with every intention of coming to work as usual the following morning. Cruddock would be most unlikely to authorise any such action. Bord would be mortally offended by it if it were taken without his authority. As he went on with his telephone enquiries automatically, Sam had a brain wave. He might persuade Lydia, as an anxious wife, to contact the police. It would be perhaps a little callous, but Lydia and her mother were familiar enough with service conditions to understand that the calling in of the police officially might drive Heathley to some excess of fury and draw a disproportionate amount of attention to what might be, after all, a misunderstanding or a mood of sulks. As he was thinking this, Sam was put through to the manager of the Grand Hotel at Flimby, and heard the man say with bored politeness that he had seen the Professor and that he thought he might still be in the Oceanic Bar.

"The Professor very rarely visits the Oceanic Bar," the voice went on, "though he sometimes has dinner here. That's why I was surprised to see him there, though of course Colonel Bord is a regular customer. . . ."

"He's with Colonel Bord?"

"They were together when I passed through the bar some little time ago; perhaps you'd like me to put you through?"

"Wait a minute," said Seagram, speaking carefully and with an authority he had not used before. "I'm a particularly old friend of both these gentlemen and I know they happen to be discussing some urgent business. Would you please be good enough just to let me know if they're still there, without switching me through."

This tone of authority without explanation was nearly always effective. The manager agreed with some alacrity that he would go and look. While he waited, Sam came to the conclusion that the two main elements of his uneasiness were now joined. Was it not a bit too much of a coincidence that there should be at once something suspicious in the activities of Bord and some of the signs of a crack-up in the character of Heathley? On the other hand, perhaps Bord, experienced, ambitious and ruthless as he had proved to be, was doing some kind of smart job on his own. Clearly it was unlike both of them to meet quite by chance in the Oceanic Bar at such a time. Like so many imaginative thinkers, Sam ruled out chance and coincidence absolutely.

When the manager returned to the telephone saying

that Heathley had gone and asking if he would care to be put through to Bord, Sam hesitated only for a moment before deciding that it was still too soon for any hint which might provoke even the mildest show-down. "I shall be seeing them both later," he murmured, and thanked the man for his trouble.

He was apprehensive. There was a little to be added to his pattern, but too much of it was still surmise. It was a relief that Heathley was evidently not making a dramatic disappearance. It was disturbing though, to hear of him in the company of the only man about whom there was real suspicion, the same individual indeed with whom the late Deputy had spent some of the unaccounted hours before his accident. Either for the best Security reasons, or for some unrevealed purposes of his own, Bord was working on Heathley. Were things fundamentally wrong with Heathley, and was Bord an influence of salvation or corruption? The Security Officer was still in the Grand Hotel. There was still an opportunity for Sam to make that recon-naissance of the late Deputy's quarters. His only mistake was that, when he had already risen to go to fetch the key, he went back to the telephone out of humanity to tell Lydia not to worry, that Heathley was no further away than Flimby, that probably the Memsahib was right and he might well be back at work by morning, even if he were in no mood to return home.

The Deputy had lived in one of the more modest self-contained service bungalows which, because of the extension of the Sick Bay, stood a little on its own. It was screened by a natural thicket of gorse bushes which nobody had ever troubled to trim. As the service bungalows in this quarter were more used by transients than by permanent staff with settled families, no gardens had been developed. This isolation and relative privacy compared with most of the dwellings at Port Amberley had suited the Deputy's taste, both for melancholia and for the pursuit of his hobby which had been bird-watching.

Seagram, picking it out as the only building which was unlighted, parked his vehicle outside the Sick Bay and made his way along one of several paths through the rough grass and the gorse bushes. By the back door, of which he had the key, there were a number of bottles. He stooped and struck a match. There was nothing remarkable about them except that they showed that the late Deputy had had a catholic taste for whisky. He was just about to strike another match, to find the keyhole, when lights went on inside. He dropped the match and waited. There was no sound but the sad wind from the marshes, teasing the gorse and sending yellowish-grey clouds across the moon. Sam held his breath. While he had the ultimate authority of the Director himself to inspect the bungalow, it would be awkward to have to explain his presence to any of the Security Guards, whose duty it was, of course, to report to Bord.

Sam himself was quartered in a bungalow of similar pattern. He could tell that the person inside was in the large front room which was used as a lounge. Then a nearer light went on, and he knew that the person was coming through to the kitchenette. He ducked under the light which poured through the panel of the back door and moved cautiously round to the side of the building. But in doing so, he tripped over empties which lay half concealed in the damp grass. As he steadied himself, he heard an answering clatter of bottles from within the kitchenette.

He made up his mind then to cut across to the gorse

bushes and wait. From there he might even get enough of a glimpse of this nocturnal visitor to satisfy his curiosity. It was rather more than curiosity, anyway. He took a couple of cautious steps forward through the straggling grass, with the intention of breaking through to the path. As he did so, the back door of the bungalow opened quickly, the light was switched off and the door slammed. He turned round just in time for his face to come into the full beam of a torch. "Good God, Seagram, what on earth are you doing up here?" said Bord, in his crisp regimental voice.

"Hello there!" Sam said, with a lightness he was far from feeling. "They told me you were off the Station, Dennis, otherwise I should have come along with you."

"If you start roaming about places I've told my patrols to keep an eye on, you'll get a bullet in your calf, old man. The chaps are a trigger-happy bunch; it would just suit them to have a pot at an unauthorised ghost coming out of a dead man's quarters."

"It's rather an irregular moment for you to inspect, isn't it, Dennis?"

"If you choose to come here at night, I suppose I'm entitled to," Bord parried. "But seriously, Sam, I wish you'd have a word with me before you do this sort of thing, particularly as my guards don't all know you by sight yet."

They had begun to walk round to the front of the bungalow where Bord left his car. "I'll let you have a look in the morning if you're really interested in the Deputy's books and things," Bord went on. "By the way, did you walk here or. . . ."

"I left my vehicle in front of the Sick Bay." Sam pointed to the side-path which had brought him through the gorse to the back door. "I didn't quite figure out which was the best way in here."

230

Bord stopped. "In that case," he said, "I can't give you a lift, and your best way is probably back on that path over there." It was an easy-going dismissal, indicating that any further explanations would be left till the morning. I'd have taken you in now, Sam," he added, "but it's getting late, and I'm a bit weary myself. . . ."

"Wouldn't you like me to give you a hand with those bottles?" said Sam, lighting a cigarette and trying to read the labels of the three bottles in the crook of Bord's arm.

The Security Officer swung away. "I can manage very well, thank you. It's just the remnants of a case of drink I was sharing with the Deputy." He cleared his throat, controlling his temper. "I've been over at Flimby for a break this evening," he went on, but his voice still had a defensive edge to it. "Saw old Heathley over there at the Grand, by the way. Fairly knocking it back he was too, between ourselves. Then when I got back here, I realised that I'd nothing in the house for a nightcap. So I thought I'd just get my share of the case before the lawyers begin making inventories of things to-morrow. So long, Sam." His eyes were masked by the darkness, but Sam had the feeling that they were watching him intently. He meant to say something about Heathley, anything which might prolong this nervous defensive conversation which might reveal so much, but Bord turned without another word. Sam waited long enough to see him stow the three bottles into the back of his car and drive off slowly.

Bord had acted casually enough, once he had bitten back his annoyance. But Sam suspected that he would turn the car again to make sure that his own vehicle drove off from the Sick Bay. He went back slowly, giving himself the slight satisfaction of keeping the

Security Officer waiting. He drove toward his own quarters, but when he came to the curve by the Wind Tunnel Block, which was circular, he accelerated off the main roadway and drove quickly round the building. As he emerged again, he nearly collided with Bord's car coming fast round the curve.

In his own quarters, he asked the telephone night enquiry operator if there were any messages. He was told that Brian Jackson had just called and had emphasised that he was telephoning from a call-box and that it was no use trying to ring back. He had left a message that their mutual friend was all right.

So Brian had seen or heard of Heathley. Sam Seagram mixed himself a nightcap and began pacing up and down his quarters. He did not feel justified in telephoning Lydia at that hour with such a vague message. It was late, in fact, to expect any further action, but too early to sleep. He would think things over and stick by the telephone. If he could only probe the mystery of Bord, perhaps, after all, his uneasiness about Heathley might be assuaged.

In the small hours he fell asleep, stiff and cold in his clothes, by the silent telephone.

CHAPTER XXI

BRIAN's telephone call to Sam had been made hastily because Heathley had been standing a few yards away on the other side of the lath and plaster wall of the village inn just down the road from Chestnut Lodge. Brian had gone there with his brother Richard to talk over the funeral arrangements with the Little Sonding builder whose family had buried the dead in all the Sondings for many generations.

It was a tradition in those villages for the male members of the family to discuss details and prices with the undertaker in some neutral territory. The undertaker, unemcumbered by mourning women, was able to develop a sombrely grand line of sales talk about coffins. The male members of the bereaved family were able to fortify their sorrow and, they supposed, to drive a harder bargain with the undertaker than would be quite decent in the presence of the dead.

Brian had been glad enough to fall in with this. He had been moved by the dignity of his father lying in state in the front parlour and by the dearth of sorrow and self-pity in the household. It was typical of the dark people, even in an age in which they drove tractors, watched television with the avidity of a secret vice and held their own in the great markets of London, that they should take an almost pagan pride in their dead. It was a pride as old and open as those bitter wolds which they had turned in the course of centuries into rich market gardens. Brian drew strength from this sparse death ritual of his own people. Few of the customary condolences were exchanged. The women gave themselves up quietly to an orgy of cooking. The male task was to ensure an unostentatious funeral furnished with the best of everything, and until it took place to provide a barrel of the best in the front porch, or any convenient spot almost within reach of the corpse's own dead hand.

In the inn, as a preliminary, among friends of the family and people in the know, there was a ritualistic and, for the most part, silent exchange of drinks in which the undertaker played a discreet part. Brian, exhausted by the events of the day, and regarded by many of his family's neighbours as one who was almost outside the secretive routine of Sonding village life, had fallen into a mood of tranquil preoccupation. He was content with being at home, with being among people who were able to meet even death on their own terms. For one who had been under such stress, who had to acknowledge physical fear, who had been plagued by ideas and theories, who had been so suddenly engulfed in the tenderness of love, the decorous noise of the inn was wonderfully soothing.

Then Heathley had pushed his way through the doors and had stood there, blinking against the light, swaying as if he had had too much to drink. Many of the older men and the regulars had greeted him with "Good evening, Professor. . . . Nice to see you, Mr. Heathley. . . . Well, if it's not our old cricketing champion. . . ."

Heathley looked through the smoke haze straight across to Brian as if he expected him to be there. The look was at first so fixed that Brian wondered whether Heathley really saw him. He thought of trying to shrink away out of sight. With the announcement of his appointment impending, and the disagreement which there had been between them, Heathley was surely the last man he ought to meet on this particular evening.

Heathley, nevertheless, came toward him with a preoccupied look on his face, a look which he sometimes bore when he was concentrating. He spoke as if they were both already in the midst of a conversation. "Whatever we are, or whatever we've become, it's people like old George Jackson who know their own compass and live within it who are the people who most matter. I've spent too long in some great echoing sewer, ornate, utilitarian, dirty, essentially confining. I shall never go back that way again. I've come out of it and smelt the sea and the land. I've been fortunate enough to recollect what human dignity is, whether it be in a small compass or a large. Your old man knew his compass and his dignity filled it. Perhaps I myself, and certainly you, may discover in ourselves some infinitely greater compass. Have a drink with me, both of you, Richard and Brian. I was in Flimby to-night, alone and miserable and . . . I suddenly thought of old George lying there dead. Forgive me, you two. I just made up my mind that I wanted to pay him my last respects."

It was curious that it was Richard, the slow and inarticulate likeness of old George, who managed to grope at once towards Heathley's meaning. Without embarrassment or hesitation, he said: "The old man thought a lot of you, and I'll be very pleased to take a drink. And, when we've had a drink, Mr. Heathley, the family and I would be happy for you to take a look at the old man just for luck."

Because of Seagram's telephone call, Brian was studying Heathley to see if he were drunk. For the sake of everybody, including Heathley, he rather hoped that he was. He had seen Heathley merry on occasions, but it had always seemed inconceivable that such a man should get drunk. While his brother was speaking, Heathley's hand fell on Brian's shoulder. "You're looking at me, Brian, as if you're trying to guess what sort of a night-out I'm having. That's the sort of look you're giving me! If you weren't lucky enough to be so rooted here in the Sondings, I'd accuse you of having given me a Port Amberley look. Even when he didn't approve of me, which was often enough, your father never looked at me quite like that—and your father was a man who understood absolute values."

"It's handsome of you to talk about the old man like that. Proper handsome," Richard said, giving Brian no chance to answer. "The Guv'nor wouldn't have understood a word you were saying, but he'd have liked to have heard you say it."

"You don't think I'd ever have dared to say it to his face, do you?"

There was great laughter. It was the sort of double talk which went well with the occasion. Sonding people knew how to hold their liquor. Those of them who knew Heathley respected him because he had always taken his drink at a good pace, but discreetly, and held it too. It was useless for Brian, in a bout of self-consciousness, to scowl at him. Heathley was in tune with the mood of the company where the undertaker sat with the bereaved, and where men played darts and drank with rather more than their usual verve.

As Heathley's hand kneaded his shoulder, Brian, for once, felt that he did not quite belong either to the Sondings or to that rootless world which his own people called "down yonder." He was touched by Heathley's generous appreciation of his father, which might have sounded so strange in any other company. He was so touched that he could not trust himself to add a word to what his brother had said. Respect and gratitude for everything that Heathley was and everything that he had been in his life flowed through his nature only to be stemmed by the intolerable guilt of knowing of his own appointment as Deputy and by the furtive prompting of the strange telephone call he had received.

"It's good of you to come, Heathley," he managed to say at last. "After all, it's been a hell of a day, hasn't it? I'm not much good at expressing such things, but I'm sure you know from Mrs. Loose how the old man respected you, behind your back, whatever he chose to say to your face."

Heathley gave the impression of listening, but he almost ignored what Brian had said with such an effort. "I'm the one who's been awakening recently, Brian, to a new perception of human values. I'm beginning to understand now what I never saw at the time. Old George never got much beyond his own acres and the London markets, but he was a big man because he related everything to the things he knew. It could be the same with you or me—but what's inhibiting us?"

The rhetorical question hung, mystifying and ominous, with the tobacco smoke beneath the rafters. Somebody brought the drinks which Heathley had called for. He had not overdone the generosity. He was not buying his way in. He knew the people of the Sondings too well for that. He paid without any flourish. He had treated most of the company, but tactfully. He was a real gentleman, and nowadays, gentlemen were scarce. The group around the under-taker appreciated that. He was old George's friend.

Nothing much had ever been said about it; but look how he had played cricket and look what he had made of old George's son. There was a momentary silence because, without a word being said, they were acknowledging that they were drinking old George's health in Heathley's beer.

Brian was sufficiently rattled to choose that moment to go to the telephone. He had supposed that he could slip out unnoticed, but he went into the passage where the telephone was, with his ears burning. Out of sheer weariness and perplexity, he had contrived in that clumsy exit to draw attention to himself. Heathley had looked up with annoyance, as if Brian had trodden on his tie. Richard had jested uneasily about flying being bad for the bladder. The company drank in silence because of that question of Heathley's which nobody had understood and which only Brian could have answered. The silence followed Brian round the corner. He lowered his voice and gave the message furtively, hastily.

Heathley was not himself, but it was also plain enough that he was not drunk. Another domestic tiff with Lydia might well explain his solitary mood which might be little different from that which had made him refuse to play golf last Wednesday. Or it might be a continuation of the aggressive self-justifying state of mind which had been building up ever since the test was abandoned, and which had found a brief embarrassing outlet in the presence of the Minister.

Brian paused for a moment before he went back to join the party to ask himself whether it was not perhaps an act of disloyalty to have telephoned at all. He had been impressed by the urgency of what Seagram had said. Had it not been for his dread of Heathley's reaction to his promotion, he might have taken

Heathley aside and told him the gist of what Seagram had said. As it was, it seemed to be only honest to give some hint to Heathley about the anxiety he was causing.

He put a bold face on it, therefore, when he went back and said: "I'm sorry. I suddenly realised that I had promised to telephone Port Amberley. I should have done it half an hour ago."

"I can't imagine whom you find to talk to at this time in the evening," Heathley said sharply, causing smiles among the company.

Brian winced, but went on boldly. "I had to speak to the Night Enquiry Operator to pick up a message and, by the way, Heathley, they're very anxious to get hold of you. I believe the Director has been asking for you."

"And who told you that, may I ask?" said Heathley, slamming down his drink so that some of it spilt on the deal table.

"Oh, they just asked me if I happened to know where you were, and I'd said I'd be seeing you and was there any message. . . ."

It sounded unconvincing and Brian knew it. Heathley only needed to go to the telephone and speak to the Night Enquiry Operator to expose the message as a half truth at best. Probably by this time the night switchboard staff had some vague instruction to get in touch with the Security people or with Lydia if Heathley came through. When Heathley rose to his feet Brian moved over quickly toward him and began: "If you should ring up, perhaps you'll. . . ."

"Do you think I'm some piddling little yes-man, moving around on the end of a string, Brian, or what? I've done my job for to-day, and so have you, not just for others, but for our own satisfaction. I shall resume

239

work when I choose, and I shall talk to Cruddock in a language we can both understand in broad daylight. I came here to do honour to old George and to breathe some sweet clean air, not to toady on the telephone to a lot of. . . ." He broke off and raised his voice. "We'll have another pint of beer, Richard, and then, if you'll allow me, I'll come back with you and pay my respects. Brian and I very nearly made the mistake of talking shop then."

Outside in the street, the chilly night smelt of the turned earth and of the sea, as the ragged procession moved up the hill toward Chestnut Lodge. Without any specified arrangement having been made, they were expected by the women. Mrs. Jackson and her sister, in their best black, with their aprons off, were hovering in the kitchen with plates full of sandwiches and cakes. There was a discreet but ample tray full of glasses belonging to the house and borrowed from neighbours, on the first landing of the stairs down which old George had insisted upon travelling alive. Among the flower-pots in the porch, was a barrel of beer tapped and ready for drawing. Old George himself was laid out among the best furniture in the parlour, where the curtains were drawn and two oil lamps had been turned down low. There were no candles or flowers, for Sonding people abhorred any ostentatious or wasteful ritual.

They straggled in, by twos and threes, and moved about informally, some in the porch, some in the parlour, by the deathbed, some in the kitchen. The two old ladies assisted by Lucy the daughter who had married well, deftly handed round food. The men drank and talked, not loudly but not in hushed voices. Old George would have found it very proper and very discreet. In an age when food and drink were even more plentiful, he had done just the same for his father. The lamps were turned up. There were undercurrents of decently restrained laughter. It was an occasion of respect in which sorrow took only a second place. Had it not been for the presence of Heathley, which undermined his self-confidence, with an embarrassed shame which he had done nothing to deserve, Brian might have been at his ease. Heathley lightly said: "I suppose it's the will of God that you and I should have spent the early part of the day testing a human theory to its breaking-point only to learn a lesson in human values in the evening. Sorry if I was a bit edgy just now when you reminded me of Port Amberley. I don't want you to think that I've had too much drink or that I'm some sort of nervous wreck. I'm not excusing myself to you or to anybody else. I don't even expect you to be on my side. You've already got a greater potential than I shall ever have. Probably you're going to realise it sooner rather than later. Probably it's a thousand times greater than that which your old dad ever had. If only you can realise it as he did. . . ." He made a gesture towards the sheeted figure on the bed. "I'm not saying this out of sentimentalism but because I think we can afford to be outspoken in front of old George. Do you understand what I'm driving at?"

Brian had rarely failed to understand Heathley's synthesis of facts. When the time came for him to differ from Heathley, he had done so with reluctance and respect. But this prophetic mood of Heathley's, expressed as if he were some creature from another world, authoritative, naïve, mystifying, made a mere emotional impact on him. He could feel what Heathley was driving at. Coming on top of the knowledge of his preferment over Heathley, it was intolerable. There

241

were tears in his eyes when he mumbled: "You're too generous, Heathley. I owe everything to you." He did not know where to begin, but he felt that at all costs he must say something of which he would not be ashamed when to-morrow came and he would be sitting in the Deputy's chair. If only he could have had the courage to blurt out the truth. If only he could have demonstrated his personal loyalty to Heathley by doing that. Yet he was the one person who must not tell Heathley. Whatever assurance he gave and whatever sympathy he added, the news coming from him could only appear cruel and vindictive. "Whatever happens in the future, Heathley," he managed to say, "I want you to know that I shall never cease to be grateful to you for coming here and for saying what you've just said." His voice cracked a little and Heathley gave him a long enquiring look in the lamplight, for it had sounded like a farewell speech. But it was inevitable now, Heathley was thinking, for people to appear to be different, for was not he himself moving out of the grooves of his old life into a new realisation of himself, where even the torment of Lydia's confession could not touch him? He had sensed by this time that Brian Jackson would intensify his opposition to him over Phase II. It was for this reason, he imagined, that Brian was behaving with a restraint which looked so like embarrassment. Physical and moral stamina also entered into it. There was no doubt that Brian had had to force himself to take part in the air test. He had been shaken by it as an experience—and who wouldn't be? Apart from the physical strain, his convictions had evidently been torn this way and that. Brian was strong, highly trained and intelligent, but had he sufficient resilience? Brian had come back to the shock of his father's death and had managed to play his part among his own people with a certain preoccupied dignity. But how would this former pupil of his, who was now his equal, have stood up to the shock of having the loyalties of his private life swept away? Who but he, Heathley, had the unique stamina to rise above an event such as that. He smiled at Brian and said: "You look as if you're about all in, Brian. I must be going."

"You're going back to. . . ." Brian hesitated, wishing he had not asked.

"I'm going to have an hour or so in my office, and I might look in and see what the nightshift are doing with the prototype. After all, I may need it to-morrow and I'm feeling as fresh as a daisy."

"Isn't it a bit late, Heathley? After all, the night-shift knows just what to do, and I expect you'll be seeing the Director first thing in the morning."

"Don't worry about me, Brian," said Heathley, childishly pleased to have made the younger, man talk like a fussy uncle. He moved round the room saying good-bye. The other visitors left with him. Brian heard Heathley's car as he was helping the family to tidy up, and his mother pressed him to stay the night. Heathley had been right about one thing at least. He was just about all in. He was so exhausted physically and nervously that his mother's voice seemed to come from a long way off.

What was the use now of going back to Port Amberley? Why not let everything ride now? He would need all his strength for the ordeal which would follow his appointment as Deputy. He decided not to go back to his quarters at the Station, but, to the amaze-ment of his family who regarded a telephone as a piece of commercial equipment to be used sparingly by day and not at all by night, he insisted on calling up Port

Amberley once more. He hated himself again for doing so, but, in his state of dazed fatigue, it seemed to be a duty, a duty attached to his new responsibility as Deputy. He asked to speak to Seagram. The Night Enquiry Operator said that he had instructions to take all the Major's messages. "Well, just tell him as soon as you can that Professor Heathley is on his way back. He left me a few minutes ago," Brian said warily, and turned back to the stairs where his brother Richard was waiting, amazed by the triviality of the message.

"I don't see why you need do that, Brian," he said, "after all, the Professor himself will be down yonder inside a quarter of an hour."

"A matter of routine," Brian snapped back, and just in time checked himself from adding something about Security.

Richard shrugged his great market-porter's shoulders and sat down on the stairs, unexpectedly, instead of turning to mount them.

"There's something more than the old man's death on your mind, I can tell that, Brian, though for once you've said nothing. Maybe we've been too busy. Maybe it's something happening down yonder which I wouldn't understand." Richard turned a pipe between his teeth. His country voice sounded like Brian's. "I reckon you might sleep better if you said what was on your mind."

In candlelight, Brian sat at the foot of the stairs and talked about Ilse, for it was that which he really needed to say. He knew now that he would be bringing her home here to Chestnut Lodge after the funeral, to meet his people. His tired voice, speaking less, it almost seemed, to Richard than himself, used simple words. Richard must know that Ilse had never had a home. Richard must know how he had come to depend upon Ilse's support.

When at last they went up the stairs, all Brian's uneasiness had vanished. He had brought something of Ilse's composure with him into his home. By talking of her, he had subdued his sense of shame regarding Heathley. He stumbled into his room resolving to think it all out but, before he could undress, was blessed by deep dreamless sleep.

CHAPTER XXI

DENNIS BORD would never have attained such distinction in the Service had it not been for his ability to descend from the giddiest heights of intuition to a classical devotion to detail.

He returned from Flimby a man of high destiny, one to whom such ordinary values as safety and peace of mind were unknown. His success not just as a matter of luck, it was the natural result of enterprise and hard work. He was covered all along the line, though the activities of Seagram were still to be watched, and perhaps countered. It was only his detailed knowledge and perception of what made the wheels go round at Port Amberley which had enabled him to turn a chance encounter with Heathley into a wonderful opportunity. He had done well before he met Heathley, but only in the negative sense of acquiring knowledge. The encounter in the Oceanic Bar offered the positive achievement which he had, in his most exultant moments, promised himself.

He was prepared in every respect to take advantage of the meeting. From the moment of Heathley's stumbling out, Bord had alerted himself for the chance of a lifetime. In the man's moments of tragedy was the promise of the kind of action which would be superlative and decisive. Whether Heathley returned to Port Amberley that night or not, was of less consequence than the certainty that Heathley would go back in the end. He might be shattered personally but he would return because he was the begetter of M.7. His visionary sense of destiny was already landing him outside conventional patterns of behaviour. He was at his most vulnerable. He had discovered and fallen in love with his own genius. It was personal unhappiness, this fatal illusion. It was a blind vanity compounded of frustration and misery which had attacked him, forcing him off balance and, in Bord's reckoning, making him momentarily fertile.

Here was triumph. It was his own persistence, his relentless search for a crack-up which might be fertile, his flexibility combining to discover in Heathley a loyalty which might be stolen. Bord dedicated himself to this opportunity with a fanatical fervour tempered with what he considered to be majestic self-control.

The Night Enquiry Operator regarded it as a routine check when Bord appeared in person and sifted through all the messages which had passed that evening. The Security Officer paid particular attention to everything concerning Seagram and Jackson, and gave instructions that all further messages were to be referred to him, and that Major Seagram was not on any account to be disturbed. The Night Enquiry Operator treated these instructions as part of a mystifying Security régime which he would never dare to try to understand. When Bord idled for a few moments, like a good officer, accepting a cup of switchboard coffee and making enquiries about the family, the Night Enquiry Operator was relieved, as he was meant to be, by a feeling that there was nothing urgent about Bord's nocturnal activities and that Security, which never slept, was simply carrying out a routine exercise.

Bord delighted himself by holding his excitement in check long enough to cross-examine the man and find out that his own Duty Security Officer, as well as

Felix Tatham, had asked to be advised when Heathley returned. After the encounter in the Oceanic Bar, he had supposed that there would be a measure of official anxiety about Heathley. Had it not been for that, and his own knowledge of Heathley's domestic catastrophe, he himself might have had to set in motion the Security machinery which would check on Heathley's movements nationally and, if necessary, bring him in. He returned to his office and demanded routine reports from the Deputy Security Officer and all patrols, assuming responsibility for any further messages which might come in about Heathley's movements. Then, because such calls frequently provided him with advance information and hints of higher policy, he telephoned his Headquarters in London, using the special line.

He discovered that London, as he had hoped, had been particularly satisfied with the information he had passed and the action he had taken, over the Deputy. He then went on to suggest, in the most tactful way, that he himself, on behalf of Cruddock, would be grateful for any immediate information of Heathley trying to contact the Minister or higher officials in the Ministry. Bord put through this personal enquiry which he knew would go down in the unofficial records, in order to make sure that his own reputation for alertness would be protected in the unlikely event of Heathley in his present madness driving to London to browbeat the Administration or simply to give himself over to dissipation.

The results of this manoeuvre were more rewarding than even he, with the devil's luck on his side, had dared to hope. His carefully chosen words were quite unexpectedly interpreted when the voice at the other end said: "You're expecting another outburst from the Professor, are you? The Minister apparently mentioned to the Chief this evening that Heathley might take the appointment rather badly. It's not really our pigeon, of course. The Minister was discussing it with the Chief Press Officer who will make the announcement, and the Chief just happened to be there. . . ."

Bord took a deep breath and murmured non-committally, "That's why I mentioned this. I quite agree that it's not our pigeon. But the Professor's certainly not in a tractable mood and I like to take precautions." He left it at that. He knew only too well how to let them suppose that he knew every detail of everything that went on, so he paused and was rewarded again.

"It's be a bit of a knock, I suppose, as Jackson is a much younger man."

Bord's heart thumped, but his voice said: "Not so very much younger." Then he added: "Well, old boy, I mustn't wait on. It's a very busy time down here just now. Just bear in mind what I said about Heathley. The Chief might like to know in the morning. It may not be important but it's just one of those occasions when this Department can do a little extra to help the Management. So long!"

It was, of course, important now, vitally important, to know where Heathley was. He cursed himself for having let the man stumble away from the Oceanic Bar, supposing that this would give him a far stronger return approach when the bitterness of what he had said had had time to sink in. He had been preparing himself for a decisive come-back ever since that moment. He must be sure now that nothing prevented the meeting taking place. Could he justify a Security and police search which, localised and unobtrusive, would bring Heathley's movements up to date? Bord reached out for the telephone, but as he did so the Night Enquiry Operator came through with the message addressed to Seagram which Brian had described to his brother as a matter of routine, saying that Heathley was on his way. By hating himself but doing his duty, Brian unconsciously filled the cup of Dennis Bord's triumph.

The Security Officer used one of the bottles he had brought away from the Deputy's quarters to measure himself out a triumphant libation. The only uneasiness in his mind as he drank lay in Heathley and Jackson having been together. The one certainty which went with the toast, however, was that he was on the threshold for decisive action. He reached the main gate just in time to receive Heathley in an unhurried manner as if he himself had just arrived.

"When I saw the lights behind me, I wondered who it could be at this time of night. I'm glad it's you, Heathley. There's something I want to talk to you about."

Heathley frowned and fidgeted with the gear of his car. He tried to veil his irritation by saying with a show of good humour: "The trouble with you, Bord, is that you always have something to say."

Bord spoke quickly, noticing that Heathley was already in gear. "Sorry if I may have seemed a bit tight in the Oceanic this evening, Heathley, but I'm not taking back anything I said. Anyway, I've been at work since then."

"You said a moment ago you'd just driven in," Heathley showed traces of irritation.

Bord, taking no chances, opened the door of Heathley's car and said: "You don't imagine that my job's limited to Port Amberley, surely?"

Heathley shrugged his shoulders. "Well, I must get

on," he murmured, showing no interest whatever in the scope of the job. "I'm going along to the office and then I may look in to see the nightshift working on the prototype." He was master of himself now. The visit to High Sonding had shown him how much he had in reserve.

"You wouldn't like me just to let your wife know you're back?" Bord said.

"You? Why ever should you?" Heathley scowled, for the thought that Lydia might be waiting up had not entered his mind.

"I could get one of the gatekeepers to 'phone through," Bord said, making little of it, adding, with a jab of meaning, "I thought probably you wouldn't want to."

Heathley bowed his head. He was not, after all, immune from this anguish. "Better let them ring through and say I'm working," he growled, half letting in the clutch so that the car gave a tremor as if it were trying to move of its own accord.

"I'm sick of talk," Heathley burst out, "I'm going to work." He let the clutch make more than a polite jerk forward.

"Heathley, old boy, I think I've made it pretty clear where my sympathy lies."

"You have, and I'm grateful. I was upset at the time but I've remembered everything you've said. I'm grateful to you for having said it. But now I'm going to work."

"You're going to work on your project, aren't you? Because it's the only thing in the world which is important? It's the only thing in your life which makes sense. You're going to devote yourself to it, aren't you? I'm speaking as your friend, Heathley, as one who recognises your genius. It's my destiny to serve men like you." Bord's voice became staccato, hitting Heathley's nerves with the precision of a drill. "What I want to say is something which directly concerns your work."

"In that case, I suppose I can't ask you to say it here?" Heathley said impatiently. "We'll meet in the morning."

"I'm not going to say it here, Heathley, and in my view it's too important to keep till the morning. I'll drive over to your office if you like, or, better still, you come into mine which is on your way. It won't take long to say and we can have a drink at the same time."

"I don't want a drink," Heathley said, revving up the engine, "but I'll look in for a minute if you say it's important."

Bord closed the door and said: "I'll put your message through and follow you right along." Had Heathley noticed that his vehicle was still pointing toward the main gate instead of inward to support the lie that he had just arrived? Heathley could wonder but he would soon have other things to think about.

A few minutes later, the Memsahib was turning to Lydia saying, "There you are. I told you so. Go to bed, darling, and let the man work himself silly. I told the man on the gate to let me know the moment he came in. One more sniff of the smelling salts, darling, and you'll feel better even if it does make you cry."

As Lydia sniffed the bottle and, crying, went off to sleep, Heathley and Bord entered the office together.

"Thank you," said Heathley, "I'm not drinking. I had several glasses of beer with the Jackson family at High Sonding."

"With Brian Jackson?" Bord said and, ignoring the first part of the remark, placing a glass by Heathley's elbow.

252

"Brian was there, of course. We were just paying our last respects to the old man. I knew him quite well and I just happened to drop in."

"Brian Jackson 'phoned through to Port Amberley and reported that you were there," said Bord, sipping his drink.

"Brian reported that I was. . . . You mean he telephoned? Now I come to think of it, he did telephone. . . . Who did he report to?" The words choked him. For the second time that evening he thumped the table.

"It's my duty to deal with messages of that kind," Bord said. "I take it that Jackson was a little concerned that you had left the Station rather abruptly."

"What in hell has it got to do with Brian Jackson?"

"I imagine that he's particularly concerned with your behaviour just now."

"I've not noticed it. In any case, it's no part of his business to report my whereabouts like a bloody spy when I've called in to pay my last respects to his own father." Heathley began to shout. "Let's get this straight, Bord, before you manage to upset me again. . . ."

"I'm not trying to upset you. You must know that. If there are sides to be taken, I'm on yours. Brian Jackson, for all I know, was simply exercising his new authority as Deputy."

It was, of course, a knock-out. Heathley leaned back under it and lost himself in the pale depths of those eyes which were swimming before him.

He had ignored the appointment of the Deputy's successor. It had seemed insignificant, almost irrelevant, to the grandeur of his present conceptions. The appointment was, after all, just part of the administrative machinery. Like Lydia, and most of the more

253

senior members of the staff, he had taken it more or less for granted that he would succeed to the Chair.

At some other time, when there were less critical events than Phase II on hand, he might have given it more thought. It was an appointment of strategic importance both in the light of personal prestige and of the work in hand. Yet until this moment he had been too wrapped up in taking advantage of the late Deputy to worry about the succession. That was the measure of his disinterestedness; but it also weighted the blow which Bord, with careful precision, had struck.

There was silence in the office. Then Heathley picked up the brandy in front of him and gulped it down so that it stung inside him. In a minute or two, he might recover the stature of the god he had been when he had walked into the room. For the moment, his head sagged over the empty glass, looking down at the dregs which epitomised Brian's deception. Was it possible that within a few hours a man should listen to his wife talking as Lydia had talked and should then have fallen as low as to be the subject of telephone checks by a pupil and friend whom he had acknowledged as his equal?

"How do you know that he's going to be appointed Deputy?" he grunted, without raising his eyes.

"You needn't believe me, if you don't want to. I thought perhaps you knew about it already. It's my business to know things."

Bord picked up the glass that Heathley stared at. As he refilled it, he said: "I may have made a mistake to blurt it out like this. I didn't mean to take you unawares. If I did, then it seems to me that I'm doing you a service. It never does any harm to have some advance information. If you really had no idea of this, I'm proud to have passed it on. Have another drink, man.

I can see that it's been rather a shock." He cleared his throat apologetically but harshly. "It's grape, Heathley. A drop of brandy never hurt anybody, and the thing about this one is that it has absolutely no after effects."

Heathley shivered, took the glass; then shook his head and put it down.

"Drink it, Heathley!"

All of a sudden, Heathley was drinking it, and warmth was returning. His thoughts reassembled in the pale watery reaches of the eyes of Dennis Bord. He had quite unexpectedly obeyed the man's command, and he felt better for it. The man hastened to relieve him of any anxiety on that score. "I only want to help you. A man like you can be betrayed and it hurts; but the essential you cannot be betrayed if you are true to yourself, your mission, that which you, and you alone, know to be right. They can't touch you that near. Drink up, man!"

Bord laughed, a little wildly perhaps, but he was just stepping out of character. He was a god who would speak to a god on equal terms. He would deign, for the time being at least, to be on equal terms. It was not the moment to reveal his full character; but it was not too soon to force the pace by using every advantage. "I imagine you drove the Deputy to his death, Heathley, because. . . ."

"I had nothing to do with it." The words jerked out of Heathley as from a man on the rack. "The man was a damned nuisance, but. . . ."

"You were the one I had to protect from the enquiries. You'd better know that now. It's all been settled. But you were the person who could have benefited from that particular accident. You of all those who happened to be in the vicinity. There were only yourself, Ilse Leon and, of course, the new Deputy, Brian Jackson. . . ."

"So you think that I . . .?" Heathley saw it all piling up against him. Because his mouth was dry and his spirit was desperate, he accepted the third drink, gulped some of it and said: "All right, suppose I did kill the Deputy?"

He said it because it was the easiest thing to say. He said it because he wanted the yellow fires of this man's eyes to flare up and give him the reckless courage he needed. Courage? It was more than that. He was still a master man in spite of the losses he had sustained. Perhaps even because of the losses. Perhaps he was purified. This might be his ultimate expression, his importance which an administration had tried to contain, which a woman had failed to appreciate. . . .

"Perhaps you killed the Deputy for the best reasons, Heathley. . . ." Bord was teasing now. The room which had veered away in an anaesthetic trance came swivelling back. He was making nightmare efforts to contradict. All he said was: "I was simply making a rhetorical point when I said *suppose I did kill the Deputy*. Now you're making me say I killed him."

"Didn't you?" Bord laughed.

Before he knew what he really meant, Heathley was saying: "What if I did?"

"It would have been a matter of expediency," came Bord's answer with lightning incisiveness. "If I hadn't been so completely at one with such a motive, I might have acted differently."

Heathley pulled his great frame together as if he had been dozing in front of the fire. "You seem to be half threatening me and half trying to implicate me. I don't get the drift of this conversation at all."

256

"The drift of it is surely that the death of the late Deputy has been explained and even justified."

"I tell you, I didn't. . . ." Heathley roused himself, but Bord silenced him with a gesture. "Don't let's bother about that. I've only told you this to prove that I at least have been on your side all along. You've been using me without knowing it, and you'll need me again, Heathley. You'll need me perhaps sooner than you think. You'll certainly triumph, Heathley, but for the time being you may well be in a fix."

"For the time being, I shall be in a fix—of course." As he found himself repeating the words, Heathley shed his doubts and scruples in a splendid simplification. The fix he was in was really an ignoble mesh of administrative detail.

No wonder his vocation had never been understood by those armed with such deception as Brian Jackson had used that evening. His quality had been misunderstood even by Lydia, whose deception still hurt when he dared to think of it. In this over-simplified world, stripped of its everyday values, he found a sudden happiness in the abstract consideration of M.7. He had created it, though naturally he had used the work of others. It was his contribution, nevertheless, to humanity. It was above administration and petty personalities, above the small cunning of those who had been nearest to him.

"You're thinking, Heathley, that you have only one loyalty and that is to what you've created for the benefit of the human race."

Heathley started. "I wasn't thinking that in so many words. But. . . ." He was looking into Bord's eyes again. He found there sympathy, understanding but, above all, the encouraging stimulus of excitement.

"But that's what you should think. M.7 is really

yours. It represents your authority. Why not take it out of range of all this?"

"Why not take it out of range of all this?" Heathley found himself repeating, and the idea of his authority surged through him like a great light. He stood up and cleared his throat. He faced the man, who, saying so little, had yet become his companion in this supreme realisation of himself. The man who had served him by proving the deceit and disloyalty which would have enmeshed him. The man who had simplified so much in so few words. Heathley made no open response to these thoughts. He strode toward the door and said: "A few hours' work and I shall be ready for the next test, which, as far as I'm concerned, will be decisive."

"And if they stop you?"

"I hope I'm big enough to sink my own feelings and to submit to Brian Jackson's authority . . . up to a point."

"To a point! But there are circumstances in which, surely, you must recognise your own authority."

"I shall recognise my own authority, too. I shall carry out the test."

"That's what I meant," Bord murmured. "You'll carry out the test. You'll be in command and I suppose it's unlikely that you'll choose Jackson to go with you."

"It's unlikely that Jackson will offer to come again," Brian snorted. "It takes stamina. I shall go alone."

"But you could take a companion."

"I'd thought of it."

"So had I, Heathley. I've proved, I think, that I'm on your side. Surely I can demonstrate that confidence to the extent of being your companion—whatever happens, whatever you may decide."

258

Heathley looked at his watch. He experienced an acute excitement, the reckless uncomplicated excitement of a boy planning a school raid. "If you still feel like that in two hours' time," he said, "come down to my office and we'll talk."

"I shall feel like that in two hours' time. I'm with you, Heathley, all the way."

CHAPTER XXIII

LYDIA, in the bedroom she had painted pink for warmth, Brian Jackson, in the steep attic of his childhood, Sam Seagram, in a room which reminded him sparsely that he was on duty, were each awakened early in the morning by thoughts of Heathley. Each of them was a little ashamed to have slept at all that night. The morning for each of them declared itself as a state of emergency.

"I ought to have tried to see him when he came back last night," Lydia said, as the Memsahib, wearing a kimono covered with dragons, paddled around her bed.

"Nonsense, Lydia. The fellow at the gate said that Heathley was going straight to his office and didn't want to be disturbed. He's a straightforward fellow, too. His children are attending my Sunday school. In any case, I think you ought to be pleased that Heathley sent through any message. After all, in Malta your father simply went off and played polo."

"You're right, Mem. It means everything, of course, that Heathley thought of sending a message when he got back. After last night, I realise that that means everything."

In Chestnut Lodge at High Sonding, Brian, hearing the distant clutter of cups, went to the crooked stairs and called down that he was ready for some tea. He was met by his aunt wearing her working apron. She came toward him whispering indignantly. "Do remember your poor father's down there below."

"He can't hear us," Brian answered recklessly.

"But the daily girl can," the little aunt sniffed, handing him the cup she had poured, after the manner of the women of that household, as soon as she had heard him stir, and concealing with doleful aplomb a delighted curiosity about Ilse.

In his quarters at Port Amberley, Sam Seagram, longing for half a pint of orange juice, picked up the telephone. The Night Enquiry Operator had gone, he discovered, leaving a message with the switchboard that he was not to be disturbed. It appeared that Colonel Bord had taken over such calls as there had been, having carried out a routine inspection of the switchboard during the night. In the course of a call or two, Sam learnt that Heathley was back and had spent several hours at work with the nightshift on the slipways. As they had gone off duty, some of the men on that shift had complained at the main gate about having been driven by Heathley.

Had Bord and Heathley been together again on the Station? That was Seagram's starting-point for the day. He blamed himself for having slept, for this information, gleaned from the switchboard staff and ever-garrulous gatekeepers, hinted at some former collusion between Bord and Heathley. Cruddock, it seemed, was equally uneasy, taking the precaution to go to the telephone in the Director's own office when Sam called to make a progress report.

Cruddock said: "I'm arranging a staff meeting this morning just as soon as people can be got together. The longer I delay the announcement, the more diffi-cult things are going to be for Jackson. If Heathley is still in that strange defiant mood of his, I'm afraid that we shall have another scene, but I'm determined to do everything to ensure that Phase II goes forward smoothly, even at the risk of a serious upset with Heathley. You see the point, Sam, don't you?"

"Sure, I see the point, Hereward, and I think just as soon as you get your meeting organised, I'm going to ask you for authority to take over the Security of the whole of this Station for the time being."

"But, my dear Sam, that would cause panic. You know, as well as I do, that I'd have to get authority on the highest level and, rightly or wrongly, the Minister went off with a very high opinion of Bord. Your facts would have to be very strong indeed. They would need to be conclusive. Anything which amounted to suspicion with a man who is recognised as being about the most efficient Security Officer in the service would need absolute evidence, and can hardly fail to cause the most unpleasant sensation. Must you raise it now, Sam?"

"Unless it's already too late, I shall certainly have to raise it, evidence or no evidence."

"You're surely not still playing about with surmise," Cruddock said fiercely. "If you were a scientist, you'd be sacked out of hand for guesswork—dangerous guesswork."

"We're dealing with people, the unpredictable human element, Hereward, not with the ascertained facts of science. It's my view that Heathley's been tainted. Last night Bord went to the late Deputy's quarters and took away a supply of brandy which I was just about to examine."

"Surely you didn't tell him you were going to examine it?"

"It was much more difficult than that. I caught him redhanded taking the stuff away, though I had no

262

chance to see it in any detail." Sam was sweating with the effort to be circumstantial. Without further authority from Cruddock, he could do nothing. He had known Cruddock much too long, however, to rely upon getting this authority on a friendly basis, except in return for overwhelming evidence.

"Look here, Hereward," he said aggressively. "Heathley's been working away like a madman all night both in his office and with the nightshift on the slipways."

"He's entitled to keep what hours he likes, as a departmental head. Indeed, in the circumstances, I think it's the least he can do. . . ."

"Then if he and Bord. . . ."

"Look here, Sam, old friend, you're holding me up. I want to have this meeting of mine within half an hour, before there's any possibility of London making an announcement about the Deputy's appointment. I know what they are. The Minister revels in special announcements of this sort. He hates to keep things to himself in case they get overripe and spoil that progressive reputation of his. Come to the meeting, Sam, and, until we see how things are going, keep your present status. If you really think there's anything you can do meanwhile to make some sense out of what you keep hinting at, I'll review it on the spot."

Seagram gave up. With this present status, there was nothing he could do. When the Memsahib telephoned a moment later, suggesting that he come across to take some coffee and speak to Lydia, who was still distraught, it seemed at least one way out of the hiatus. There was time to do it before going to the Control Room for the meeting.

So in less than five minutes, the Memsahib was

angrily asking him to observe what the east wind had
done to the prunus, and he was trying to say something
adequate as he looked at Lydia. In the end, he cut
through the small talk. "I've not got much time, ladies.
Heathley's back, as you know, and I'm glad for your
sake. There's to be a conference over at the Control
Room. I expect I'll see him there."

"Just as I said it would be," the Memsahib purred.

Lydia shook her head though. "I wonder if you will.
I've an idea you won't."

"Now that's interesting, Mrs. Heathley, ma'am.
Why do you think that?"

Lydia was very still as if she were listening again.
"The children have just told me that his chief
mechanic, Dan Little, called while Mem and I were in
the kitchen seeing to breakfast. He'd been sent to
collect my husband's flying log book which he always
keeps on a shelf in the hall. It isn't the first time Dan's
been sent to pick it up. Arthur won't go into the air
without it. I believe it's some sort of regulation that
he's always supposed to carry it, but it means much
more than that to him. It's a kind of talisman. He's
not superstitious about anything else. He's never
admitted even to being superstitious about the log
book. But I know it can only mean that he's carrying
out another test."

"Presumably we shall find that out at the meeting.
Everybody's got to be there."

"He can't be very fit for a test," Lydia spoke with
a stillness not born just of anxiety but foreboding. "He
can't be very fit after what happened yesterday and
then working all night."

"Of course he isn't," the Memsahib declared. "But
he's the sort that never undertakes a job unless he
knows he's fit, and by now he's probably coming to his

264

senses. If Cruddock's wise, he'll realise that and talk things over."

"In any case," Sam added his word of consolation, "it's pretty obvious that the outcome of the meeting will be to scrap this kind of test."

Lydia frowned. "Do you think that Heathley's the sort of man who'll go back on it now?"

Sam glanced at the clock and decided that even though there was so little time, it was more honest to tell them now rather than to allow the news of the appointment of the new Deputy to leak out after the meeting and reach them through the medium of gossip. He said: "You're not going to like what I'm going to say, Mrs. Heathley, but it's better that I tell you now in order that you may be ready to meet any repercussions. The new Deputy has been nominated, and it's an appointment which can hardly fail to affect Heathley."

"It isn't Arthur?" Lydia gasped as if she had been struck.

"It's Brian Jackson."

It was Lydia's burden that she, more than anyone, best knew how devastating this news would be to Heathley. She alone fully recognised how completely he would be taken by surprise, how he had hardly deigned even to think about the succession, so convinced was he that he would succeed. Many others might have had doubts and theories. She had even had some vague doubts herself. Heathley, however, had dismissed it all as something he could not afford to worry about.

This was the one moment she ought to be with him. By saying something now, she might make amends for everything. In the hysteria of her own selfishness, she had struck a blow and seen him crumple. If only she had known that this other blow was to fall. "I must go to him," she whispered. But, even as she tried to stand up, she swayed and fell.

Sam did what he could; but it made him late for the meeting. He promised to come back when it was over. But, in his heart of hearts, as he raced across toward the Control Room, he knew that he was unlikely to be able to fulfil that promise.

CHAPTER XXIV

THE fact that the Director's conference was called in
the Dome left no doubt in anybody's mind about it's
significance. Only departmental heads and higher
executives had been summoned, but they included
among them everybody responsible for the planning
and operation of M.7. The results of the first test,
Heathley's outburst, which by now was common
knowledge, and the appointment of a new Deputy had
created a ferment of speculation even among the most
level-headed. Though Cruddock had acted at the
earliest opportunity, he had not been a moment too
soon, he thought to himself, as the staff, subduing
themselves with an effort, assembled round the horse-
shoe table.

He had asked Brian to call for him at his office; and
on the way to the Control Room he had briefed him.
However self-assured and competent Brian might be,
this meeting would be an ordeal. But, as Cruddock
said, it was an ordeal best faced at once and in public.
It was unique in his experience, he pointed out, for a
new appointment to be made at such a critical stage
in the practical work on a project. Yet the whole future
of M.7 depended upon a Deputy with a clear view of
policy and a firm hand in carrying it out. Cruddock
admitted that the conference had been precipitated by
Heathley's behaviour. "I'm not going to refer to it,
but between ourselves, Brian, I'm still mystified. I
would have been only too willing, for instance, to have

observed the courtesy of telling him privately about your appointment. But there, this attitude of his must have a cause and, if by any chance that cause comes to light during this conference, so much the better, however uncomfortable it may be. I believe in plain speaking and plain dealing. . . ." Cruddock was steaming himself up. He liked a private rehearsal before presiding at meetings. The briefing of Brian was serving a double purpose. It was doing them both good.

Brian had made an attempt to talk about Heathley, to express the gist of that meeting of the night before which still haunted him; but Cruddock had not listened. He had cut him short, insisting upon a ceremonious handing over of the Deputy's key to the Dome. When they arrived, he had guided Brian to the seat on his right. He greeted the more senior members of the staff by their first names in a manner which he imagined put them at their ease. Then he took out his pencils and began to doodle furiously, glancing from time to time at the clock.

The horseshoe table began to fill up, not according to any pattern, though most people had been quick to notice Brian's position on the Director's right. Nothing was said, but Brian himself became acutely self-conscious because of what was left unsaid. If only Cruddock would start the meeting!

Brian was, in fact, so occupied by this unexpected attack of nerves that he was almost the last to notice that by some instinctive understanding among those present, the seat on Cruddock's left had been left empty for Heathley. Surely Heathley was not going to cut this conference? He would be mad if he did. Brian forgot his own discomfort in his concern for Heathley. There was a subdued murmur of conversation as people noted the time furtively, anxious not to show any sign of anxiety.

Cruddock raised his head and glared about him, with an attempt at a bland smile contorting the lower half of his face. If Heathley was really preparing what amounted to an act of mutiny, Sam Seagram's presence was all the more important and he noted with fury that there was no sign of Sam. He pressed a button and spoke to Kennedy, whose shift it was again as Duty Controller on the Upper Deck: "You might get somebody to ring through to Major Seagram, Controller. I particularly wanted him to be present at this morning's conference. By the way," he added, with heavy casualness, "we also lack Professor Heathley."

"He's been doing a local test with the prototype, sir," came Kennedy's voice.

"But surely notification of this meeting was passed on to him?" barked Cruddock.

"It was passed through the moment we had it, sir, and acknowledged. We thought the Professor was bringing the craft straight in, but. . . ."

"Pass through a message from me recalling the craft to base at once." Cruddock dropped the key and looked round again without the smile. He said: "Well, gentlemen. I shall begin. . . ." Then the door opened, and Sam tiptoed in.

"You're late, Major. But you'd better sit here." Cruddock indicated the empty place on his left.

Sam astonished the company by both disobeying and answering back. He made no attempt to sit down. Instead he voiced what was in everybody's mind. "Why isn't Professor Heathley here?"

"He's on his way back from a local test. Now, for heaven's sake, sit down, man, and let's get started."

But Sam spoke out of turn once more. "If you don't

mind, sir, I'll go below and consult your Duty Controller. It's essential for security purposes that I contact both Professor Heathley and Colonel Bord."

Cruddock threw down his pencil violently. "This is too much, Sam." Seagram turned away toward the door with the amazing remark: "I can't help it, Hereward. That's the way it is."

The people round the table stirred in spite of themselves. During the short time that Sam had been at Port Amberley, he had played his part well. This was the first indication that he was on familiar terms with the Director. Cruddock had never been called Hereward even by his wife in public. He was alive to this himself and grinned his embarrassment.

"That's one cat out of the bag, gentlemen. Though Major Seagram was attached to us as Personnel Liaison Officer, I'd better reveal at once that his status is rather more than that. He is, in fact, making an overall security survey not only of this Station but also of all trans-Atlantic channels of information. I shall be glad if every member of this meeting will give him all the assistance they can. It happens that he's a very old friend of mine and we worked together for many years in Washington, but you mustn't let that deter you. Now I think it's quite obvious to you all that this is an emergency conference called in very exceptional circumstances. I believe in plain speaking and plain dealing. . . . The success or failure of the M.7 project lies, in my view, right here on the table in front of us. For that reason, I intend to begin by naming the new Deputy Director. . . ."

Within five minutes, Brian had surprised himself by his cogent summing up of the M.7 programme. What added such weight to his words was the fact that he had been out with Heathley the day before. What was overwhelmingly convincing in his treatment was that he said nothing which denigrated Heathley's research or practical handling of Phase II. He spoke factually and lucidly, with an authority which nobody could deny. He said at once that Phase II must revert to the orthodox method of approach. The unorthodox trial had proved not only that there was danger in testing the human capacity to the limit of endurance, but that there was a great risk of navigational error. The navigational fixes could never reach a degree of accuracy which could ensure that the testing craft would remain within the limits of friendly territory when travelling at supersonic speeds. His first action as Deputy, therefore, was to cancel that part of the programme categorically and immediately.

As he finished speaking, lights flickered on the panel in front of the Director's seat. Cruddock saw them but ignored them while he said: "I concur with the policy expressed by the Deputy. He has my full support. It would obviously have been more satisfactory if Professor Heathley had been present, but I wish the meeting to know that, even if he had been here, our decisions would have been the same. I propose to issue instructions that all prototypes are to be brought ashore and beached, whether Professor Heathley is working on them or not." He pressed the switch down. "What is it, Controller?"

"Professor Heathley, speaking from the prototype craft which he has on local test, has just stated that he is preparing to carry out the next air test in the series."

Cruddock said: "Wait!" and dropped the key. Then he turned to Brian and said with weighty emphasis: "I must leave it to the Deputy to decide this. I'm glad in a way that it should happen at a moment when we're all assembled here. . . ." He was skilful, as usual, in underlining collective responsibility. He was skilful also in exploiting his well-tried principle of the delegation of authority.

Brian did not wait for any second asking or for the views of the meeting. There might well be some who still supported Heathley's line of approach, but it was now his duty to form a decisive policy. He no longer thought of Heathley as a friend, protector, colleague, or even as the man who had brought tears to his eyes not many hours ago. The issue was clear enough in abstract terms. The folly of a further test without discussion was manifest. The fallibility of Heathley's line of approach had been proved. He lifted the key and said: "This is Jackson speaking, Controller. I have taken charge of this project, following my appointment as Deputy Director. Please signal Professor Heathley that all tests are cancelled until further notice. The Director and I would like to see him the moment he returns."

He turned to address the meeting. He was pale beneath his Red Indian colouring. It made him look pasty. "It's the last way that I would have chosen to break the news to Heathley," he said, for the first time showing emotion, "but now perhaps the Director will allow me to run over the programme in detail in order that no time shall be wasted by the rearrangement of work."

Cruddock, however, found in this a golden opportunity for intervention, to point out the obvious. He paid some handsome compliments to Brian. Then he elaborated upon the concern which existed in the highest quarters about the success of M.7. He was only just launched on this when the door opened again and Sam Seagram said: "Sorry to butt in, Hereward, but

I'm afraid I've got to ask you for emergency powers. I want your authority for Colonel Bord to be suspended and detained."

The Director stood up, as did many of the others, but Brian, suddenly drenched with the memory of his encounter with Bord outside the Dome, cut across the confusion. "Where is Bord?"

"Kennedy and I have been trying to find out. All that we know is that he took out one of the Security launches to meet Heathley as he was returning from his local test."

Brian jumped to the key. "Has my message to Professor Heathley been acknowledged, Controller?"

"Acknowledged, and that's all."

"You mean that no answer was given? What do the plots show?"

"The craft surfaced for a short time and we believed it to be engine trouble, but now she appears to have put about. We're trying to make contact with the Professor to ask his intentions, but he doesn't answer."

"I shall speak to him myself," Brian said. He and Cruddock stood together. The others spread into groups, like people standing about in a road accident. The atmosphere changed from that of a conference called to consider weighty decisions to that of a council of war dominated by a single sudden explosive event.

"Gentlemen, I'm authorising Major Seagram to take full charge of all Security measures until this unauthorised test has been stopped and we return to normal. I shall be glad if you will go to the routine positions you occupied during the first test. The Deputy and I will remain in supervisory control here."

"Before you go, gentlemen," Seagram added, "I think you'd better know the preliminary precautions I've taken. This Control Room is sealed and the guard will have instructions to let nobody in or out without reference to me. There'll be no telephone calls except for those authorised by the Deputy. This will apply also to the Experimental Block, and there will have to be a special check on the main gate."

Cruddock frowned. It seemed to him that Sam was overdoing it. He said: "Surely, Sam, this is just a matter for alerting the Control Room only until we have Heathley safely back? We don't want to arouse unnecessary speculation."

"It's not just Heathley I'm worrying about, it's Bord. I'm issuing instructions to the Security guard to use their side-arms if necessary, if he resists, but to get him at all costs. We've sent out all the speed boats."

"But Sam, this isn't America. . . ." Cruddock was pleading now. There was sweat on his forehead. "You can't start shooting on the assumption that a man who is a trusted and responsible Security Officer has suddenly turned traitor."

"This is the twentieth century, Hereward, and it doesn't matter which country it's in. Treachery no longer moves by countries and, once it starts, it moves damn quickly."

Brian had been speaking to the Controller again. He turned to Cruddock and said: "Heathley still refuses to answer and the plots show him to be heading out at speed. The Doctor has got an urgent message for you, Seagram. He says you're expecting it. Shall I put him through?"

"Since its probably the evidence you're looking for, Hereward, I'll talk to the Doc right now."

He took up the telephone receiver and spoke. He said: "You confirm its presence in the brandy? Right. Only weakly, but it's there? That's all I want to know, Doc, but keep working at it."

He put back the receiver. "I shall have to go below to see to these routine precautions. I wish to God I'd forgotten I was in peaceful old England and taken the precaution of knocking Bord down last night when he was collecting his bottles. I wish to God I'd worked on surmise and let the evidence look after itself. The moment Kennedy told me that Bord had gone out in Heathley's direction, I got every available man to work on his office, and, of course, within a few minutes I had a report back from Captain Grover that they'd found some phials of stuff in his top right-hand drawer. Don't ask me what it is, but from my knowledge of the way these people operate after we picked up that couple in Rome, my guess is that it's one of those things the newspapers call a truth drug. In Rome they used it to loosen people up. They did the same thing in Miami and the Doc's just confirmed that there are traces in the drink which the late Deputy took so copiously before he had his accident."

Cruddock said: "You don't think Heathley. . . ."

"Heathley may have had a drop last night to loosen him up but it's obvious that he hasn't had a course of it."

As Sam left the Dome, Brian said: "I'm going to talk to Heathley myself." He leant forward to the microphone. "Controller, will you please put me on to the plain language circuit to the prototype."

In the Control Room, everybody had gone to their posts. There was customary quietness but with it a tension which was like the air being sucked out of the place. The organisation was running just as smoothly as it had done in the first test, but for the fact that there was no commentary from Heathley at the controls. The automatic data flowed in steadily as the various channels opened up. The navigational and radar staff was standing by ready to take over control of the craft from base as they had done to bring in Heathley and Jackson the day before, if Heathley chose to use the master switch.

Brian's warm country voice began to bridge the silence, speaking to Heathley unemotionally in the jargon which was second nature to them both. Sam Seagram paused on his way across the Upper Deck to listen. As he did so, the news came through that the speed boats had discovered the Security launch which Bord had used. It was empty.

Did that mean that Bord and Heathley had had an assignment? Did it mean that he would have to issue an order for Heathley also to be detained—by force if necessary? On his way down to the entrance, he could hear Brian's voice speaking to Heathley, persuasive, level, and easy. Ilse looked up from her work, her lips moving as if she were able, by repeating the words, to add some force of her own to what Brian was saying.

At the entrance, Captain Grover, an Assistant Security Officer, was waiting for instructions. Sam walked out with him into the pale sunlight of the Control Room car park. He was giving him orders to put a guard both on Heathley's office and, unobtrusively and tactfully, on both sides of his home, when Lydia called to him. She got out of the small runabout she used for shopping. She walked unsteadily and he hurried to meet her. "You promised you'd come back to tell us what was happening, but I guessed the sort of thing that was happening, so I came to find you. Has Heathley done something violent? Has he gone off somewhere?" Sam took her by both hands, drawing her away from Grover back toward her car. "He's done nothing violent, but he's defying orders."

"And he's gone off?"

"He's gone off. We're trying to get him back."

"But it's all my fault . . . it's what I said. . . . The worry and frustration of it all . . . and then this monstrous thing of appointing somebody over his head. . . . If only I'd known. . . ."

Sam called across to Grover telling him not to wait. He knew that he would have to tell Lydia about the precautionary measures he had ordered. He knew he could not in any case leave her alone in her anguish, numbed, in the driving-seat of the little car. He knew, too, that it was not all her fault.

CHAPTER XXV

IN the prototype Heathley stiffened as if he were taking a salute when Brian's first orders as Deputy announced that all tests were to be cancelled till further notice. He recognised the urgency in Kennedy's voice as it relayed the message. He prodded the switch which sent back an automatic acknowledgment of the signal and, as if he were speaking to himself said: "That settles it." He had not slept since he last sat at the controls. His face had gone bluish grey with stubble and grime. Some of the time he was not quite sure whether he was talking or thinking.

Bord, in the seat beside him, said: "There now. That leaves you in no doubt about your so-called friends back there. What future would it have held for you?"

The words may have sunk in, but Heathley gave no sign of having heard them. His hands hovered over the instrument panels. There was a sensation of movement and speed as if they were disembodied, moving independently of the earth and the elements. Heathley said: "You'd better try on the pressurised mask. We shall need it before long." His manner was matter-of-fact, impersonal, as one member of a crew to another. He slipped the plastic hood over his head and demonstrated its self-sealing collar. He went on talking through the speaking attachment, explaining the simple methods of communication while the hood, which he himself had invented, was being worn.

They heard repeated requests for acknowledgment and information coming through on the circuits from Port Amberley, but Heathley made no further acknowledgment. When Bord struggled out of his hood, Heathley was studying navigational data, singing to himself, and, in the midst of his singing, repeating the phrase which had cropped up with last night's brandy: ". . . so we'll take it out of range of all this. . . ."

Bord rocked himself to and fro in the seat, tapping his right hand against his pocket and the gun which he had had no occasion to use. These were moments of glory which alone were worth all the long years of bitter self-discipline. This approach to the final stages of his achievement was worthy of his long singleness of purpose. Nobody but he could have had the vision to hold to that purpose with such flexibility, exploiting such luck. He rocked himself to and fro because it was so painful in these sweet moments of triumph to go on acting the part of an ordinary unheroic efficient man. When he heard Brian Jackson beginning to talk on the circuit, he was glad that he had not been too hasty in pressing Heathley into making decisions. At the moment, nothing more specific had been indicated than that Heathley would take himself, and his creation, the M.7 prototype in which they were riding, "out of range." No destination had been discussed— except by implication. Watching Heathley's face work like that of a man under torture, as he listened to Brian's sober pleading, Bord carefully slid the list of secret emergency call-signs from the inner pocket. "I hope you're enjoying this little speech from your former pupil and friend, Heathley."

Heathley started and abruptly switched off. "One will learn in time to ignore such things," he said with an ugly hard grimace which was supposed to be a laugh. But what was so unexpected and did not go with the laugh at all, was a little boy's tear in his right eye.

Heathley's first frenzied reaction to Brian's voice was giving way to a new calm. It was essential that this calm should not be followed by any weakening. The craft was building up speed. Heathley's hands travelled with assurance from one instrument to another. Bord mastered his excitement and said: "I've got the call signs here, Heathley, and you may like to know that I'm a trained radio operator. But I shall need a little training in the peculiar methods you employ on this ship."

Heathley looked at him blankly. "When the time comes, we'll deal with them," was all he said. He made no attempt to take them. They seemed to have no immediate meaning in the over-simplification of his exhausted mind.

"But surely, Heathley, the sooner we give them notification, the better. You'll need instructions where to come down. They have only the briefest intimation of our coming."

Heathley seemed surprised. "They know we're coming?"

"I let them know, of course."

"But. . . ." Heathley attended to the instrument panels. He was frowning. Bord watched him in amazement. Was this the first time that Heathley had considered practical details? Had he really been so obsessed with his project and with himself that when the crack-up came his only thought was to take it "out of range"? Bord was momentarily afraid. His hand returned to the gun in his pocket. Had the crack-up just meant madness? Was it conceivable that he would be denied his own supreme glory, now when everything had been achieved but the mere hand-over of the century's greatest treasure? "It was merely a matter of routine to let them know, of course, Heathley. Naturally I have my ways and means."

"You're well organised then?" Heathley said between his teeth, leaning forward over the panel.

"I've given a lifetime to the job. I've spared no detail. Where your work and life are concerned, I've spared nobody." His eyes misted over. His control was slipping. But now he no longer cared.

Heathley was saying: "I didn't know you had it in you, Bord. To me all this is a kind of revelation. I'm flattered when you speak of greatness, but when you speak of work I think I understand what you're driving at. The work is more important than the individual. Creative work cannot be measured against mere human happiness. . . ." Was Heathley intent on the panel or so overwhelmed by the revelation which Bord, now the master of his destiny, had just made?

It was the moment of victory this. A sudden submission of Heathley, his allegiance and his creative genius. Bord need contain his excitement no longer. His voice was rising. "Within my own sphere, I have my moments of greatness too. It is because I've attended to every detail which would serve your purpose and my purpose. From the moment when the late Deputy became useless and dangerous to us both, and I disposed of him. . . ."

Heathley raised his head quickly. "So you killed the Deputy, and yet you tried to make out that I. . . ."

"I was merely drawing you out, Heathley, leading you on to your destiny."

"And you just killed that man in cold blood?"

"A mere expediency, Heathley. We're not stopping for trifles like that. The life of a single bumbling old man. . . ."

281

"But in the eyes of God. . . ."

Bord laughed hysterically. "Who are you to be talking God stuff, Heathley? I got that out of my system years ago. In a man of your authority, it's ridiculous. There's only one power in the world. The controlled power of humanity, controlled by men of destiny like you and me." The voice grated to a standstill. There was a pause. Heathley switched on the Control Room circuit. Brian was talking again, pleading, Bord grabbed his gun. "Cut that damn thing off, Heathley, and tell me that you believe what I've just said. Repeat it after me, Heathley."

Heathley switched off the circuit and his hands, ever assured, flicked over the controls. Without looking round, he said: "We're about to enter the high-speed phase of the flight. Fix your straps and the pressurised mask. We shall be accelerating in thirty seconds from now."

The hand which had held the gun was fully occupied. Then Heathley's voice came through over the communication circuit. "Settle in your seat. It's a bit unpleasant at first but you'll soon get used to it. Ready! Now!"

The craft juddered, then steadied. There was no sensation of violence, only a throbbing swooping movement which seemed to lift them out of time and space. For a few moments, Bord felt that his head would burst. Fiery worms of high-pitched sound went boring through his senses. The images on the radar screens became blurred. Bord was not a coward but he knew when to let fear overwhelm him. He relaxed and almost lost consciousness. Then, as soon as his discomfort began to ease, he fumbled again for the call-sign sheet. The high-pitched sounds fused together in a steady tone. When Heathley said: "You need a little stamina for this sort of thing," the clarity of his voice in the hood came as a surprise. Bord at first found it difficult to speak at all. Then he managed to say: "I've got the call-signs here, Heathley. Just tell me how to operate the circuit so that I can let them know. . . . We don't want to run into trouble."

Heathley's voice came back, resonant and calm, over the circuit: "Wait! I'll ask for those when I want them." Then, with what seemed almost a defiant gesture, he brought in the Control Room circuit. At first the voice from base was plangent and distorted. Heathley fingered the dial until it became a soft whisper: "Heathley, darling. I shall go on talking until you answer. I don't mind who overhears us. I want you to know that I love you. You and you only, Heathley. Come back, for God's sake. Giles and Elizabeth were asking where you were this morning. What shall I tell them this evening? I shall go on repeating this until you answer. I had a silly flirtation, Heathley. I don't care who hears me say it. I told you about it because I wanted to bring you to yourself. Because I loved you and only you. I want you to realize that I didn't know of your other trouble. I've come here into the Control Room now to say this. I don't care who hears me. I shall go on saying it until you answer. I love you Heathley. . . ."

Bord leaned sideways in his seat. "Switch it off, damn you," he said, and his right hand clumsily lunged out with the gun. "They're even using your wife, Heathley, the wife I saw on the pier at Flimby. . . ."

"Never believe a word that anybody else has told you, Heathley. My life depends on you. We were married in the eyes of God, and in the eyes of God I've remained faithful. I shall go on saying this. . . ."

"There you are, the God stuff, Heathley." Bord was

283

croaking. "You can't afford to believe it. You won't believe it. Not now. You're dedicated to the greatest mission in your life. Or are you going to be just another traitor shot for the good of the cause?" His voice, competing with Lydia's whispered pleading, broke. "You think you've got complete control and that's where you're wrong. I'm not afraid of death, if you die first. But I don't want to sacrifice you. You're too important, Heathley."

Too important? What was it old George Jackson used to say: *Aren't you going to make God angry?* By his silence now he was crossing the last frontier, the cruellest frontier of all—and beyond it the desert land without God, without love, without honour, where men killed you expediently and spoke casually of it. Heathley's voice boomed out like that of a man just making a great discovery. He spoke, not to Bord, not to himself but to the world of God. "I'm going to talk to my wife."

Bord leant forward and grabbed Heathley's left hand as it moved to the circuit switch. "I'll give you your last chance, Heathley. Here are the call-signs. Here's your future. The glorious future of M.7. If you talk back now to Port Amberley, I'm going to kill you."

"Another kill in cold blood, eh!" It was the quietness of cunning now, of a man accustomed to danger. "And why are you going to kill me and destroy yourself, may I ask?"

"You're a traitor," screamed Bord. "A traitor to. . . ."

"But I'm not. I'm not a traitor, my friend. I'm one who's just finding out what treachery really is. Give me that call-sign sheet."

"So you've chosen life," Bord sighed, handing him the sheet, clumsily because of the hood. "You've chosen. I knew you must." The triumphant sigh was punctured by a shrill dying whistle. The shining plastic of the hood sucked inward and wrapped itself about Bord's face as the pressure stove it in, suffocating him.

Heathley reached for the Control Room circuit switch, but paused. He still held in his hand a length of the lead of Bord's hood which he had wrenched off the panel which fed it. The man had half risen before he slumped back over the far side of the seat.

What was he going to say to Lydia? He had escaped back into life and this lead which he had broken, bringing death to the man beside him, was the nightmare evidence of what he had done. He threw it down, and automatically checked over his instruments. He studied the radar screens and the automatic navigational fixes. He set in motion the deceleration equipment and initiated a turn. For a few healing moments, he was absorbed by the necessities of airmanship. By the time he raised his hand and cut in to the Control Room circuit, his diseased sense of destiny, his identification of himself with absolute power, had vanished. He gave a call-sign to make sure that they would hear him. He tried to talk naturally but all that his dried-up mouth could manage was: "This is Heathley, Lydia. I'm coming back."

He heard Lydia saying "Heathley" over and over again and he fancied he heard her crying. He could not make himself say another word. Orders, suggestions, warnings, questions, flowed in over the circuit. He used the automatic acknowledgment signal and said nothing. Then he switched off and began to think. This was the loneliest hour in his life. Within it he made discoveries which the years of abstract thinking had denied him.

He had shrunk to man-size in the presence of Lydia's

broken whispered message. He had not only found love again but honour . . . a tarnished word which did not fit the exact vocabulary of science. A word tinged with jingoism, but because of Lydia's whispered love, he had killed for it. It had come into his head for want of a better word. Lydia would understand it without any explanation. Lydia would understand that she was an end in itself.

He thought no more about Bord until he reached conditions where the pressurised masks were no longer necessary. He took off his hood and then with clinical care removed Bord's. The man had died mercifully and quickly in his moment of imagined triumph. Heathley felt neither pity nor sorrow. It had been a necessary part of his own suffering to carry out this execution. Bord himself had treated life lightly enough. His death by violence was surely no more contrary to moral principle than had been the death of old George Jackson fearing the anger of God in peace in his own bed.

Heathley had tested himself to the limits of human endurance only to learn the humility which told him what was man's and what was God's. He had been luckier than some in grappling with the devil in person and killing in self-defence. He fought back fatigue now and his real stamina reasserted itself—the stamina which old George Jackson had been so quick to recognise. He would face the music, but first he would dispose of the devil.

Beneath the lemon-coloured sky of early afternoon, Heathley alighted in a taut sulky sea, almost within sight of land but near enough to the position of the morning rendezvous with Bord, which already belonged to a nightmare past like some incident in a dead war. He weighted the pressurised hood with one of the emergency cylinders and let it go, then, at the very moment when, back in the Dome, Lydia slid sideways into the seat they had kept for him at the horseshoe table and Ilse, leaning over to comfort her, placed her free hand over Brian's—at that moment when the Control Room plotters excitedly reported his arrival out there among the marker buoys in one of the desolate experimental target areas, Heathley heaved the mortal remains of Dennis Bord out through the hinged side blister of the craft. He said a prayer: "May you learn something from old George Jackson about the anger of God before you meet your Maker," he croaked, not knowing that he spoke aloud.

He looked about him methodically before closing the blister. He found Bord's gun and threw it out too. He had at least simplified one issue for everybody concerned. He was returning to disgrace and to love. To prolonged investigations but also to forgiveness. He would suffer for what he had done, but he would be able to bear it because of what he had learnt and because of the undying memory of Lydia's voice desperately whispering her faith in him.

They would find Bord. They would piece together his story. There would be a verdict. No doubt the affair would be hushed up. What leak there had been would be stopped. Everyone would be screened again. Security would reassert itself. The essentials of M.7 were safe. At the end of Phase III, no doubt, the project would be given a name and proclaimed by the Minister —or by one of his political successors.

Heathley boosted the power, lifted the circuit switch and spoke in the level voice he always used on tests. "Test complete," he said. "I'm coming in."